Lies and Solace

Love at Solace Lake, Volume 1

Jana Richards

Published by Jana Richards Books, 2018.

This is a work of fiction. Names, characters, places, and incidents either are the product of the author's imagination or are used fictitiously, and any resemblance to actual persons living or dead, business establishments, events or locales, is entirely coincidental.

Praise for Jana Richards

A LONG WAY FROM EDEN

"Jana Richards has penned a poignant romance that will have you believing in the power of love." N.N. Light's Book Heaven

SEEING THINGS

"Seeing Things is a book that will keep you at the edge of your seat." Alice Klein, Sime-Gen Reviews

THE GIRL MOST LIKELY

"Loved this book! Jana Richards writes with great wit and a sharp eye for detail, making her characters and story feel absolutely real." Jill Blake, Goodreads Reviewer

Prologue

HARPER LINDQUIST STOOD on a wooden crate and handed her grandfather a wrench, watching in rapt attention as he disassembled an outboard motor. She was fascinated by the inner workings of the motor and the way Grampa Bill knew how to coax life back into the old beast.

Grampa raised an eyebrow at her. "Don't let Grandma see those dirty hands. Make sure you clean up before you go back to the lodge."

Harper held up her hands to inspect them. They were covered in dirt and grease gathered under her nails. She stopped herself from wiping them on her T-shirt. The last time she'd done that Grandma had scolded, saying she should be more like her little sister Scarlet. Scarlet never got dirty or ruined her clothes. Harper had been hurt and embarrassed when Grandma called her a filthy little hellion. She said that at ten years old, she should be learning to bake, not hanging out in her grandfather's garage like a grease monkey.

But Mom had defended her, telling Grandma it was just an old T-shirt and could always be washed. She'd kissed Harper and helped her scrub the grease from beneath her nails. As much as she loved her grandparents' fishing lodge in northern Minnesota, she'd be glad to go home to Minneapolis, away from Grandma Dorothy's critical eye.

But as the summer dragged on, she began to worry that they were never going home.

"Grampa, is Daddy going to live with us again?"

Grampa Bill heaved a sigh. "I don't know, child."

Harper frowned. That wasn't the positive reassurance she'd been hoping for. Daddy had moved out of their house in the spring, leaving a huge hole in her family. In the months before he left, Harper had heard arguing between her parents and had caught snippets of words and phrases she didn't fully understand, like "unfaithful". And some she did, like "divorce".

When school let out for the summer, Mom packed their things, bundled her and Scarlet and baby Maggie into the car and drove to the lodge. Mom said they'd stay there until she worked some things out. Harper had no idea what that meant, but she'd been ecstatic when Daddy had shown up unexpectedly today.

Harper ached to have him back home. She wanted things to be the way they used to be, when Daddy used to kiss Mom and play with her and Scarlet. He was often away for work, but when he was home he was the best daddy ever.

"Why doesn't Daddy want to come home? Doesn't he love us anymore?"

Grampa Bill laid his big hand lightly on her head, sadness etched in the weathered lines of his face. "Harper, your daddy will always love you, no matter what. But sometimes adults have problems they need to work out. Your mom and dad are talking. That's a good thing. Maybe that means they're both willing to try."

Harper nodded. She hoped they tried real hard so they could all go home together.

Willy Eklund, Grampa's handyman, stumbled into the garage, his breathing labored and his eyes wild with fear.

"She's in the water! He hit her!"

"What are you talking about?" Grampa asked.

"Miranda! She was arguing with her husband, and then he hit her with one of the oars. Miranda fell in the water and he jumped in after her, but I never saw either of them come up again."

Miranda? Mom? The wildness in Willy's eyes scared her. Why would Daddy hit Mom? Were they okay?

"Where did you see them?"

"Around the point. I was on the shore, picking blueberries."

"Get a boat ready, quick. We're going out." Grampa turned to her and she could see he was scared. Her stomach clenched like when she was going to throw up. If Grampa was scared, it was really bad.

"Run to the lodge. Tell Grandma what happened. Tell her to call the police. Go!"

She nodded and ran, tears streaming down her face.

Fear made her stumble on the path and skin both knees. They *had* to be okay. They just had to be.

Chapter One

Twenty-Two Years Later

HARPER WOKE ABRUPTLY, groggy and unsure what had disrupted her sleep. Then she heard it. *Bang, bang, bang.* Someone was pounding on the front door of the lodge and ringing the doorbell over and over.

She groaned and threw back the covers, shivering when her bare feet hit the cold wooden floor. As she slid her feet into slippers and threw on her robe, she checked her alarm clock; twelve-ten a.m. Who could be at her door at this hour in the middle of a January blizzard?

Whoever it was, she couldn't let them freeze on her doorstep. Tying the belt on her robe securely, she hurried to the door.

As Harper tried to open the heavy wooden front door, the howling wind ripped it out of her hands and sent it crashing against the wall. A cold gust blew snow into the foyer, instantly chilling her to the tips of her worn slippers. A snow-covered man stepped over the threshold and, struggling against the wind, pushed the door shut. He brushed the snow from his dark hair as he turned to look at her, and Harper's breath caught in her throat. Whoever he was, with his dark brown eyes and chiselled cheekbones, he was easily one of the best-looking men she'd ever seen.

"I'm really sorry about this," he said. More snow fell to the floor as he brushed off his overcoat. The smell of wet wool and citrusy aftershave filled the small foyer. "I hit the ditch this afternoon on my way here to our meeting, and I had to wait for hours till a snow plow came by and pulled me out. I haven't seen a blizzard like this in years."

Harper blinked at him. This was the guy she'd waited on tenterhooks to meet all afternoon, the guy who held the future of her lodge in his hands. "Are you Ethan James?"

"Yes. You must be Harper Lindquist."

"Yes." She conjured up a polite smile. "Welcome to Solace Lake Lodge."

He pulled off his gloves and extended his hand. "Thank you. I'm pleased to meet you, Ms. Lindquist. Again, I'm sorry to wake you at this hour. This wasn't exactly how I'd hoped to begin our business association."

It wasn't the way she'd wanted to begin either. She'd been corresponding by email with him for two weeks, ever since he'd responded to the ad she'd placed in the Minneapolis *Star Tribune* looking for an investor willing to put up the money necessary to bring the lodge back to life. She'd been thrilled when Ethan James told her his employer, Hainstock Investments, wanted him to visit the lodge to investigate its possibilities. He'd told her Mr. Hainstock himself was very excited about her property.

"When you didn't arrive by four, I assumed you'd decided to postpone the meeting because of the storm."

He grimaced. "Unfortunately, I wasn't smart enough to do that. I tried calling you, and then discovered I didn't have cell service. I'm really sorry."

She'd been crushed when he didn't show. She'd spent days planning her presentation, cleaning the lodge, even deciding what to wear.

Get over it, Harper. There wasn't anything she could do about it now. But perhaps she could still salvage the meeting. Time to play the gracious host. "No problem. I'm glad you made it here safely. Can I get you anything? Are you hungry?"

His smile was almost comical in its relief. "Starved."

She couldn't help smiling back. "That I can do something about."

She hung his damp overcoat on the coat tree near the door, taking in the designer label. The elegant dark grey suit he wore obviously didn't come off the rack at Suits-R-Us. It fit him perfectly, from his broad shoulders to his narrow hips. Even after hours stuck in a ditch, Ethan James looked like he stepped off the pages of *GQ*.

She, on the other hand, looked like a homeless person. Despite telling herself to buck up, she couldn't resist a glance down at her ancient pink chenille robe, worn fuzzy pink slippers, and pajama bottoms emblazoned with images of Mickey giving Minnie a smooch on her mousy lips. Her hair was likely a tangled mess and she could feel crusty things in the corners of her eyes.

Great.

Sadly, the homeless part was frighteningly close to the mark. If she didn't convince Mr. Hainstock's representative that Solace Lake Lodge was a viable investment opportunity, she really would be homeless.

Harper squared her shoulders and plastered on a smile, trying to forget about her less than professional appearance. Instead, she channeled the confident air of the businesswoman she was striving to be. "Why don't you follow me into the kitchen and I'll fix you a snack."

"Thanks, that sounds great. Do you mind if I use your washroom first?"

"Of course. Right down this hallway and to the left."

"Thanks."

While he headed toward the bathroom, Harper hurried to the kitchen. Her mind whirled with excitement and trepidation. With Ethan James in the lodge, at least she had a fighting chance to save her home.

After washing her hands, she opened the fridge and pulled out the roast beef that she'd sliced earlier in anticipation of serving him lunch. She buttered a couple of fresh buns, and reached back into the fridge for mustard, dill pickles and the plate of carrot and celery sticks she'd prepared. At least her previous work wasn't going to waste.

Hopefully, none of her preparations would go to waste. She mentally rehearsed the pitch she'd memorized.

Eco-tourism is the way of the future. By investing in the Solace Lake Lodge, Hainstock Investments could get in on the ground floor.

This had to work. She'd make it work.

When Ethan stepped into the kitchen, she gestured for him to take a seat at the table. She put the sandwiches on a plate and set it on the placemat in front of him. "Would you like coffee?"

"I'd love some. Can I help you with something?"

"No, I'm fine. Why don't you go ahead and eat?"

While she measured coffee grounds, she watched from the corner of her eye as he pulled the blue and grey silk tie from his shirt collar and stuck it into the pocket of his jacket. He opened the top three buttons of his immaculate white shirt, and Harper's mouth went dry at the sight of the small triangle of tanned chest.

Embarrassed by her reaction, she spun away, busying herself with finding cream and sugar. Had it been that long since she'd seen a man as attractive as Ethan James?

Definitely. There weren't a lot of unattached men her age in this part of north central Minnesota. And certainly none who looked like Ethan James. Minnewasta, some ten miles down the road, was a great little town but not exactly a breeding ground for good-looking men. The town's population of fifteen hundred, which hadn't changed much since she'd started elementary school there as a ten-year-old, were salt-of-the-earth kind of people but decidedly average looking.

By the time she had herself under control and brought coffee to the table, Ethan had already devoured his food.

"You look like a guy who could use some apple pie."

His brown eyes lit up. "I never say no to apple pie."

Harper grabbed the pie from the fridge and cut it into six even pieces. After placing one piece on a plate, she warmed it for a few seconds in the microwave before bringing it to him.

"Bon appétit."

"Thank you."

He dug into the pie with obvious enjoyment. It occurred to her that with the blizzard blocking the roads, Ethan was likely going to be a guest at her table for several more meals. She did a quick inventory in her head of the contents of her freezer and pantry and hoped they'd be adequate.

She refilled both their coffee cups and got him another piece of pie. The way this guy ate, running out of food was a distinct possibility.

Ethan finished the last bite of his dessert, then wiped his mouth with his napkin. "That was great. Did you make it?"

"No, I'm not much of a pastry chef. The cook at Miller's Golf Resort down the road made it and gave it to me. I work there part-time. She's always giving me food. Says she's trying to fatten me up."

Harper averted her gaze. That tidbit of embarrassing information had spilled from her mouth too easily. It had to be the late hour.

"When you see her again, tell her it was delicious."

Hoping her cheeks weren't as red as she thought they were, she turned back to face him. "Well, I'm supposed to see her tomorrow, but with this storm, I'm not sure either of us is going anywhere."

His dark brows furrowed in a frown. "I guess not. Like I said, I hate to impose, but do you think I could spend what's left of the night on your couch?"

"I think I can do better than that. I have plenty of room. This is a hotel, after all." She tried to keep her smile upbeat as she added, "At least it used to be."

"Thank you. I'll leave as soon as the weather clears."

"There's no rush. You can stay as long as you need to."

"You're very kind."

"Actually, I'm more practical than kind. If you stay here long enough, maybe I'll be able to convince you to recommend investing in my lodge. I need you alive and unfrozen, Mr. James."

Something flashed in his eyes before he looked away. But then he laughed softly, and she thought it must have been fatigue that made her think she'd seen a trace of guilt on his face.

"I'd kind of prefer that myself," he said.

She liked the sound of his laugh. Despite the impression of privilege and power given by his expensive suit, his laugh was genuine and unpretentious. Hope blossomed in her heart. Ethan James seemed like a decent guy. With luck, he was a guy with the ability to look past all the lodge's faults to see the possibilities she saw. "Can I get you anything else?"

"Thanks, no, I'm fine. But it's been a long day. If you don't mind, I think I'd like to take you up on that offer of a room now."

"Of course. Do you have anything with you, any luggage?"

He shook his head. "No, nothing. Not even a toothbrush. I'd planned on a two-hour meeting, not an overnight excursion."

"I think I can rustle up a few things, maybe even a toothbrush."

"Thank you. I appreciate your hospitality."

"You're welcome. Mr. James—"

"Please, it's Ethan."

"Ethan," she repeated with smile. "I want to thank you for coming here and considering the investment potential of the lodge. It means a lot to me."

He nodded, but said nothing more. Ethan James was her last hope. None of the banks she'd contacted would lend her money. If he and Mr. Hainstock decided Solace Lake Lodge was too big a risk, it was all over.

Harper pushed down her fear and made herself smile. "If you follow me, I'll show you to your room and find you a few things."

She led him up the stairs to what had once been the best room in the lodge. It still had the best view of the lake, but everything else about the room screamed shabby, with none of the chic. The area rugs were worn and faded, and the wooden floors had long ago lost their shine. The bedspread and matching curtains hadn't been replaced since before her grandmother died some ten years previously. They'd been washed so many times that the once vibrant blues and greens were now faded and dull.

As she entered the room, she lifted her chin slightly, refusing to be embarrassed. The room was spacious, and she made sure it was always scrupulously clean. She had nothing to be ashamed of.

Except maybe...

"I'll bring you an extra blanket and a space heater. With this wind, it's going to get cold in here tonight."

"Thanks." Ethan opened the door of the closet and then closed it. "Where's the bathroom?"

"Down the hall, third door on the left."

He looked surprised. "Oh."

"There's extra towels and soap in the bathroom." Even to her own ears, the promise of soap and towels didn't sound like much to get excited about.

But then that was why he was here – to help make the lodge something a lot of people *could* get excited about.

"I'll be back in a moment."

She fled back down the stairs and hurried to her own quarters on the main floor. Lifting the heavy lid of the large, old-fashioned trunk in the corner of her bedroom, she rummaged through the clothes and other items stored there until she found a man's robe and pajamas, a T-shirt, a couple of flannel shirts, and a pair of jeans. Though normally practical to a fault, she hadn't been able to part with some of Grampa Bill's old clothes. Somehow, giving them away meant he was really gone. Harper lifted a flannel shirt to her face and inhaled. Even though she'd washed the clothes before putting them away, she swore she could still detect the faint scent of her grandfather's favorite pipe tobacco. The thought made her smile.

After finding a space heater, an extra quilt, and a new, still packaged toothbrush along with a mini tube of paste from her last visit to the dentist, she hauled everything back up the stairs to Ethan's room. The door was open, but she stopped on the threshold, feeling uncomfortable about walking in unannounced.

"Ethan?"

He turned from the window where he'd been staring into the darkness and stepped toward her. "Here, let me take that from you."

His fingers brushed hers as he reached for the space heater. A tingle of awareness made her shiver. She lifted her gaze to his, blinking rapidly. "Well, I should be going. Goodnight. I hope you sleep well."

"You too. Thank you, for everything."

She nodded before turning around and hurrying back down the stairs. A moment later, she retreated into her own room and closed the door. She stared at the lock, her hand hovering above it. After a moment's hesitation, she turned it. Locking the door made her feel slightly ridiculous, as if she believed she was so irresistible Ethan wouldn't be able to keep his hands off her. As if she had to worry about him ravishing her in the middle of the night.

What would it be like to make love to him?

Harper tossed the ridiculous notion from her mind, embarrassed by the direction her thoughts had taken. The only thing she wanted from Ethan James was his belief in her project.

And lots and lots of money.

Chapter Two

ETHAN THREW THE EXTRA quilt on the bed before plugging in the space heater and turning it to high. Harper had been right about the cold; the room was freezing. He could feel the wind blowing in around the window frame. It was a wonder snow hadn't drifted in.

This old log lodge was too far gone to be saved. He knew Harper Lindquist wanted money from his company to renovate the lodge, but that wasn't going to happen.

Ethan ran a hand over one of the massive logs forming the outside wall of the bedroom. The place did have a certain north woods rustic charm. But he was only interested in the land the lodge sat on. If Harper accepted his proposal, the building would be torn down, putting it out of its misery. She'd likely be disappointed, but there was no helping it.

He sifted through the clothes Harper had left for him and wondered who they belonged to. Her husband? A lover? He dismissed the thought. The clothes looked slightly old-fashioned, something an older man would have worn. Her father perhaps.

Whoever the clothes belonged to, he was grateful for them. He slipped on the pajamas and robe, leaving his socks on for extra warmth. After finding hangers in the closet, he hung up his suit and dress shirt. He should have known he'd be overdressed for his meeting. Even from her emails, he could tell she was an informal sort of person. He smiled when he thought of her wholesome, fresh scrubbed beauty. Despite the blonde braided pigtails and the rest of the pixie-like exterior, he sensed that a strong, passionate woman lurked beneath the pink chenille robe.

But he wasn't there to speculate on her personality. In the morning, after a good night's sleep, he'd tell her that Hainstock Investments was only interested in her land and had no use for the lodge. End of story.

He turned down the blankets on the bed. He should have made his intention clear in his emails, or maybe he should have talked to her on the phone. But he believed he needed to make his case in person. Now, he wondered if he'd unintentionally misled her into believing Hainstock Investments might be interested in loaning her the money to renovate this old heap. Judging by what she'd said earlier about convincing him of the possibilities of the lodge, he was afraid he had.

He took the toothbrush and paste to the ancient bathroom and brushed his teeth. The bathroom was even colder than his bedroom, his socks no protection against the icy floor tiles. When he was done, he marched back to his room and climbed under the covers. It was freezing. Several minutes passed before he stopped shivering and warmed up sufficiently to relax under the crisp, white sheets.

As he drifted off, a jab of guilt assailed him. Not only had he misled her about why he was there, he hadn't told Harper who he really was. He didn't like deceiving her, but he'd learned from bitter experience that when people knew his true identity, they treated him differently.

He wanted his relationship with her to be completely untainted by the truth.

THE NEXT MORNING, AFTER a quick shower in the frigid bathroom, he dressed in the clothes Harper had given him and went downstairs in search of coffee. He found Harper in the kitchen flipping pancakes. She looked very different this morning. Her long blonde hair hung loose around her shoulders and cascaded down her back in tumbling curls. She turned to him with a smile. The cobalt color of her sweater brought out the vivid blue of her eyes.

"Good morning. I hope you slept well. Were you warm enough?"

"I slept very well. The extra quilt and the heater did the trick."

Despite his guilt, he'd slept like the dead. The quiet of the lodge reminded him of the inn his family once owned in Wisconsin. So did the cold.

She appeared relieved. "I'm glad. Breakfast's almost ready. I hope you like pancakes."

"Love them."

"Good." She put two pancakes on one plate and four on the other, then added a generous portion of bacon to both. She handed him the plates. "Here, you take these and I'll bring the coffee. I thought we'd eat in the dining room this morning."

She placed the coffeepot, a couple of mugs and a pitcher of maple syrup on a tray and headed for a side door. Ethan followed. He was unprepared for the sight that greeted them when they entered the dining room.

A wall of windows overlooked what appeared to be a snow-covered lake. Through the blizzard, he caught glimpses of majestic evergreens on the opposite shore. The storm obscured much of the view, even as it added a wild beauty to the scene. The swirling snow made frothy peaks that changed minute by minute in the howling wind.

He set their plates on one of the tables of the lodge's dining room and stared out the window. "Wow."

"Beautiful, isn't it?" Harper said.

He glanced back at her. "Yes."

Her lips turned up in a satisfied smile. "That's why I brought you here. Why don't we eat before our food gets cold? Coffee?"

"Please."

She filled their mugs, then sat in the chair across from him. "You should see it in the summer. The lake is a hundred and twenty acres of sky blue perfection, and so clear you can see to the bottom. It's a great fishing lake, full of walleye and largemouth bass. Birds of every description sing in the trees, and butterflies and insects fly from wildflower to wildflower. It's a little piece of heaven and I plan to keep it that way. It's eco-friendly all the way."

"So you said in your emails." She'd written that she wanted to use sustainable practices in renovating and maintaining the lodge. Ethan swallowed a delectable piece of pancake and put down his fork. Time to come clean.

"Ms. Lindquist—"

"Please. Call me Harper."

"Harper, before any more time goes by, I have to tell you that my company will not be investing money into your lodge for renovations."

A gamut of emotions – disappointment, confusion, desperation – flitted across her face. She carefully set down her coffee cup. "Then what are you doing here?"

"I have a proposition. I wanted to talk to you about it in person."

She turned her head to stare out the window, her mouth pinched, and her brows drawn together. For an uncomfortable moment, he thought she was going to cry. *Damn it.* He'd been stupid not to tell her the truth upfront. But when she looked at him again, her eyes were dry, her face composed.

"What's your proposition?"

"My company recently purchased Miller's Golf Resort. You said you worked there."

"Yes. I work part-time in the dining room, and I help with the accounting. I know the Millers have been trying to sell the resort for a while. They want to retire."

"Yes. Hainstock Investments made them a good offer and they accepted."

"When did this happen?"

"A few days ago. The final papers haven't been signed yet, so they probably want to wait until that's done before they tell the staff." Ethan paused and sipped his coffee to quench his suddenly dry mouth. "When we saw your ad at the same time we were negotiating with the Millers, it seemed like the perfect opportunity."

One of Harper's eyebrows rose delicately. "The perfect opportunity for what?"

"To expand the resort. Your land is adjacent to Miller's, and you've got a much bigger lake. We'd like to purchase your property so we can build a second golf course and construct vacation condos on the lake. We'd be very careful to use eco-friendly products in all phases of construction." He named a figure for the land he knew was well above the market price.

Harper looked unmoved by the generosity of his offer. "And what about the lodge? What are your plans for it?"

"I'm sorry, but we don't have any plans for the lodge. We'd have to tear it down."

She abruptly pushed back her chair and stood. "You could have saved yourself the trip. If you're going to rip down the lodge and cut down most of the trees for a golf course, I will never sell this property to Hainstock Investments. I'd rather give it away to the nature conservancy I've been working with for the last few years." She threw her napkin on the table. "And since your company is the new owner of Miller's, you can tell them I quit."

He stood as well, lifting his hands in surrender. "Harper, wait. Let's talk about this."

"There's nothing to talk about." Her hands fisted at her sides as she turned to stare out the window at the storm. She gave a sardonic laugh. "I can't even tell you to get the hell off my property."

He wasn't surprised she wanted to get rid of him. "I've got four-wheel drive on my truck. I should be able to make it at least as far as Miller's."

She sighed and shook her head. "You've already been stuck once. The storm's worse now."

That was true. It was lucky he'd only driven into a snow-filled ditch rather than a steep embankment, or perhaps into a tree. He didn't relish going back on the road, but by the set of her shoulders, it was obvious she didn't want him there. Damn, he should have checked the forecast before he left Minneapolis, but he'd been too excited about the possibilities.

"It's best if I go. I don't want to upset you any further."

"No, that's crazy. You don't have to do that."

Harper gripped the back of her chair with both hands and stared at the floor for what seemed like hours, but was probably no more than a minute. Ethan waited, not sure what he should say or do. Then she straightened and lifted her gaze to his, her blue eyes issuing a challenge. She gave him a half smile. "I've got a proposition for *you*."

He blinked at her, confused at this sudden turn. "What do you mean?"

"Stay here until the storm is over and listen to my proposal to renovate the lodge. If I haven't convinced you by the time the blizzard lets up that it's a solid business idea with the potential to make money, then I promise I'll consider your offer to buy my land."

"Are you serious?"

"Very. Can you promise you'll listen objectively to my proposal, without letting any preconceived ideas get in the way?"

What did he have to lose? "I promise to listen objectively and if I'm convinced your ideas have merit, I'll take them back to Hainstock Investments." He folded his arms across his chest. "And what about you? Will you listen objectively to our ideas for your property?"

She took a deep breath and nodded. "I promise I'll listen as long as your ideas take the environmental health of my property into account."

It was certainly better than being thrown out into the snow. He extended his hand. "I believe you have a deal, Ms. Lindquist."

She stretched out her hand to shake his. Her lovely mouth curled into a wide smile, transforming her from merely pretty to exquisite. "Please, call me Harper."

HARPER SPENT A COUPLE of hours giving Ethan the grand tour of the lodge. He wanted to inspect every room, every closet, every little cubby-hole the lodge had to offer. Ethan James was nothing if not thorough.

Thoroughness was one of the attributes of the company he worked for, or so her research had told her. So was honesty. When Ethan had first contacted her, she'd gone to the library in Minnewasta to use the internet to find out all she could about Hainstock Investments. From everything she'd read, the company and its founder were straight shooters. Though they'd been around for less than five years, they were already well known for their ethical investment practices. Knowing that had calmed Harper's fears.

When Ethan got down on his hands and knees, stuck his head under the kitchen sink, and rattled a few pipes, she laughed. "I already told you the kitchen and all the plumbing in the place needs to be redone. I've shown you the estimates from the contractors. What do you think I'm trying to hide from you?"

He pushed himself to his feet. For a big man, he was grace in motion. "I don't think you're trying to hide anything. I just want to check things out for myself." He grabbed a piece of paper towel from the roll on the counter and wiped his hands. "From what I can tell, everything you're saying is pretty accurate. You're not trying to sugarcoat the condition of the place. It's about as bad as you say."

Ouch. It was one thing to know things were bad, but quite another to have bad news confirmed. Harper closed the door of the cabinet beneath the sink. "I want to be upfront about everything. I believe it's best to know the truth. It's the way I like to do business."

He winced, then quickly looked away and fiddled with the faucet. *Odd.*

"Once we start ripping things apart, we'll probably find even more problems. That's what usually happens during a renovation."

A thrill of excitement skittered across her nerve endings. "So, you're going to tell your employer to invest?"

He held up his hand. "I didn't say that. I was speaking in general terms, hypothetically. Don't read anything into it."

Her elation took a nosedive. “Fine. Why don’t we take a break? How about some coffee and cookies?”

“Sure.”

As she measured coffee grounds into the basket, her cell phone rang. A quick check showed her supervisor was on the line. “Hi, Mary. How’s it going?”

“Oh, it’s great, if you like blizzards and empty restaurants. That’s why I’m calling. There’s no point in you coming to work. Even if you could make it through the snow drifts, there’s no customers here to serve anyway.”

Harper frowned. She was supposed to start work at Miller’s at three o’clock, and she counted on her paycheck as a waitress to supplement her income. “You sure? I could take the snowmobile. It’s not far.”

“No, please don’t do that!” Mary said, the alarm in her voice loud and clear. “I’d be worried sick about you. And really, there’s no point. The place is dead. No one’s going to drive out here in a blizzard. I promise I’ll make it up to you later with extra shifts.”

“What about tomorrow? I’m scheduled for the dinner shift again.”

“We’ll have to see what the weather’s like tomorrow and take it from there.”

Harper did a quick mental calculation of her current bank balance, knowing it was fast depleting. Most of her income came from doing the books for several small businesses in the area, including Miller’s. But the money required to keep the lights on and the heat running in the lodge meant she needed the extra work.

“I’ll talk to you tomorrow. Bye, Mary.”

"Bye. Stay warm."

She ended the call and stuck her phone back into the pocket of her jeans before putting another scoop of coffee into the basket. As soon as Ethan left, she'd turn the heat down. It cost a fortune to heat the old place, but she needed to keep the furnace working or run the risk of letting the pipes freeze. And frozen pipes tended to burst, causing damage that was far more expensive than a mere heating bill. If that happened, she might as well lock the doors and walk away.

Panic coursed through her veins at the thought. If she couldn't convince Ethan and his company to sink money into the lodge, it was game over. The roof couldn't withstand the spring rains, and she couldn't afford a new one. She'd have no alternative but to sell to Hainstock Investments or donate the land to the nature conservancy. Either way, the lodge would be history.

She'd be letting her grandfather down. This place had meant everything to him. And where would she go?

"Harper? Is everything okay?"

Ethan's hand on her shoulder brought her back to the present. She was so tired of handling everything on her own. Her sisters tried to understand, but they didn't have the same attachment to the lodge that she did. And they were far away. She was so tired of being alone.

For one wild moment, she wanted to fling herself into his arms and take comfort there. Instead, she made herself stand tall. She had no choice but to see this venture through to its conclusion. Alone.

Harper swallowed back the tears that were dangerously close to the surface. "Yes, everything's fine. That was my boss at Miller's. I was supposed to work in the restaurant today, but with the blizzard, there's no business. So I have the day off."

His lips quirked in a grin. "I thought you quit."

She couldn't help but laugh, and some of her tension eased away. "I changed my mind."

"You don't sound particularly overjoyed about having the day off."

"Well, I could always use the money." She shrugged, trying to make light of the situation for his benefit. "Who couldn't?"

"Harper, what would happen if my boss decides not to put money into the lodge? What if he decides Hainstock really only wants the land?"

Was he telling her it was hopeless? She tried not to let her disappointment show. Squaring her shoulders, she looked him in the eye. "Then I'd have to leave. Whether I sell to you or donate the land, the lodge would be torn down or fall down on its own. It would be the end of everything my grandfather built here, everything he believed in."

He nodded, but the expression in his dark eyes didn't give any indication of which way he was leaning. "Come on, let's finish making coffee and take it into the lounge. Maybe it's warmer in there."

"Why don't you go ahead? I'll bring the coffee when it's ready." She needed a moment to compose herself.

"Okay." He walked across the kitchen, then turned back to her. "Whatever happens, you're going to be okay. I've known you for less than a day and I already know you're a strong person. You'll find your way."

At that moment, Harper didn't feel the least bit strong. But somehow it helped knowing Ethan believed she was.

This time her smile was genuine. "Thank you."

Chapter Three

ETHAN WATCHED HARPER expertly stack wood in the lounge's fireplace, a smaller replica of the one in the dining room. Using kindling as a starter, she soon had the fire blazing. He had never much cared for wood burning fireplaces because of the smoke and ash, but this one was very welcome as it threw blessed warmth into the room. As she busied herself pouring coffee from a carafe, he wandered around the lounge. It was a small, cozy room at the front of the building that had probably served as the lodge's bar at one time, judging from the wooden counter on the opposite side of the room and the glass shelves on the wall behind it. There were a couple of old sofas and upholstered chairs placed strategically in front of the fireplace.

Harper handed him a coffee cup, then shut the glass-paned French doors leading into the lounge, trapping some of the heat. Finally, he was able to peel off one of the two flannel shirts he was wearing. He'd needed the warmth of both of them, as well as the T-shirt, until now.

He sat down in one of the upholstered chairs and set his coffee cup on the side table next to it. "Thanks for the loan of the clothes, by the way. They fit pretty good, and they're a hell of lot warmer than my own clothes."

"You're welcome." Harper sat in the armchair next to his. "They belonged to my grandfather. He was tall, like you. After he died, I didn't have the heart to donate all his clothes."

"I'm sorry. When did he die?"

"About a year and a half ago, but he'd been sick for some time. He was never really the same after my grandmother died ten years ago. He lost interest in the business, and bookings started to slide. I tried to convince him to modernize so we could attract more than just die-hard fishers to the lodge, but he wouldn't budge. Without Grandma, he didn't care anymore. Bookings have dwindled to a few of Grampa's most loyal clients in the summer."

"Did you always live with your grandparents?"

Some emotion he couldn't name flashed in her eyes. "Since I was ten. My parents drowned out there on the lake, and my sisters and I came to live with them."

"I'm sorry."

Her smile was tinged with sadness. "Don't be. For the most part, we had happy childhoods here. But I always wondered what might have been if our parents had lived."

Ethan fought the urge to gather her in his arms and hold her tight. She shouldn't have to be alone this way.

Instead, he wrapped his hands around his coffee cup to keep from reaching for her. The impulse to protect her surprised him. Was it her sad history that affected him so profoundly or was it something about Harper herself? "How many sisters do you have?"

Her smile this time was much more relaxed. "Two. Scarlet is thirty, two years younger than me. She lives in

Chicago and works for a PR firm. She's some kind of marketing genius, or so she tells me. Maggie is the baby of the family. She's twenty-four and is a marvel in the kitchen. She graduated from cooking school a couple of years ago, and she's worked in restaurants in Minneapolis since then."

"And you stayed here."

"It's where I want to be."

"Do your sisters help with the expenses of running the lodge, like the heating and maintenance?"

"No. They've got their own lives to live."

That surprised him. "Aren't they part owners of the lodge as well? I'm sure I read that in your proposal."

"Yes, they are. When Grampa died, he willed the lodge equally to the three of us. I think he was hoping we'd work together to run the place. But Scarlet and Maggie have their own dreams. They've offered to help with expenses from time to time, but I've refused. The lodge is my responsibility."

He thought about arguing with her. Logically, if her sisters were equal owners of the lodge, they should share equally in the expenses. Instead, Harper bore the weight of the entire burden. It made no sense.

But from the stubborn set of her chin, she didn't want to hear his logic. She reminded him of his sister, Lydia. As the oldest, she, too, had taken on far more than her fair share of responsibility for the family.

It wasn't his place to shine a critical light on Harper's family. Lord knew his family had enough problems of its own.

But it bothered him that she believed she had to do everything without assistance.

Time to change the subject. "Are your sisters married? Any kids?"

"No, we're all single, no kids. Scarlet's been engaged a couple of times, but both times she got cold feet at the last minute and called off the weddings. And as far as I know, Maggie has never had a serious boyfriend. At least no one she's introduced to me. What about you? Do you have someone significant in your life? What about kids, brothers and sisters?"

He tried very hard to forget about Bree, his former girlfriend, but she lingered in his memory like a bad smell. "No significant other. I've got an older brother and sister, which makes me the baby of the family. I'm the same age as you, thirty-two. I don't have any kids, but I've got two nieces and one nephew. My sister's daughter and son are sixteen and twenty-one respectively, but my brother's little girl is a preschooler. I still get to spoil her."

"You're lucky." She sounded wistful, but then she tilted her head and gave him a grin, as if pushing aside the emotion. "Little known fact about the Lindquist sisters. Our mother named us after characters from books set in the South, or in my case, a famous Southern writer, Harper Lee. Scarlet's name came from Scarlet O'Hara from *Gone With the Wind,* of course. My baby sister Margaret Catherine was named after Maggie Cat in *Cat on a Hot Tin Roof.*"

"Kind of unusual for a family from Minnesota."

"That was our mother. She was one of a kind."

Though she smiled, her sadness touched him once more. He'd lost his mother as a young man and that had been hard enough. He couldn't imagine being orphaned at ten.

"Your grandparents did a good job of raising the three of you. You sound very proud of your sisters."

"I am. I just wish..." Her voice trailed off and she looked away.

"What do you wish, Harper?"

She turned back to him, the wistful expression evident in her blue eyes once more. "I wish they lived closer. I wish I could pop over to see them anytime I wanted to. And when I'm really dreaming big, I wish the three of us could work together here at the lodge to make it the success I know it could be."

"That's a nice wish."

She shrugged. "Pie in the sky. If I told Scarlet what I just told you, she'd tell me to suck it up and quit dreaming."

Ethan chuckled, amused by her. "She sounds like my brother."

"Oh, yeah?" She tucked her legs beneath her and settled back against the cushions of the armchair. "Tell me about him."

Ethan shifted uncomfortably, unsure how much to disclose. "Not much to tell. He's two years older than me and like I said, he has a daughter who'll be turning five soon. He works as a contractor and a carpenter, he's opinionated and brash, and tends to be overprotective of his family. Especially me. For some reason, he hasn't figured out that I'm not twelve anymore."

The amusement in Harper's laughter warmed his soul like the fire warmed the room. "Sounds like a man after my own heart. I know exactly how he feels. It's hard for me not to be overprotective, too."

He feigned annoyance. "You don't know what it's like being the youngest in the family. And it's not only my brother. My sister Lydia is twelve years older than I am. Growing up, it was like having two mothers."

"Are your parents still alive?"

"No, they're gone now. Mom died of breast cancer when I was eighteen, and Dad died seven years ago."

"I'm sorry."

"Yeah, so am I." He missed his mother every day. His father's passing had been a relief. The old man had been a hard person to love.

"Where did you grow up?"

"In northern Wisconsin. My parents owned a small inn in a resort village."

Harper leaned forward, her gaze intent. "Is that why this place interested you?"

"Perhaps initially. But like I said, I'm only willing to invest money if it makes financial sense."

She tilted her head. "You mean investing money on behalf of your employer, don't you?"

Crap. Way to go, idiot. "Yes, of course. But the company relies on me to make a sound recommendation based on facts and figures. I take that very seriously." He needed to turn the conversation back to her before he slipped again and revealed more than he intended. "How long has the lodge been in your family?"

"Over seventy years." Thankfully, she settled back into the chair and a smile lit her eyes. "My grandfather's family farmed west of here and when his father, my great-grandfather, returned home from World War Two, he used the G.I. Bill to purchase this property. His father was furious because he wanted him to use the opportunity to buy some good farmland. But great-grandfather didn't want to be a farmer. He wanted to hunt in the woods and fish in the lake, and live a quiet life. He named the lake after the solace he found here and brought his wife and his five-year-old son, my grandfather, here to live. He made a modest income guiding other fishers and hunters. My grandfather said his father had been a POW during the war, and he needed the solitude and peace."

"Did your great-grandfather build the lodge?"

"Yes. Grampa made some additions and modifications, but essentially it's the same building my great-grandfather built in the fifties."

No wonder Harper was fighting so hard for the lodge. Three generations of her family were attached to the land, the lake, and the building. He fervently hoped her plans for the lodge proved economically feasible.

The thought stunned him. Twenty-four hours ago he was sure he'd tear down the building and now he *wanted* Harper to convince him to save it?

She set her coffee cup on a side table. "Would you like more coffee, or are you ready to look at the blueprints and estimates for the renovations I've had drawn up?"

He got to his feet. "I'm ready."

"Brace yourself," she said with a rueful smile. "Those estimates aren't for the faint of heart. The costs are pretty steep."

Ethan grinned. "Bring it on."

MUCH TO HARPER'S RELIEF, Ethan didn't seem fazed by the staggering estimates she'd secured for the renovations. Not like she'd been. To her everlasting shame, she'd actually wept in front of the plumbing contractor when he told her how much it would cost to fit each of the ten guest rooms on the second floor with its own bathroom. The expense still overwhelmed her.

She watched as Ethan unrolled the blueprints on one of the dining room tables and thoroughly examined them. She'd had an architect draw up blueprints for the renovation of the lodge, using the money she'd made by selling the last pieces of her father's rare stamp collection to pay for it. The stamps had been collected by her great-grandfather, added to by her grandfather, and passed to her father when he was twenty-one. Guilt for selling the collection still plagued her. They'd been the last physical link she and her sisters had to him.

For the hundredth time, she brushed aside the guilt. She couldn't afford to be sentimental. The stamp collection had allowed her to send her sisters to school and helped her with her grandfather's care when he was sick. Now, they were providing a future for the lodge.

At least she hoped they were. She still had to convince Ethan the lodge was a sure bet.

"What do you think?" she asked tentatively.

Ethan straightened. "The estimates to get this place up and running again are enormous. But it's nothing I didn't expect."

"So no surprises. That's good, right?"

He shrugged. "Depends how you look at it. It's not the costs so much as the future income potential of the lodge that concerns me. There's no point sinking money into the place if we can't make money in the future. I'm worried the lodge is too small. There's only ten rooms upstairs, and if you put in bathrooms, you're going to lose at least two bedrooms."

Harper's excitement dimmed, but she refused to give up. "Being a small, boutique hotel is the whole point. The other resorts in the area are doing well, and there's no reason to believe a revamped Solace Lake Lodge couldn't be profitable, too. We've got a bigger lake and a better beach than many of the other resorts."

"Miller's Golf Resort has dozens of rooms."

She was prepared for his counter arguments. "Sure, but they cater to an entirely different kind of clientele. They host golfers in the summer and snowmobilers in the winter. If we emphasize the eco-friendly nature of this place, we'll attract a whole new crowd."

"I suppose it's possible."

"I *know* it's possible," Harper said, warming to her subject. Too anxious to sit any longer, she got to her feet, nervously tugging on the cuff of her shirt. "We can cater to couples who want a romantic getaway, and to people wanting a chance to commune with nature. Eventually, I'd like to build a spa where clients can have a massage or take a sauna. Or maybe even hire estheticians to give facials and other beauty treatments. The problem with the lodge in my grandfather's day was that it was essentially a man's kind of place. We rarely had women staying here. And only the hardiest of ice fishers ever turned up in the winter."

The flicker of interest she saw in Ethan's eyes told her he was really listening to her ideas. "I agree. The only way a place like this can survive is if it's a year-round resort."

"Yes, exactly. We can create cross-country ski trails through the forest and clear some of the snow from the lake for a skating rink. I know horse drawn sleigh rides are popular in the winter at the other resorts. There's a guy who lives about ten miles from here who runs dog sled teams, and he said he'd be interested in partnering with us." With one finger, she tapped the binder containing all her cost estimates and ideas. "I've detailed all my plans in here."

He opened the binder and began leafing through the pages, his attention lingering for a moment on the information she'd collected about the different species of birds found on the property. "I'll consider all your ideas carefully."

She blinked, surprised at being taken seriously for a change. Even her sisters didn't truly believe the lodge could be saved. That's why she hadn't told them about making contact with Hainstock Investments. Better to ask forgiveness than beg for permission. "Thank you."

He gave her a brief, distracted nod, before lifting another set of blueprints, the ones belonging to her new luxury cottages. "If I understand correctly, you've already built two of these cottages. Is that right?"

She pointed out the window. "Yes. See out there, across the lake? There have always been cottages in the woods about a quarter mile from the lodge. But they're old and uninsulated, and not in very good shape. Last spring, I tore down two of them and built two winterized cottages with hot tubs and every modern convenience. I'd hoped they'd appeal to people who wanted a wilderness experience without losing their Wi-Fi connection. That is, whenever I actually get connected to the Internet."

He followed her gaze through the swirling snow. "And? Were they popular?"

"Not as popular as I'd hoped. But I'm convinced that was because I didn't have the money to advertise. Scarlet helped me place a couple of ads on radio stations around the state, but it wasn't enough."

She'd taken a gamble and lost. Instead of using the last of her cash reserves to repair the crumbling roof, she'd built the two luxury cottages in the hope they'd attract enough business to allow her to fix the roof. They hadn't.

Ethan crossed his arms over his chest. "But despite their inability to draw interest, you want to build more high-end cottages? Isn't that throwing good money after bad?"

Harper swallowed her nervousness, afraid he suspected her plan was nothing more than a pipe dream. She couldn't lose him now, not when he was so close to being on her side. Lifting her chin, she gave him a confident smile. "I don't believe so. Like you said, we'll need the extra capacity for guests. And I think some guests will prefer the privacy and convenience that a self-contained cottage can provide."

After a moment of hesitation, he nodded. "Okay, I'll go along with you there."

Harper breathed a sigh of relief when he resumed flipping through the pages of the binder. Maybe she still had a chance to win him over, however tenuous.

Ethan stopped at a section in the binder regarding the lodge's restaurant. "You want to create a restaurant in the lodge that uses organic and locally sourced products as much as possible. Wouldn't that also add to the costs?"

"It might, but it would also set our restaurant apart from others in the area."

She reached over to turn to the next page in the binder and their fingers touched, sending a spark of awareness up her arm. Harper's breath caught at the sensation. But when she dared a look at Ethan, he appeared unaffected by the bolt of lightning that had struck her. Stepping back, she cleared her throat before resuming her sales pitch, her heart racing.

"I've detailed information about restaurants in the area along with their menus in this section. To be honest, much of the local fare runs toward the fast-food end of the spectrum. Serving organic, locally sourced food also goes along nicely with the eco-friendly and sustainable vibe I want to create. But mainly, I want people to come to this resort because they've heard about the fabulous meals we serve."

Ethan nodded, but said nothing further. She couldn't tell whether he was excited about her plans or if he was simply humoring her. He was very good at concealing his thoughts.

She cleared her throat once again. "There's something else I want to discuss with you. If we decide to go into partnership with your company, my sisters and I must retain a majority ownership in the lodge. I won't give up more than a forty-nine percent interest. We need to control what happens to the lodge."

Ethan's brows lifted. He straightened to his full height and stepped away from the table. "Hainstock Investments would have to put a lot of capital at risk to renovate the lodge. We would need to protect our investment."

"My sisters and I are taking a big chance, too. If the project fails and my sisters and I have to sell our fifty-one percent to you, you'd still have the land. But it won't fail. Even at forty-nine percent ownership, it's still a sound investment for you." She gently pushed the binder toward him.

"My employer may not feel that way."

She stood her ground. "I'm sorry, Ethan, but that's my bottom line. I did lay out my terms in my proposal to you."

"Yes, you did, but we assumed the terms would be negotiable."

"You know what they say about assumptions." Harper took a deep breath. She was dead serious. She wouldn't give up complete control and let the lodge be turned into something she didn't recognize or want. It would be far less painful to sell the whole thing quickly and walk away.

Ethan's lips twitched into a smile. "I believe it's something about being an ass."

She released the breath she'd been holding. "Something like that."

"I can't promise anything, but I'll make your wishes known to Mr. Hainstock."

She almost fainted in relief. Some tough businesswoman she was. "Thank you."

A strong gust of wind howled down the chimney, making Harper shiver. Snow slammed against the windows of the dining room. "I think the storm is getting worse. I hate to tell you this, Ethan, but I don't think you're going to be able to leave here today."

"No, it doesn't look like it."

"You're in luck. It just so happens I have another vacancy. Or ten. And I've got at least another day to convince you the lodge is a sure bet."

He gave her an amused expression. "You don't give up, do you?"

"No, I don't."

He chuckled and shook his head. Harper was beginning to enjoy the way his lips turned up at the corners when he smiled, as if he knew a secret he wasn't sharing with anyone but her. He had a beautiful mouth, with beautifully shaped lips that looked soft and inviting. She wondered how they'd feel pressed against hers...

"I'm sorry to impose on you this way."

It took a minute to register what he was saying. She blinked a couple of times to clear her wayward thoughts.

"It's no imposition. Unless, of course, we run out of food. Then I'll have to send you out on the lake with an ice auger and a fishing line to catch our supper. Just warning you."

"Duly noted." His dark brown eyes shone with humor. "Let's hope it doesn't come to that."

"Lucky for you, I laid in a supply of canned soup and microwave popcorn before the storm. That should sustain us for days."

"Sounds...delectable."

Harper laughed at the look of dismay on his face. Even if the blizzard abated tomorrow, he wouldn't be able to leave right away. It might take a day or two for the snowplows to clear the roads.

Strangely, she was no longer worried about being isolated at the lodge with him. She didn't know why, but she felt safe with Ethan. In fact, she didn't care if it took a week for the snowplows to arrive.

"WHO HAS MOVIES ON VHS tape anymore?"

Harper lanced Ethan with an indignant glare as she loaded the movie into the old machine. "Someone who appreciates old technology and can't afford a new DVD player. Besides, it still works and I have all these old VHS movies. I can't throw them out."

Ethan rolled his eyes. "Wouldn't you like to watch a movie that was made after 1995?"

She sat beside him on the sofa and turned to him with laughing eyes. "I appreciate the classics."

"Oh, yes, the eighties were the golden years."

Harper laughed, picked up a bowl of popcorn from the coffee table, and threw a couple of fluffy white kernels at him. "Hush up. *Ferris Bueller's Day Off* is about to start."

"I'll give you the Reader's Digest version. He skips school."

"Shhh."

They watched the movie, though Ethan spent more time watching Harper than he did a young Matthew Broderick. After eating a few handfuls of popcorn, then passing the bowl to him, she picked up a basket filled with yarn sitting next to the sofa and began to knit something in baby blue. Her knitting needles clicked rhythmically as she watched the movie. She rarely glanced at her hands, seemingly knitting by remote control. He was content for the moment to munch on popcorn and watch her.

When the movie ended, Harper hit rewind on the remote. "Would you like to watch something else?"

"Why don't we talk for a while?"

"All right. What would you like to talk about?"

You. He gestured to the blue yarn on her knitting needles. "What are you making?"

"It's a baby shower gift for a friend who's having a boy." She held it up for him to see. "It's a sweater, or at least it will be."

He could see it taking shape. Exquisitely tiny stitches lined up in perfect, even rows along the body and the sleeves of the miniature sweater. "Cute. You're very talented."

"Thank you. I enjoy making things." She reached into her basket. "I've already finished the matching hat. I hope the kid's head isn't too big for it."

She passed the diminutive hat to him. The soft baby blue yarn was like silk in his hands. Like the sweater, the hat's stitching was perfect and even. The tiny rosettes that attached the two blue satin ribbons that would tie under the baby's chin were finished with delicate care.

He handed it back to her. "It's beautiful. I'm sure your friend will treasure it."

"Thank you." With a smile, she took the hat from him and gently placed it back in her basket.

"What was it like growing up here?"

Her needles began to click once more, her attention focused on her task. "It was fun. In the summer we had a whole lake to swim and boat in, and in the winter we had a gigantic skating rink. We're only about ten miles from Minnewasta and about thirty from Brainerd, so we weren't too far from civilization."

"Did your sisters love it here as much as you did?"

Though she gave a negligent shrug, there was no mistaking the regret in her voice. "As children they did. But as they grew older, they wanted something more."

"And you? What did you want?"

She put down her knitting and stretched out her arms to encompass the room. "All I ever wanted was this."

Fascinating. Though she'd put together a solid business plan for the lodge, the bottom line for Harper was completely emotional. Ethan had an overwhelming desire to make her dreams come true.

But he couldn't give money to every pretty girl who asked for it. He'd found that out the hard way. If he said yes to her project, it had to make complete financial sense.

Ethan was brought up short by that thought. Was he seriously considering it?

He shook his head, forcing his thoughts back to the present. "Have you ever lived away from the lodge?"

"Yes. When I finished high school, I moved to Minneapolis for a few years to go to college and get an accounting degree. My grandfather insisted that I learn a trade."

"He sounds like a wise man." Perhaps he'd been aware that the lodge was nearing the end of its life and wanted Harper to be prepared.

She picked up her knitting once more. "He was. I thought accounting would be good, practical knowledge for running the lodge, but it's turned into my main source of income the last few years. In addition to working in the dining room at Miller's Resort, I help with the books there. I also do the books for a number of small businesses in Minnewasta and area."

"So, if things don't work out with the lodge, you have something to fall back on."

Her needles abruptly stopped clicking. She looked up and met his gaze. "Yes, I suppose. But bookkeeping isn't a passion for me. It's simply a skill. And I hated living in the city. This is where I want to be."

"Things don't always work out the way we want them to."

Pain flashed in her eyes before she looked away and began knitting once more. "No, they don't."

He hated to cause her any distress, but she needed to be prepared for bad news. As much as he liked Harper, if the lodge didn't have the potential to make money, there would be no deal. Period.

He wished he could tell her the truth. That the decision to invest was completely his. That he was Ethan James

Hainstock, owner of Hainstock Investments and head of the Hainstock Foundation. With the help of his sister Lydia, a financial planner, and her husband Graham, a certified public accountant, he'd formed both organizations five years ago when he'd won over a hundred and seventy-five million dollars in one of the biggest lottery wins in Minnesota history. It had been the best thing that had ever happened to him. And the worst.

Since then, he'd been inundated with requests for cash from both worthy causes and nefarious schemers. Some of the most egregious attempts to separate him from his money had come from those he thought he could trust the most.

Now, anyone wanting to get close to his money, or him, would have to work hard to win his trust.

Chapter Four

THE NEXT MORNING HARPER hunted through the collection of winter clothing at the lodge until she found a snowmobile suit big enough to fit Ethan's tall frame, eager for him to experience more of her property. After they both dressed in warm boots and hats and gloves, she led the way to the garage. Time for a little road trip, or in this case, a little off-road trip.

She tugged on the handle of the overhead door once, then twice, with no result. What she'd give for an automatic opener that would lift the door with a push of a button. The stupid door kept slipping off its tracks, which made using the garage difficult. Most of the time she kept her truck outside because it was too hard to open and close the door.

Bracing her feet, she gripped the door handle one more time and pulled as hard as she could. She was rewarded with the squealing sound of metal rubbing against metal as the door began to lift.

Ethan grabbed the bottom of the door and pushed it up the rest of the way. "I think you need a new garage door."

"I've needed a new garage door for about ten years."

The open garage door revealed her pride and joy, two snowmobiles. They were far from new, but regular maintenance and loving care kept them humming along happily. Harper handed Ethan one of the extra helmets she kept on the shelf at the back of the garage. "Wanna go for a little spin around the property?"

He grinned like a kid ready for an adventure. "Absolutely."

She grinned back. "Good. I'll drive."

He pulled the helmet onto his head and hopped on the back of the sled. Harper started her machine and drove it out of the garage and into the yard before heading toward the lake. The wind had calmed, but it still held enough fury to whip snow against their face shields as they zipped across the frozen lake. She tried not to be distracted in her mission by the closeness of his body tucked in behind her on the machine. But she couldn't help but be aware of him, especially when he lightly grasped her waist as they took a steep curve.

After crossing the lake, they drove through the forest, the shelter of the trees giving some much-needed protection from the wind. Following a path she'd known since childhood, Harper guided the snowmobile up a steep embankment and through deep snow toward the two cottages she'd built the previous summer. To her, the cottages were modern and luxurious, but she wasn't sure if Ethan would agree. Simply looking at his clothes, it was obvious he had more experience with luxury and wealth than she did.

Harper pulled up in front of one of the cottages and cut the engine. Nerves made her stomach flutter uneasily. Ethan got off the snowmobile and removed his helmet.

"Pretty spot," he remarked, looking down toward the lake.

Harper removed her own helmet. The two cottages sat on a hill overlooking the lake, affording a panoramic view. "Aside from the view from the lodge, this is the best aspect on the property."

"Yeah, I imagine it is."

When Ethan turned toward the cottage, Harper turned as well, following his gaze. She hoped he saw the beauty and the potential she did when she came up here.

"Like I told you, there were a couple of old cottages here. I had these new ones built on the same spots. The space between the cottages, and the trees between them, provide complete privacy. Grampa once told me he'd chosen this spot because he wanted visitors to feel like they were the only people on the planet when they visited. Like his father, he was a person who valued solitude."

Childhood memories flooded back, overtaking her. How her grandfather had loved this place. And how she'd loved him.

Harper swallowed, suddenly aware that Ethan was staring at her. She blinked a couple of times before finding her voice. "I'll show you the cottage."

She led him through the heavy snow and up the stairs to a spacious front veranda currently covered in more than a foot of snow.

"In the mornings, this is a lovely spot to drink a cup of coffee and listen to the birds. In the evenings, guests have a wonderful sunset view." Harper hoped he could see the picture she was trying to paint. "Last summer, I set up this veranda with a couple of Adirondack chairs and a small table for snacks and drinks."

"Nice."

"This is also a very sunny spot." She pointed to the steeply sloped roof. "Right now the cottages are powered by the regular electrical grid, but I'm hoping in the future we can retrofit them for solar. This roof catches the sun most of the day and is steep enough that the snow slides off easily. It's the reason I choose this design."

He nodded in acknowledgement. She waited for him to say more and when he didn't, she slipped off her heavy gloves and pulled the key from her pocket. "Why don't we go inside and take a look?"

Not waiting for an answer, she used her foot to push away some of the snow from in front of the door and then unlocked it. Ethan followed her in, closing the door behind him and removing his boots on the rug. She did the same, trying to ignore the butterflies dancing in her stomach.

"This cottage has two bedrooms, with an open concept kitchen and great room, and a four-piece bath. The vaulted ceiling gives a feeling of space even though the footprint is actually quite compact. The kitchen is fully outfitted with dishes and appliances, and the bedrooms and bath come with linens, towels and extra blankets and pillows." She pointed to the sofa. "The sofa pulls out into a bed, so the cabin can sleep six. There's enough room for families to be comfortable, but couples wanting a romantic getaway will still find it cozy. The cottage next door is exactly the same." Whether Ethan appreciated the cottage or not, she was damn proud of what she'd accomplished.

She'd spared no expense in kitting out the two cabins. The counters in both the kitchen and bathroom were granite, each with a marble backsplash, and the wood-burning fireplace in the great room was tiled in slate. The furniture was chosen for its style as well as its durability, which meant it had cost more than she'd wanted to spend, though she'd been assured it would hold up well over several seasons of use. She was hopeless at decorating, so she'd made a deal with the owner of the furniture store; Harper would do her taxes for the next two years in exchange for the owner's help in selecting the furniture and all the decorating bits and bobs. Harper had been pleased with the outcome.

She hoped the furniture would have a chance to prove its worth. A quick glance at Ethan gave her no clue what he was thinking. She forged ahead.

After showing Ethan the bedrooms and bathroom, she pointed to the sliding glass doors next to the fireplace, hoping she could finally get a reaction out of him with her favorite part of the cabin. She smiled nervously. "I think you're really going to like this."

She opened the curtains, drawing them back with a flourish, to reveal a large snow-covered deck. "There's too much snow to go out on the deck right now, but you can see how big it is." She pointed to her right. "That big lump over there under the snow is actually a hot tub. In summer, there's plenty of room for a dining table, a grill, and a couple of lounge chairs on the other end. The best thing about this deck is that it's completely concealed by the trees and bushes. Guests can commune with nature *au natural,* if they're so inclined, without worrying about prying eyes."

Ethan's lips quirked in a smile. "I'm sure they'll appreciate the privacy."

"My guests last summer said the deck and the hot tub were their favorite features."

"The cottage is lovely. It's beautifully decorated, and I think it's got everything a guest could need."

Harper frowned, her stomach clenching. "I sense a 'but' coming on."

"It's very generic. There's nothing that screams 'only available at Solace Lake Lodge'. You could probably find this same cabin at a hundred different lakes in Minnesota."

She winced and turned away. Unable to afford a truly one-of-a-kind design created specifically for this spot, she'd purchased the architectural plans online. He was probably right in saying this exact same cottage could be found anywhere.

She would not shrink from her duty to save the lodge. She squared her shoulders. "Of course I would have preferred a unique design for each cottage, something that conforms to the exact terrain of each spot. That's where your investment comes in."

"What did your guests do here last summer?" He opened a couple of cupboards and pulled out one of the drawers.

"Most of them hung out on the beach or fished in the lake. I have a couple of boats I let them use. My guests came here for the serenity they couldn't get in the rest of their lives. But it's not enough. Some guests are going to want something more active or interesting to do. I believe that to make this place truly unique, there's going to have to be unique things to do."

"Like what?"

The skeptical note in his voice put another knot in her stomach, but she kept talking. "If we truly want to cater to the eco-friendly crowd, we need to offer bird watching excursions, nature hikes, guided fishing trips, and interesting classes, like lessons on making compost."

Ethan's eyebrows lifted. "Making compost? Seriously?"

Harper kept her gaze level with his. "What I'm trying to illustrate is that in addition to facilities, we also need programs and activities."

She sat on one of the stools at the kitchen island. If she was going to advertise Solace Lake Lodge as an eco-friendly resort, then they had to play the part. But it would require money. "I'd have to hire knowledgeable staff, buy equipment."

He folded his arms across his chest and leaned against the counter next to the sink. "Yes, that's true."

"I've been reading up on eco-friendly tennis courts that use recycled and sustainable materials rather than petroleum products. They're nicely cushioned and they even last longer."

"Sounds perfect."

"Sounds expensive." Harper drummed her fingers on the granite counter. She inhaled deeply. *In for a penny, in for a pound.* "This is why the investment from Hainstock is so important. I don't have the money or the expertise to do any of this on my own."

Ethan nodded. "I know."

"There's so much potential to make the lodge totally different from places like Miller's Golf Resort. Not everyone wants to golf. I'm sure there's a market for what I want to build, but I need help."

He nodded again but said nothing more. Harper tamped down her frustration. She wanted him to love this project as much as she did, to be as excited about it as she was. His lack of response made her want to scream. But he wasn't going to show his cards until he was ready. Until then, she'd keep pushing, selling.

Did she want him to share her enthusiasm simply because of the money, or was her motive more personal? An investment by Hainstock would mean Ethan would remain in her life, at least for a while.

Harper shook her head to refocus. She'd known the man for less than two days. "Let's go back to the lodge. It's time for lunch."

With another nod, Ethan put on his boots and followed her outside to the snowmobile. Harper headed back to the lodge, detouring onto the highway to see if it was drivable. With snowdrifts as high as five feet in some places, it was clear that it wasn't.

Good. She'd have more time convince Ethan that Solace Lake Lodge and Hainstock Investments were a perfect match.

And if she was honest, she'd admit she wasn't ready for him to leave.

AFTER DINNER THAT EVENING, Harper brought a tray with a pot of tea and a plate of cookies into the lounge. Ethan helped himself to one of the chocolate cookies. The delectable combination of fudgy dark chocolate and white chocolate chunks melted in his mouth. "Mmm. The chef at Miller's has outdone herself once again."

Harper poured the tea. "I'll have you know I made these cookies myself."

"Really?"

"You don't have to sound so shocked. I do have some cooking skills. My grandmother taught me to bake cookies."

"Did she teach you to knit, too?"

Harper set her teacup on the table next to the sofa and tucked her legs beneath her. "Yes. She insisted I learn a few feminine skills like baking cookies and knitting. When I first came here to live, I spent a lot time with my grandfather learning to take apart outboard motors and snowmobiles. I think she was afraid I'd turn into a mechanic. The thought horrified her."

Ethan took a sip of the hot tea. Harper didn't look like any mechanic he knew. Not with her long blonde hair falling in waves over her shoulders and her delicate fingers with their pink enamelled nails daintily picking up her teacup. "Did she have anything to worry about?"

"I seriously considered small engine mechanics as a career at one point, but I was still enough of a girl that I didn't like the idea of permanent grease stains under my nails. These days when I do engine work, I use latex gloves to keep my hands clean. My grandfather would laugh at me, but Grandma would approve." She frowned as she took another sip of tea. "It wasn't often she approved of anything I did."

He wondered about that statement but decided to leave it alone, not wanting to upset her. "You actually work on outboard motors?"

"I can do routine maintenance stuff like changing oil, checking spark plugs, and winterizing. If there's anything more complex, I have to talk to a real mechanic."

Despite her humility, Ethan was impressed. She fascinated him – a woman who could knit a delicate bonnet for a newborn while changing the oil on a two-stroke engine. "Your grandfather must have been proud of you."

She flashed him a self-deprecating smile. "I was the grandson he never had."

"I'm sure he didn't think of you as a boy." Ethan certainly didn't. Tonight, with her blue eyes watching him with feminine interest, he couldn't think of her as anything but a beautiful, desirable woman.

He shifted uncomfortably in his chair. He needed to reign in thoughts like that.

"Maybe not. I remember my mother telling me that he'd tried to interest her in the running of the lodge and in small engine maintenance, but it wasn't her thing."

"What was her thing?"

"Mom loved to travel. My father took her to Paris for their honeymoon, and she raved about it. She promised to take me one day, but she died before it could happen. I've never made it to Paris, but I've always wanted to go. To see what made it so special for her."

She took a sip of her tea, her gaze unfocused as if lost in memories. "She was an interior designer. I remember how beautiful she made our house in Minneapolis. She loved to sew things like pillows and curtains, and she made Scarlet and me several dresses. Drove me crazy because I didn't want to be dressed the same way as my little sister. I don't think she ever made matching outfits for all three of us. Maggie was too young when she died, not even two."

"It must have been tough to grow up without her, without both of your parents."

"Yeah, it was. Our grandparents tried their best, but it wasn't the same."

"I'm sorry."

"Thanks, but it's ancient history. I survived." She bit her lip. "Out of the three of us, I think Scarlet took their deaths the hardest. I sometimes think she still hasn't recovered."

He cocked his head to look at her more closely, alerted by the note of sadness he heard in her voice. "What do you mean?"

"She comes across as this tough dynamo, this hard-nosed business person, but inside that independent façade there's a vulnerable little girl." She looked up, a conspiratorial grin on her face. "Scarlet wouldn't like me talking about her."

"I promise I won't tell her."

"I appreciate that."

"What was your dad like?"

A genuine smile lit her eyes. "I adored him. When he was around, we all laughed. He loved to take us places, like the beach or the playground. But he worked crazy hours and traveled a lot for his job as a corporate lawyer, so his time with us was limited. I sometimes wonder, if he'd known how short our time together was going to be, would he have spent more of it with us?"

"I'm sure he wished he could have been with his children more often. Men often feel they have to trade time spent with their families for earning a living."

"Yes, you're probably right. I know he adored my mother. That's why I've never understood..."

Her voice trailed off as she turned to stare into the fireplace. Her sadness reached out to him and made his heart ache.

"What don't you understand, Harper?"

She blinked, as if she'd momentarily forgotten he was in the room. "I'm sorry. All this talk about my parents is bringing up old memories."

"I didn't mean to upset you."

"You didn't, truly. I have a lot of wonderful memories of my parents. The thing is, I've never understood what happened to them, to their marriage."

"What do you mean?"

"Something had gone wrong. In the spring of the year they died, my Dad moved out of our house. When school was out for the summer, Mom brought us here to the lodge. I think she needed to get away, to think. Sometimes she would leave us with our grandparents and go away for a day or two, just driving she said. Other times, she'd take her canoe out on the lake. She loved this lake and knew every rock and shoal. Sometimes her friend Abby from Minnewasta would go out on the lake with her. But more often she'd be all alone, drifting on the water."

"It sounds like she had some things to think through."

"Maybe. I was too young to make sense of everything I saw. I know she and my grandmother argued, but they were careful not to let me hear what they said. I was afraid we were going to stay at the lodge forever, but when I asked Mom, she kissed me and said everything was going to be okay."

"Do you think she planned to work things out with your dad?"

"I know he wanted to work things out with her. He showed up unexpectedly at the lodge and I was sure everything was going to be the way it was before. We were going to be a family again."

"Is that when they had the accident?"

Harper's gaze skittered away, but not before he saw the pain in her eyes. "Yes."

"Accidents happen, and sometimes we don't know why."

"Yes, I suppose they do." She didn't look convinced. The expression on her face spoke of deep sadness.

Ethan linked his fingers together to keep from touching her. They were contemplating a deal that could potentially be worth millions and if he made the investment in her lodge, their business partnership would continue for years. A personal attachment to Harper Lindquist was something he couldn't afford. He needed a clear head to make his decision, one uncluttered by lust or tender feelings.

But it was damn hard. He wanted to hold her, to comfort her and tell her everything would be all right. Unfortunately, he couldn't promise that any more than her mother had been able to.

Harper rose from the sofa and moved around the coffee table. "It's getting late, and I'm really tired. I'm going to bed, but please feel free to help yourself to anything in the kitchen."

He got to his feet. "Thank you. I'll let you know in the morning what I've decided to recommend to my company."

She nodded and gave him a tight smile. "Good night."

"Good night."

She left the room and closed the French doors behind her. Ethan sat once more, resting his head back against the cushions of the sofa. Though her parents had died over twenty years ago, Harper suffered their loss as if it happened yesterday.

He thought of his own parents, especially his father, something he tried not to do too often. Harper had been right when she'd guessed the lodge reminded him of the inn where he'd grown up in Wisconsin. His father had squandered the inn, drinking away any profits until it was lost. Perhaps a part of him wanted a second chance. Maybe in some deep recess of his psyche he thought that if he invested in Harper's lodge, it would be like returning the inn to his mother. The inn had been in her family for years, and she'd been devastated when they'd lost it. She'd given up after that, succumbing to her cancer within a year. Ethan had never forgiven his father.

His cell phone rang, jerking him from his thoughts. The sound surprised him since the phone hadn't rung since he'd arrived at the lodge. When he pulled it from his pocket, he saw his sister Lydia was calling. "Hey, how are you, Sis?"

"I'm fine. The question is where are you? I've been trying to call you for days."

"Sorry. The cell phone reception is a little sketchy out here. This is the first time my phone has worked."

"Where is 'out here'?"

"Solace Lake Lodge. I came out to meet the owner and talk about buying her land, remember? I've been storm-stayed ever since."

"For two days?"

"What can I say? It was a hell of a blizzard. It's over now, but the roads are still blocked. I'm here until the snowplows dig us out."

"Did you secure the land?"

Ethan cleared his throat. "We're still negotiating."

"What's the owner like? What was her name again?"

"Harper Lindquist." He hesitated a moment, carefully weighing what he said to his sister. "She's a good business woman."

"Really? How old is she? We tried to look her up on social media, but we couldn't find anything. The lodge doesn't even have a website."

"She's my age. Early thirties."

Lydia went silent, and he thought they'd lost their connection. Then he heard her make a derisive sound in her throat. "I suppose she's pretty."

Harper's beautiful smile and soulful eyes jumped into his mind's eye. He tried to keep his voice unaffected. "She's attractive enough."

Lydia huffed into the phone. "I don't want you to get sucked in by another pretty face. I knew Graham and I should have come with you."

"Come on, Lydia. Give me a little credit, will you?"

"You haven't always made the smartest decisions when it comes to women. I worry about you, you know."

"I wish you'd stop. I'm a big boy now. I can look after myself." He took a deep breath to calm himself. He loved his sister, and she loved him. She was fiercely loyal to her family, a mama bear ready to pounce if anyone messed with her brood. It was her legacy from their dysfunctional family. Lydia had been thrust into the role of mother to him and Cam whenever their real mother had been too preoccupied by their father's drinking. It was a role she still took to heart.

"I'm sorry," he said. "I love you."

"I love you, too. I'm sorry to be such a pain in the ass."

He chuckled. "At last, something we can agree on."

"Ha, ha." He heard her take a deep breath. "So. When do you think you'll be able to wrap up negotiations for the land?"

"Soon." He didn't like lying to Lydia, but he didn't want to talk about the possibility of investing in Harper's lodge over the phone, especially when he knew she'd be opposed.

"Okay. Give me a call when you get back to the city, will you? I'd like to know you're not frozen in some snowbank."

"I promise I'll call. Goodnight, Lyddie."

"Goodnight, E."

He ended the call and put the phone back in his pocket. Lydia would not be happy when she found out what he was doing. Not only would an investment in Harper's lodge increase the scope of the project, it would put a lot of money at risk. But his sister would object most to the emotional connection he was building with Harper. Lydia would say he was letting his feelings cloud his judgement, and he wasn't sure he could argue with that. His heart told him to help

Harper, no matter what. But he couldn't, wouldn't, let his heart overrule his good judgement.

There was no doubt Harper was a remarkable woman. She'd raised her younger sister and looked after her ailing grandfather, while at the same time running the lodge and earning a living. She was hardworking, straightforward and honest, not to mention beautiful. *God, she was beautiful.*

He'd known other beautiful women but he'd never experienced this overwhelming protectiveness towards them. Nor the sense of closeness after knowing them only a couple of days.

There was something about Harper Lindquist, something that touched his heart. One look from her and he wanted to give her everything she asked for. Why did he feel such a pull toward her?

He sat in silence, thinking of Harper, until the flames in the fireplace turned to smoldering embers.

Chapter Five

THE SNOWPLOWS HAD ARRIVED during the night, clearing a path to the lodge. When Harper got up to make breakfast at seven-thirty, Ethan was outside shoveling snow from around his truck. Apparently, he couldn't wait to leave. Her shoulders slumped as she made for the kitchen.

She filled her coffee maker with water and measured the grounds. Of course he was anxious to leave. A meeting that shouldn't have taken more than a few hours had lasted for nearly three days. He wanted to return to the city. He had a job and a life to get back to.

And perhaps a woman he'd neglected to mention.

He'd said there wasn't a special woman in his life. She wanted to believe he was the kind of man who wouldn't lie. And the kind of man who would honor any commitments he made to a woman. Not that he'd done anything with her to disaffirm those commitments.

No, she had no reason to believe he'd lied to her. She'd sensed a connection with him, an emotional bond that felt ridiculously real, considering they'd just met. He'd listened to her, laughed with her, understood her problems.

Who am I kidding?

With a disgusted shake of her head, she turned her attention to making breakfast, beating butter and sugar together with more force than was probably necessary. She added the rest of the ingredients for her blueberry muffins, then spooned the batter into a muffin tray and slid it into the pre-heated oven. Even if there had been some sort of connection between them, neither of them could act on it. They could be embarking on a potentially huge business deal, and they both needed to remain neutral.

Assuming Ethan had found merit in her proposal. He'd promised to tell her his decision this morning. Her stomach clenched in nervous anticipation. She busied herself washing up the dishes she used to make the muffins. The small task and the warm water eased some of her tension.

A short time later the front door opened and she heard Ethan stamp his feet on the rug to shake off the snow. A minute later, he entered the kitchen, rubbing his hands together.

"Man, it's cold out there."

"You need something warm to drink."

Harper poured him a cup of coffee. Their fingers brushed as she handed him the cup, and sparks of electricity shot up her arm. Her gaze collided with his. In that split second she thought he, too, sensed the simmering energy between them. But she was afraid to give voice to whatever it was that had passed between them. Afraid that she had misread the look and would embarrass herself. She pulled her hand away and lowered her gaze.

"You've been busy." She hated the husky note in her voice.

"Yeah. I'll take off after breakfast."

She made herself smile as she took a couple of plates out of the cupboard. "It's been fun having company. Most of the time I'm rattling around alone in this big old place."

Ethan propped one hip against the cupboard. "You're pretty isolated here. Is it safe for you to be alone all the time?"

"I'm fine. The Millers are only a few miles down the road, and I've got lots of friends in town I can count on. Besides, nothing ever happens around here."

He sipped his coffee, saying nothing, but the concerned look in his dark eyes told her he didn't buy that statement. It warmed her heart to know he worried about her, even if there was no cause.

The timer dinged and she tore her gaze away from his to take the muffins out of the oven. "I'm out of bacon and eggs. I hope you don't mind blueberry muffins for breakfast."

"Of course not. They smell delicious."

"Good. Everything will be ready in a couple of minutes."

While the muffins cooled, she sliced a cantaloupe, the last piece of fresh fruit in the lodge. If Ethan had stayed any longer, they would have had to dig into her reserves of canned goods.

She wouldn't have minded eating canned peaches if it meant Ethan was with her.

She pushed aside the thought. He was leaving, and there was nothing she could do about it.

To her horror, tears prickled the back of her eyes. She couldn't cry in front of Ethan. It was stupid to cry. Harper kept her back to him, grateful when she was able to get herself under control once more. She hoped Ethan hadn't noticed her distress.

She arranged a couple of muffins and some slices of cantaloupe on the two plates, forcing herself to smile as she turned to him. "How about one last look at the lake from the dining room?"

"I'd like that."

The sun was beginning to rise over the trees. For the first time in three days, the beauty of the lake was clearly visible. The look of wonder on Ethan's face excited her. He truly got this place.

"I knew the lake was beautiful, but I didn't realize how truly spectacular it was until now."

"See how the fresh snow sparkles in the sun? My sisters and I used to pretend there were diamonds buried in the snow after a storm like this. I think the beauty is Mother Nature's way for making up for the anger of the blizzard."

He chuckled. "She has a lot to make up for today."

"Yes, she does." But if it hadn't been for the storm, she wouldn't have gotten to know him.

They ate in silence. Ethan devoured his muffins and fruit while Harper picked at her breakfast, her stomach in knots. Would he recommend putting money into the lodge? If he did, they might work closely together. A relationship could develop. Her heart wondered if the feelings she thought were growing between them were real or simply blown out of proportion due to the circumstances and his kindness.

Ethan drained his coffee cup and set it on the table. "Thanks for another wonderful breakfast, Harper. It was delicious. Your grandmother taught you well."

"You're welcome." It gratified her to know he remembered the things she'd told him.

"I want to let you know I've reached a decision. You've convinced me to take another look at the lodge. I'm going to recommend that Hainstock investigate its feasibility as an eco-resort."

Harper clamped a hand over her mouth. This time she couldn't stop the tears from filling her eyes. "Oh! Oh, my goodness! Thank you. Thank you so much."

He waved off her thanks. "No thanks necessary. I was only trying to keep my butt out of the snow."

Her laughter mixed with her tears. "Maybe so, but you kept your word. You listened."

"You understand this is just a start." His expression grew serious as he reached across the table to grasp her hand. "I can't promise anything right now, only that we'll give serious consideration to your proposal. Don't let your hopes get too high."

"I understand." His words and touch brought her back down to Earth. "But I want you to know I appreciate your fairness and honesty in all this. It means everything to me."

For a second, their gazes met and held. Then, he glanced away and dropped her hand. He pushed away from the table. Harper blinked at his abruptness.

"I should head back to the city. Excuse me. I'm going to change and get ready to leave."

She nodded, unable to speak around the lump in her throat. When Ethan left the room, she sagged against her chair. This was what she'd so desperately wanted, a chance to save the lodge. And now she had it.

This was good news. She should be celebrating, jumping for joy. Or at least smiling.

Instead, she felt mildly depressed, bereft, as if she'd lost something. Ethan was in a hurry to leave. Any connection she'd imagined with him was an illusion, a product of her loneliness.

Suck it up, Harper. His interest in you is strictly business.

For one wild moment, she wished she were the kind of woman that men couldn't resist. She looked down at the frayed cuff of her shirt and the faded denim of her jeans. They were clean, but that was about all her clothes had going for them. She was plain, old Harper Lee Lindquist. Nice enough looking, but no *femme fatale*.

And even if Ethan decided he wanted something more from their relationship, she was afraid she'd disappoint him.

No one wants the oldest living virgin in Minnesota, Harper.

Sometimes she wished she'd let one of her male classmates take her virginity back in high school just so it was over and done with. But she'd wanted someone special to be her first, and none of those boys had fit the bill. Then she'd gone away to college for four years. She'd been tempted a couple of times, but had pulled back. Something had always felt wrong, or at least not quite right, and she hadn't been ready to take such a momentous step.

After her grandmother died and she was running the lodge and looking after Maggie and her grandfather, there'd been no time to date. There'd been a few unattached men her age left in the community, but they hadn't interested her. For a long time, she'd been too busy to care. Between cleaning, cooking for guests, doing the books, and helping to maintain the boats and snowmobiles, her days were full. Even maintaining relationships with her female friends who'd remained in Minnewasta had been difficult. All of them were married and having babies, their lives so different from hers.

When her grandfather became ill, she'd devoted all her time to caring for him. Scarlet and Maggie had helped when they could, but most of his care fell to her. He'd wanted to die in his home rather than in some cold, impersonal hospital, and she did everything she could to fulfill his wishes. It was only after he died and she was alone that she began to think of dating again. She'd even joined an online dating site for a while. But the results were less than spectacular.

She was beginning to think she was going to die a virgin. *Pathetic.*

With a disgusted huff, she pushed away from the table, gathered the dishes, and took them back to the kitchen to wash.

She'd just placed the last dish on the drain board when Ethan entered the kitchen, his hair still damp from his shower. He'd shaved with the razor she'd found for him and was wearing his own clothes again. Once more the elegant, well-dressed businessman. The chasm grew between them even as he stood in her kitchen. She was stupid to believe there could ever be anything aside from business between them.

She lifted her chin, determined not to let her façade slip. "I've gathered all my estimates and drawings and put them in a bag so you can take them with you."

"I appreciate that."

They walked together to the front door, and Harper lifted his beautiful overcoat from the coat tree. It still held the scent of his after-shave, and she had to resist the urge to raise it to her nose and breathe it in. Instead, she held it out to him with a forced smile. "Have a safe trip back to Minneapolis, Ethan."

"Thanks." He took the coat from her and slipped it on. "I want to thank you for your hospitality."

"It was my pleasure."

So formal. But it was the only way she could get through the next few minutes.

He picked up the cloth bag with all her information on the renovation project. "Goodbye, Harper. I'll be in touch soon."

"Goodbye." She shook his outstretched hand briefly.

He opened the front door and headed toward his truck. Harper grabbed a sweater from the coat tree and stood in the open doorway watching him leave, not quite able to shut the door on him despite the biting cold.

Halfway to the truck, Ethan stopped. For a second, he stood completely still, his head bowed. Then he dropped the bag, turned on his heel, and walked back to her, his steps full of purpose.

"Did you forget something?"

"Yeah."

He pulled her into his arms, his mouth descending on hers with an urgency that set her blood on fire. She moaned as she molded herself against him, her arms winding around his neck, her fingers tangling in his damp hair. He swept her mouth with his tongue, demanding a response. She gave herself over to his kiss, loving the sweet taste of his mouth, the clean smell of his skin, the solid feel of his body.

All too soon he broke the kiss. He grasped her shoulders and pushed away from her, breathing hard. She searched his face for answers.

"I have to go," he said. "I'll call you soon."

She nodded, unable to speak. He released her and walked back to his truck. No longer sheltered in his arms, the bitter cold swept through her. She pulled her sweater more securely around her shoulders.

Harper watched Ethan pull out of the driveway, her heart racing. When she could no longer see his truck, she closed the front door and leaned against it. The taste of him remained on her tongue and she could still smell his clean scent. Excitement and fear danced up and down her spine, fighting a duel inside her to decide which one ruled supreme.

Fear won. In one way or another, everyone she'd ever cared about had left her. She couldn't bear for Ethan to be one more person on that list.

Chapter Six

INSTEAD OF IMMEDIATELY driving back to Minneapolis, Ethan pulled into his brother Cameron's freshly plowed driveway a mile and a half outside of Minnewasta. He'd only been to Cam's new place once before, when he helped him move. Cam had rented the property and moved there a few months previously to be closer to his daughter. The lodge's close proximity to the town had first attracted Ethan's attention to Harper's newspaper ad. Minnewasta was Cam's ex's hometown, and, after they'd broken up, she'd moved there with Tessa to live with her parents.

Probably for the free rent and babysitting service, if he knew Laura.

The whine of a power tool drew Ethan to the workshop at the back of the property. When he opened the door he saw Cam feeding a piece of reclaimed lumber through the planer, his attention riveted on his task. Sawdust flew and the air filled with the sweet scent of freshly cut wood, cedar if he was any judge. His brother looked up at him in surprise and turned off the machine.

"Where the hell did you come from?"

Ethan couldn't help grinning. That was Cam. Straight to the point.

"I was in the neighborhood. How about taking a break? I could use a cup of coffee."

"Let's go to the house. I wouldn't want you to get your pretty clothes all dirty."

Once in Cam's spotless kitchen, Ethan took off his overcoat and hung it over a chair. He ran his hand over the smooth wooden top of Cam's kitchen table. "Is this new?"

Cam glanced at him over his shoulder as he filled the coffeepot with water. "Yeah, I just finished it. I made it out of wood from that old barn near Bemidji you helped me tear down last summer."

"Oh, yeah? This is pine, right?" Ethan checked the underside of the table. Cameron had attached an ornate set of wrought iron legs that looked to be as old as the barn had been.

"Yeah, it's pine. I got the legs at an auction sale for a song. Nobody wanted them."

Nobody but Cam could see the beauty in a pair of old metal table legs. Everyone else would look at the chipped paint and think they were nothing but junk. Only Cam would see life and usefulness and splendor.

"Can you make one like this for me?"

"Of course not. It's a one of kind piece. Where am I going to find another set of legs like that?"

"Too bad. It's a beautiful piece." He pulled out a chair and sat down at the table. "So how do you like living out here? How's Tessa adjusting?"

"I like it fine, especially since Tessa is thriving. Her grandparents are providing the stability she didn't get when she lived with Laura in the city."

Ethan knew Cam provided much of the stability that Tessa needed. His brother had not only picked up stakes and moved for his daughter's sake, he'd changed his life for her. "Have you found any AA meetings around here?"

"Yeah, I've been to a few meetings."

"Good to hear."

"I'm not going to backslide, E. Tessa's future is too important to me."

"I know."

Cameron's struggle with alcohol had been heartbreaking for the whole family. Ethan and his sister feared his life would spin out of control much as their father's had. But with sheer force of will, and some help from his family, Cam had quit drinking. He was determined to be a better father to Tessa than their father had been to them.

When the coffee was ready, Cam filled two cups and set one in front of Ethan. "So, are you going to tell me how you ended up on my doorstep before ten in the morning when you're supposed to be in Minneapolis, or are we going to play twenty questions?"

"No need for an inquisition, Cam. Business brought me out here." Ethan sipped his coffee, stalling as he decided how much to divulge. "I got storm-stayed in the area. I drove out before the blizzard hit to check out an investment possibility."

Cam sat across from him. "An investment possibility in Minnewasta?"

"A few miles away. An old fishing lodge. It's next door to Miller's Golf Resort." He'd already told Cam that Hainstock Investments had purchased Miller's. "The owner wants to turn it into an eco-friendly resort, but she needs money to do that."

Cam's eyebrows shot up. "She?"

Ethan tried not to squirm under his brother's penetrating gaze. "Yes, she. The owner happens to be a woman. She owns the place with her sisters."

Cam snorted in disgust. "Sisters? More women. Even better."

"Not every woman is like Laura."

He shot Ethan a warning glance. "We're not talking about me right now, we're talking about you and your inability to say no to a pretty face. I'm assuming this woman is pretty?"

A picture of Harper popped into his mind's eye. Long blonde hair, blue eyes and a warm smile set in a lovely oval face with flawless, creamy skin.

Then, there was that kiss. The one that nearly knocked him on his ass and had shaken him to his core. The kiss he couldn't stop thinking about. "Yeah, she's pretty."

"I rest my case."

"It's not like that. I'm not an idiot. I have to do a lot of research, check out the feasibility and profitability of building that kind resort before I sink a dime into it."

"I'm glad to hear it."

"I'm not an idiot." Ethan repeated the words so they'd sink into his brother's thick head. They also served to bring him down from the high he'd been on since his kiss with Harper, and reminded him to be careful. "I know I went a little crazy when I first won the money."

"You think?" Cam scoffed. "You gave money to every sob story you were told. By the time Lydia and Graham stepped in, it was nearly three million."

"They weren't sob stories. I gave money to legitimate charities who needed it, and I helped out a lot of my friends from work."

He'd been three days away from unemployment when he'd won the lottery. The pulp and paper mill he'd worked at was about to close and he hadn't found another job. Neither had a lot of his friends, many of them with mortgages and families to support. So, he'd helped them out. What was the big deal? It wasn't like he didn't have enough money to go around. Five years later, it annoyed him that his family still didn't trust him with his own money. His defensiveness over their lack of trust was equally annoying.

"And don't forget your girlfriends."

He wished he could. When word got out about his lottery win, women he hadn't seen in years started showing up at his apartment. He'd had to move and get a new, unlisted phone number, even leave the country for a while. But that hadn't stopped Bree. She'd violated his trust in the most heart-breaking way possible.

He pushed away the painful memories. "Harper's not like that."

"Harper?"

"Harper Lindquist." He told Cam her plans for the lodge. "And even if she was some kind of gold digger, which she's not, it wouldn't matter because she doesn't know who I really am."

"What do you mean?"

"She thinks I work for Hainstock Investments. She doesn't know I own the firm."

Cam stared at him. "Are you nuts? What kind of a lame-brained idea is that?"

"I'm only trying to protect myself. You're the one who keeps telling me that people are trying to take advantage of me because of the money."

"Yeah, but I didn't tell you to lie. You could have hired someone to check her out."

He could have, but he wanted to see the place for himself. The truth was he was bored. He was tired of simply investing money in far off places and projects he never saw and didn't much care about. He wanted to build something, get his hands dirty, get involved. Then, there were the complicated remembrances of his family's inn. Despite how it had ended, his family had been happy there, at least some of the time. It was hard work for not much money, but Ethan had enjoyed meeting the people who stayed with them. And he'd loved living in the country. He was tired of city life.

"I'll tell her the truth as soon as I make my decision. I didn't want the money to influence the way she treated me."

Maybe I should have thought of that before I kissed her. That kiss couldn't help but influence the way they treated each other. But he hadn't been thinking. He could only feel. Feel the way she fit so perfectly against his body. Feel the shape of her lips, the taste of her tongue. The texture of her hair as it slipped through his fingers. He shifted in his chair. Thinking about their kiss aroused him all over again.

"I still think going undercover like that is crazy."

It probably was. Harper wouldn't be happy he'd kissed her under false pretenses. Maybe she wouldn't want anything more to do with him. Even though it would be the end of the lodge, she might decide she no longer wanted to do business with him. She'd made her desire for honesty crystal clear.

But despite the risks, he couldn't regret kissing her.

"HI, SCARLET. DO YOU have a few minutes to talk?"

"Sure." Harper heard the sound of traffic and the low hum of background city noises through the phone line. "I'm on my way home. I just got on the L, so I'm all yours for about fifteen minutes."

"Good." Harper took a deep breath and then launched into the story of her plans for the lodge and her subsequent meeting with Ethan, though she didn't mention him by name. She didn't think Scarlet needed to know about Ethan's three day stay, or the amazing kiss they'd shared either. "The company originally only wanted to buy our land, but I convinced their representative to listen to my proposal and give it consideration. They're going to do their own investigations into the profitability of investing in the lodge, and then they'll let me know whether Hainstock Investments will partner with us."

When she finished talking there was silence on the other end of the line for several heartbeats. Harper held her breath as she waited for her sister to speak. One thing she knew for sure – Scarlet was going to be pissed.

"Are you saying that for months you've been gathering estimates and talking to banks and architects and this is the first I've heard of it?"

"Yes, I'm afraid that's what I'm saying."

"Why would you keep something like that a secret from me?"

"Not just from you. I haven't told Maggie, either."

"Well, that makes me feel so much better. Why didn't you tell us?"

Harper heard the sarcasm in her sister's voice, but chose to ignore it. "I needed to know if my plans were feasible before I told you. And to be perfectly honest, I knew you and Maggie would try to talk me out of saving the lodge."

"You're right about that. The fishing lodge is part of our past. It's time to let it go and move on."

Scarlet had been letting go of the lodge for a very long time. Since the day she graduated high school and moved away, she hadn't looked back. "I can't do that, Scarlet. Not without a fight."

She heard Scarlet's long, exasperated exhale of breath. "I guess there's no point in trying to convince you to sell the land and move here with me? I'd love to have you close by."

"I'd love having you close, too. I miss you. But you know how I feel about the lodge. It's the last thing we have of our grandparents. Our parents."

"Yeah, I know. What do you know about this company?"

Harper's shoulders relaxed, making her aware of how apprehensive she'd been to have this conversation. At least Scarlet was open to hearing about the opportunity. "I've done some digging on the Internet. They've been in existence for five years, and they specialize in ethical investments. That's why I was so pumped when they showed an interest in the lodge. They're a perfect fit."

"Showing an interest and investing cold, hard cash are two very different things."

"I know."

"What are they going to want in exchange for this pile of money?"

"They're going to want a piece of the lodge." She spoke fast before Scarlet could argue. "But I'm not planning to give it away. I told their representative I wouldn't consider a deal that gave us less than fifty-one percent of controlling interest in the lodge. What would be the point of giving a new life to this place if we were no longer in control of its future?"

"Good for you. I think that was a smart move. But I don't want you to be disappointed if they decide not to invest. You have to be prepared for that."

Harper swallowed and closed her eyes. "I know there's a distinct possibility they'll take a pass. As much as I love this place, I have to be realistic. Hainstock Investments is the lodge's last chance. If they don't invest, I'll have no choice but to sell." Her stomach clenched at the thought of leaving.

"What would you do then?"

"Probably find a place to live in Minnewasta. I couldn't bear to live in a big city again. I don't know how you and Maggie stand all the noise and traffic. I need someplace where I can breathe the air."

"I know what you mean. I love Chicago, but sometimes I miss the lake and the smell of the pines."

She'd never heard Scarlet admit to missing the lodge. They both must be feeling sentimental today. "It's been months since you were here. You have to come out this summer. It'll do you a world of good."

"If you're still there, maybe I will."

Scarlet's words served as a reality check. If her plans failed, by summer she could be living someplace else. Harper placed her hand against one of the massive logs that framed the lodge, feeling its warmth and strength. She pushed away the idea of leaving, refusing to deal with the possibility until she had to.

"Harper? Are you still there?"

She cleared her throat. "Yes, I'm still here."

"Are you okay?"

"Yes, I'm fine, but I'm not going to dwell on the negative." She knew her next words would get a reaction from her sister. "I told the representative from Hainstock that my sister Scarlet is a marketing whiz, and she's totally onboard to help launch a new and improved Solace Lake Lodge."

"You didn't seriously do that, did you?"

"No, I didn't," Harper confessed. "But if my plans for the lodge come together, will you help me?"

There was a moment of silence before she answered. "You know I'll do anything for you, Harper. I'll do what I can to help."

"Thanks, Scarlet. That means a lot to me."

"My stop is coming up, so I have to go. Promise me you'll keep me in the loop from now on. Let me know what happens with this investment company."

"I will. I promise."

"Good. I'll talk to you soon, okay? I love you."

"I love you, too."

The line went dead and Harper pressed the off button. *One sister down, one to go.* She punched in Maggie's cell phone number, hoping she wasn't at work. With her sister's crazy hours at the restaurant, she was never sure when it was a good time to talk.

Maggie picked up on the third ring. "Harper. What's up?"

Her sister's abrupt greeting surprised her. "Um, hey. I have some things I need to talk over with you. Is this a bad time? Are you at the restaurant?"

Harper heard her sigh through the airwaves. "No, I'm all yours. What did you want to talk about?"

The strange note in Maggie's tone caused alarm bells to ring in Harper's head. Something was going on. But before she could deal with that, she had to tell her everything she'd told Scarlet.

"Wow. Have you told Scarlet this?" Maggie asked when she was finished.

"I just got off the phone with her. She wasn't happy with me for keeping secrets."

"I suppose I should be upset, too, but I'm not. I know how you feel about the lodge, and I know you have to take this shot. I wish you good luck."

"It's not only for me, Maggie. It's for all three of us. If this plan works out the way I hope it does, it could mean a new start for us. Maybe you'll even be tempted to come home and head up the restaurant I want to build." She said the words half-jokingly to cover her deep desire for her sister to home.

"You know that's not going to happen."

"Yeah, I know." Her sister's response was no surprise. Maggie had always been adamant about her lack of interest in the lodge and her desire to live and work in a big city. She'd even talked about moving to New York, though Harper hadn't heard her mention that possibility in a while. Now that she thought of it, Maggie hadn't shared much about her career, both her present job and her future aspirations, in quite some time.

"Is everything okay, honey? You sound a little down in the dumps."

"I'm fine, Harper. Really. It's been a long day. I started work at six this morning and I just got home."

Harper didn't believe for a moment that Maggie was as fine as she pretended to be. But she didn't want to push her. "Well, the offer is always open. Assuming we have a new restaurant, or a lodge, in the future. There's nothing I would love more than having you home and seeing you happy."

There was a long pause. When Maggie spoke again, her voice sounded choked, as if she were holding back tears. "You'll need a really spectacular chef with a lot of experience. That's not me."

"Of course it's you. Maybe you don't have a lot of experience yet, but you're a spectacular talent."

"You give me too much credit."

Harper was suddenly frightened for her sister. "Honey, what's wrong? You know you can tell me anything."

"There's nothing to tell. I'm just tired, and maybe a little homesick."

"If you want to come home, I'm right here."

"It sounds like you have your hands full right now."

"Not so full that I couldn't give my baby sister a hug."

Maggie gave a laugh that bordered on the edge of being a sob. "I know. But I'm fine, really. In a mood today, I guess. I should probably go. I've got a late shift to work tonight."

Harper thought it odd that Maggie would have to work an early morning shift as well as a late shift on the same day. And since when was the high-end restaurant she'd been working at open for breakfast? Something didn't add up, but if Maggie didn't want to talk about what was troubling her, she couldn't force her. "I love you, Maggie."

"I know. Talk to you soon, Harper."

Harper ended the call worried and uneasy. Maggie was by nature strong-minded and determined, not letting anything stand in her way. The Maggie she'd just spoken to sounded depressed, defeated. Though they spoke frequently on the phone, she hadn't actually seen her little sister face to face in several months. Guilt washed over her. She'd been so preoccupied with the lodge, she hadn't recognized Maggie was having problems.

Harper closed her eyes and sent a prayer heavenward. She prayed the investment for the lodge would come through. Not only for her sake, but for Maggie and Scarlet's as well. She had a feeling her sisters needed the security of home and family as much as she did.

Chapter Seven

FOR MORE THAN TWO WEEKS, Ethan investigated the Solace Lake Lodge. He spoke to contractors to confirm the estimates Harper had secured and consulted with tourist operators and property investors on the income potential of the lodge as an eco-tourist resort. After examining the lodge for themselves, his contractors confirmed that Harper's estimates for the renovations to the lodge were accurate.

The investment experts concluded that the income potential for the type of resort Harper proposed was definitely real. She had more land and a bigger lake than other resorts in the area. Eco-tourism was becoming a hot ticket. There was nothing like the resort Harper proposed in the area as others nearby tended to cater to golfers in the summer and snowmobilers in the winter. If Solace Lake Lodge could offer something that was truly unique, they would attract attention.

However, they also said the project Harper proposed, basically fixing up the existing lodge, was too small. To make money, they needed to be able to accommodate more guests and hold events such as weddings and conferences that would bring in year-round income.

Ethan also talked things over with his family. As his financial advisors and accountants, his sister and brother-in-law were initially skeptical about the project. But being practical and savvy, and seeing his enthusiasm, they eventually came to support the venture, though they insisted on some safeguards and conditions.

Harper's ideas had real merit. Ethan experienced a surge of pride for her.

And profound relief. She would have been devastated if he'd found there was no hope for the lodge. But her reaction to the changes he needed to make to her plans worried him. She wanted to preserve her grandfather's legacy, and he got that, but his new proposal substantially changed that legacy.

He'd thought about her constantly for the past two weeks, wondered what she was doing, and if she ever thought of him. He couldn't get her, or the kiss they'd shared, out of his head.

He'd expected the feelings he'd experienced while they'd been trapped together by the storm to dissipate once they parted. Instead, they intensified. He longed to see her again, to hear her voice, to touch her. He couldn't wait to talk to her and tell her the good news that his "boss" wanted to help make the lodge something special.

His boss! He'd have to tell her the truth about that right away. He couldn't deceive her any longer. If there was to be any kind of relationship between them, it had to begin with the truth. She'd proven she was a hard-working, honest person, not someone looking for easy money in exchange for sex.

Like Bree.

Ethan thrust the distasteful memory from his thoughts. Harper was the only woman he wanted to think about right now. He picked up the phone and dialed her number, excited to give her the good news, and anxious to get her reaction.

"Hello?" Her voice was breathless, as if she'd had to run to catch his call.

"Harper, it's Ethan."

"Ethan, it's good to hear from you."

I've missed you. The unspoken words hung in the air between them.

He forced himself to remain business-like. "It's good to hear your voice, too. It's been a long two and a half weeks for me, but I had to stay focused and unbiased in my analysis. It was the best thing for my company and ultimately, the best thing for you, too. You'd only be hurt if you put your heart and soul into a venture that was doomed to fail."

Silence greeted his words. Then he heard her take a deep breath and slowly let it out. "Are you saying there's no hope for my lodge, that your company's not going to invest?" "No. I'm sorry, I've made a mess of things. I've called to tell you that after extensive investigation my company has decided to invest in the Solace Lake Lodge, under certain conditions."

"You mean it?" Her voice caught on a sob.

"Yes, absolutely. Congratulations, Harper."

"I don't know what to say, except thank you. Thank you so much." She was crying in earnest now. He wished he could be with her to hold her and kiss away her tears.

"Don't thank me yet. The money comes with some changes to your original plans. There are a few details we need to work out."

"Like what?" Wariness replaced elation and tears.

"Like expanding the project. The experts I talked to like your idea of building a spa and sauna in a separate building near the main lodge. They recommend we do that right away and make it a feature of the resort from the start. They also think that to be truly viable we need to be able to accommodate weddings, conferences, family reunions and other events like that, the kind of business that means we're busy year-round. That entails adding another building to the plans in order to hold such events. It would be separate from the lodge but perhaps connected to it in some way. And if we're hosting weddings and conferences, we'll need more guestrooms. We'd need another wing of hotel rooms added onto the lodge."

She was quiet for several minutes before she spoke. "That's a much bigger project than I'd envisioned. My grandfather's lodge would be totally changed. If I understand you correctly, it means the lodge will look much different than it does today. The business would be totally different, too. It would be some kind of event center rather than a boutique hotel."

"Yes, the business model would change, though I believe the lodge will still retain a boutique hotel feel. I've commissioned an architect to draw up plans for an expanded lodge that stays true to the original structure. I told him I want the existing lodge to remain the focal point."

"What if my sisters and I decide we want to stick with the original, smaller project? What if we don't want the lodge to change that much?"

Ethan blew out a breath. She had to hear the truth, even though it meant drastic changes for the lodge she loved so much. "We've been told it doesn't make sense for Hainstock to invest in a small ten room lodge. Eight by the time the ensuites are installed. It would be too small to generate enough revenue to justify the money needed to upgrade the place. The income potential isn't there."

Again she was silent. Finally, she said, "I see."

Ethan heard her disappointment in the terse statement. "Harper, I know this isn't exactly what you wanted, but it's the only way to save the lodge and keep it in your family."

"Isn't there some other way, a compromise of some sort? What if Hainstock only lent me enough money to build the cottages? I could keep the business going and, over time, I could make the repairs on the lodge."

"You know as well as I do that the repairs on the lodge can't be put off any longer. If the roof isn't repaired immediately, the rest of the structure is going to be compromised." He paused, weighing his words. He hoped she wouldn't be angry he'd left her little room for negotiation. "Besides, I've already brought up this possibility with our experts and board members. They feel that any half measures, like only rebuilding the cottages, would doom the lodge to failure. In order for Hainstock to invest, we have to be all in."

"So, it's Hainstock's way or nothing."

There was no missing the sarcasm in her voice. "Yes. We believe it's the only way this project can be viable."

Tense silence greeted his statement. He feared that in her next breath Harper would react out of disappointment and reject his proposal, so he spoke quickly. "You don't have to make a decision right now. Take a few days. Talk it over with your sisters and anyone else you trust. Then get back to me when you're ready. This is a big step. It deserves some thought."

She took a breath and then blew it out as if calming herself. "I suppose you're right. We'll talk it over and get back to you in a few days. Goodbye, Ethan."

The line went dead. Ethan listened to the dial tone for a moment before hitting the end button.

What the hell had he expected? Of course she was disappointed, and maybe a little intimidated. All she'd ever wanted was enough money to refurbish her grandfather's lodge. It killed him to destroy her dream.

Perhaps he'd destroyed any feelings she might have had for him as well.

HARPER WAITED A COUPLE of hours to calm down before calling her sisters. Bitter disappointment churned in her gut. To have come so close to her dream only to have it crushed hurt more than she could have imagined.

At three she called Maggie, hoping to catch her between her crazy work shifts. When Maggie answered, Harper repeated the conversation she'd had with Ethan.

"This isn't what I wanted. I wanted to keep Grampa's lodge alive, not change it into something he wouldn't recognize."

Maggie was silent for a moment. "It's not going to bring him back, you know."

"What do you mean?"

"Fixing up the lodge isn't going to bring Grampa back. He's gone."

Irritation welled up in Harper's chest. "Of course he's not coming back. I'm not delusional."

"Why did you want to rebuild the lodge, Harper?"

"So that it could be a viable business again. So that I could stay here instead of having to move away. So that Grampa's legacy could be saved the way he'd want—"

She abruptly stopped. All this time she thought she was fighting for the lodge for her own sake, and for her sisters'. But maybe deep down inside, she was trying to get her grandfather's approval. If she kept the lodge alive, she'd keep him alive.

Maggie's voice was gentle. "We can't look backward anymore. The world changes and maybe the lodge has to change with the times, too. Whatever you decide, make sure you're doing it because it's the right decision for you, not because you want to build a monument to Grampa."

"I want it to be the right decision for you, too, Maggie. And for Scarlet."

"I know. You've always looked out for us."

She tried to laugh, but her voice came out in a choked whisper. "What are big sisters for?"

"For what it's worth, I think you should take Hainstock's money and run with it. Unless you go for it, you'll always wonder what might have been."

She was right. Harper's mind drifted to Ethan. If she rejected his proposal for the lodge, would she always wonder if there could have been something between them, too?

Harper shook her head. She had to make a clear-minded decision, not one influenced by any feelings she may have for Ethan. "When did you get so smart, Maggie?"

"I've always been smart. Maybe you weren't paying attention."

Maggie's words were spoken with humor, but Harper wondered if they weren't true. She'd been so intent on being the big sister, the one always in charge, that perhaps she failed to notice her baby sister was an intelligent, capable young woman.

"Maybe I wasn't, but I'm paying attention now. Thank you for listening and for your good counsel."

"You're welcome. Good luck with your decision, Harper."

"I love you, honey."

They disconnected. Harper held the phone in her hand as she wandered from room to room in the lodge. She paused to stroke one of the massive logs in the dining room. Was she prepared to make a radical change to the lodge?

Realistically, if she didn't make the sweeping changes Ethan talked about, she'd lose the lodge forever. It was a big decision. And an important one.

After a couple of hours of pacing and soul searching, Harper dialed Scarlet's number, hoping she was home from work.

Her sister picked up after the first ring. "Hey, what's up?"

"Plenty."

She told Scarlet what Ethan proposed. "Maggie thinks I want the lodge to stay the way it is now because it's my subconscious way of keeping Grampa alive."

"What do you think?" Scarlet didn't seem surprised by the idea.

"Maybe there's some truth in it. I loved Grampa. He was the one I turned to when things got rough. Grandma and I rarely saw eye to eye. You and Maggie were always closer to her."

"I know. She wasn't the easiest person to get close to."

That was probably an understatement. "I do want Grampa's legacy to remain for the future, but there are good, practical reasons why I want the lodge to stay its present size. If it's small, it's something I can manage myself with a small staff. I know how to do it. But a resort, or some kind of event center, is way beyond my expertise. I'd have to depend on other people."

"And that scares you, doesn't it?"

"I suppose I am a bit of a control freak."

Scarlet laughed. "That's probably part of it. But if you have to depend on people, you're vulnerable to them. They can let you down. Just like when we were kids and our parents let us down by dying on us."

Harper was stunned into silence. Finally, she asked, "Where did you come up with that?"

"From a psychologist I used to see. She helped me through some stuff."

Harper's heart ached to know Scarlet had been suffering and had never once told her about it. What else wasn't she telling her? Did she and Maggie feel they had to protect her from bad things the way she'd always thought she had to protect them?

"I suppose your psychologist has a point. Not being in control is scary for me."

"We'd still own fifty-one percent of the lodge," Scarlet said. "We'd still be in control. You would simply need to hire people with expertise in the areas you don't have."

"Yes, that's true."

"On a strictly business level, an expanded lodge makes total financial sense. As an accountant, a money person, you must see that."

She grudgingly had to admit she did. "Yes."

"Good. So the way I look at it, it's a choice between selling the land to Hainstock Investments right now and walking away, or going full steam ahead and making the lodge into something new and different. You have to decide what you really want, Harper."

"Like I told Maggie, it's your decision, too."

"You're the one whose life is going to be changed, one way or the other. But if I get a vote, I say go ahead with the expansion."

"That surprises me. I didn't think the lodge meant that much to you."

"Maybe not, but I know how much it means to you. I want you to be happy, and I don't think you will be if you let the lodge go."

She was probably right. Her sisters knew her so well. Perhaps better than she knew them. "Thanks Scarlet. It was good talking to you. You've really helped."

"It was good talking to you, too. Let me know what you decide."

"You and Maggie will be the first to know. As soon as I figure it out for myself."

Scarlet chuckled. "Sounds good. Bye, Harper."

"Bye."

Harper ended the call and resumed pacing through the lodge. Every log, every beam, every floorboard reminded her of her family. The frame around the kitchen door where Grandma had recorded their heights. The tiny bathroom on the main floor that she and her sisters had fought over every morning before school. The fireplace in the dining room where her mother had etched her initials into the wet mortar as a child.

No matter how much she wanted to keep her decision about the lodge on a strictly business level, it was impossible. The lodge meant family to her. Home.

She couldn't abandon her home. But to turn it into something her grandparents wouldn't recognize was a monumental decision.

Harper walked the halls once more. She needed to make the right decision, for herself and for her family. And she needed time to make it.

ETHAN WAITED ON TENTERHOOKS for three days to hear back from Harper, knowing there was a distinct possibility she might never call. Perhaps she was making arrangements right now to donate the property to the nature conservancy. Maybe she'd decided that a larger resort wasn't what she wanted and she'd rather get out.

Maybe, but he couldn't quite make himself believe it. The woman he'd gotten to know was dedicated to her family's legacy. He couldn't see her giving up so easily.

But how would she react to his company's final condition, the one they hadn't yet spoken about? During their last conversation, they'd gotten so hung up on the expanded scope of the project he hadn't been able to bring up Lydia and Graham's recommendation. Worry gnawed at him.

When his phone rang and he saw her name on the screen, relief swamped him. Then worry. He hoped she wasn't calling to give him the brush off. "Harper, hi. It's good to hear from you."

"Hi, Ethan. I've made my decision."

No beating around the bush. He liked that about her. "What did you decide?"

"I think," she began slowly, "that I can speak for my sisters in saying we're excited about the possibility of creating a new Solace Lake Lodge. The changes aren't what I had originally proposed, but I can understand why expanding the lodge is necessary. So, I say yes."

Ethan sat down abruptly, relief making him weak in the knees. "That's wonderful, Harper. You won't be sorry."

"Don't start celebrating yet. I have a few conditions of my own."

"Such as?" He braced himself for the changes she might propose.

"However big the lodge gets, the environment still has to be our main concern. That means using eco-friendly construction methods now, and making sustainability a priority in the future."

"I agree. What else have you got?"

"I want to approve any changes you want to make to the original lodge and have input on the new structures."

So far, so good. "I think that's reasonable."

"Good." He heard her take a deep breath. "I think this means we have a deal."

Ethan cleared his throat. "That's great, but there's one more thing we need to discuss, something we didn't get to in our last conversation."

"What's that?" She sounded wary.

"My company needs a sixty percent share. We're putting a lot of capital at risk." It was one of the conditions Lydia and Graham had insisted on. They believed it was necessary in order to protect his investment. "I know we talked about a fifty-one/forty-nine split previously, but with this expanded scope, Hainstock will need to put a whole lot more money upfront."

"I see." Her voice was flat. "I'm afraid I can't do that. We have to retain majority ownership or there can't be any deal."

"Have you spoken to your sisters?"

"Yes, and they agree with me. If we no longer own controlling interest in the lodge, there's no point going forward. I guess your company will get the land after all. Send me the documents and we'll sign them."

"Harper, wait. Let's talk about this."

"I'm sorry, Ethan. There's nothing more to talk about." Her voice sounded strained, as if she was holding back a torrent of emotion. "Thank you for everything. Goodbye."

She was going to hang up and walk away. He knew her well enough to know this was no gambit, no bluff to get him to change his mind. She meant every word. This was Harper saying no.

Panic seized him. He couldn't lose her. "Wait! You can have the fifty-one percent."

"Really?" Her voice was cautious, as if she didn't quite believe him.

"Yes. Of course we wanted the controlling share, but this project is too good to pass up. We'll agree to your terms and have the papers drawn up accordingly."

"Do you have the authority to make that offer?"

"I do." His sister was probably going to give him a hard time, though.

"Are you going to get into trouble for this?"

He had to laugh at her response. Even with the future of her lodge on the line, she was worried about him. "No, I won't get into trouble." Graham and Lydia might not be happy with what he'd agreed to, but ultimately it was his company and his money. He'd take responsibility for his decisions.

"That's good. I'm glad. So, we're really going to do this?"

"Yeah. We really are."

He had to tell her truth right now. That his last name was Hainstock, that he owned the company. That he had more money than he knew what to do with, and he wanted to share some of it with her. She wouldn't be happy with him for withholding the truth for this long, but she was a reasonable woman. She'd understand. Eventually.

Wouldn't she?

"Harper—"

"I'm so lucky to have found you and your company, Ethan. You and Mr. Hainstock are men of honesty and integrity. So many business people out there are only in it for the money. They have no qualms about lying or cheating to get what they want. I hate liars. You and your company are different. You really care, and you tell the truth. Thank you. I owe you a lot."

His throat closed in shame. There was no way he could tell her the truth now.

He made a spur of the moment decision. He'd tell her the truth, but not today. He'd tell her when she'd be able to understand his reasons for keeping the truth from her.

When that would be, he had no idea.

He cleared his throat before speaking, pushing aside the guilt. "I appreciate what you're saying, but I don't deserve your thanks. I'm just doing my job."

"You're too modest."

He heard the smile in her voice and guilt piled on top of guilt. He suppressed a groan.

"I'll have the papers drawn up right away. When everything's ready, I'll be in touch. You and your sisters will have to sign."

"I'll call them and let them know. Perhaps they'll be able to come out here to the lodge for the signing. It'll be nice to have a little family reunion."

Ethan was happy for her. Whether her sisters realized it or not, Harper was keeping the lodge alive as much for them as for herself. "I'll be in touch."

"Thank you, Ethan. I appreciate everything you've done for us."

He was wrong. She would understand. He had to tell her. "Harper—"

"Yes?"

He couldn't say the words. He couldn't bear to lose her respect. "I'll see you soon."

"I'm looking forward to it."

He hoped to hell she'd forgive him for lying when he finally came clean. He hoped even harder it wasn't already too late.

Chapter Eight

AS SOON AS SHE HEARD a car pull up to the lodge, Harper threw open the front door, heedless of the February wind. She was too excited about seeing her sisters again to give a damn about the cold.

Scarlet opened the door on the driver's side and stepped out of the large black sedan, while Maggie got out on the passenger side. Harper didn't know much about cars, but this seemed like an expensive one. Since Scarlet had flown into Minneapolis from Chicago, she'd thought Maggie would pick her up from the airport and drive them to the lodge in the red Toyota she'd bought second-hand after graduating from high school. If she could afford this new car, maybe things weren't going too badly for her, and her worry for Maggie was unnecessary.

But if Maggie had bought a new car, why was Scarlet driving it?

They pulled their luggage from the trunk and made their way to the front door where Harper greeted them with hugs and kisses. "It's so good to see you both. It's been so long."
"Two Christmases ago," Scarlet said. "Remember, Maggie couldn't get the time off this past Christmas with those crazy hours she works at the restaurant."

"As I recall, Harper was working at Miller's over the Christmas holiday, too. It's not all my fault we didn't get together, so quit blaming me!"

Harper blinked at Maggie. She'd often acted as a peacemaker in her younger sisters' squabbles over the years, but she'd rarely heard Maggie lash out with such force. And with such anger.

Scarlet rolled her eyes. "What is your problem today? You've done nothing but bitch at me since I picked you up."

Harper stepped between them. "Maggie's right. The opportunity to make a few extra bucks at the resort came up last Christmas, so I took it."

She didn't add that she only did so after Maggie announced she couldn't come to the lodge because she had to work, and Scarlet subsequently decided to go to Cancun for Christmas with friends. It had been one of the loneliest Christmases of her life. She'd felt completely abandoned.

A recurring theme in her life.

She shook off the disappointment. They were all together now, and she was determined to enjoy her family. She put her arms around their shoulders. "I've been baking. Are you hungry?"

A hint of a smile touched Maggie's lips. "What did you make?"

"Your favorite, of course. Double chocolate chip cookies."

"What about my favorite?" Scarlet said with a pout. "Did you make something special for me?"

"Of course I did. There's a batch of lemon tarts just out of the oven for you."

Sometimes her sisters acted like a couple of three-year-olds. But she was willing to cater to a few whims in order to have them all together.

"Why don't you take your suitcases upstairs first? You can pick any rooms you'd like. Then, we can have tea and catch up."

While her sisters lugged their things up the stairs, Harper put the kettle on to boil and placed several tarts and cookies on a plate. When the water boiled, she spooned loose tea leaves into her pot and added water. A few moments later Scarlet and Maggie joined her in the kitchen.

"Do you still have Grandma's teacups, the ones with the pretty roses?" Maggie asked.

"Of course. Do you want to use them?"

Her sister's expression was wistful. "Yes, I think I do."

"The teacups are in the cupboard over the fridge, but I haven't used them in ages. They'll probably need to be washed."

"I'll get them for you, Shortstuff," Scarlet said, using one of Maggie's old nicknames.

Maggie rolled her eyes. "Go right ahead, Stretch."

Scarlet reached into the cupboard and retrieved three teacups and matching saucers. Maggie and Scarlet washed and dried them while Harper set napkins, forks, spoons and containers of milk and sugar on the kitchen table. Then she poured tea into the clean cups, using a strainer to catch the leaves.

Maggie wrapped her hands around the cup Harper offered her. "This reminds me of Grandma. You remember how much she loved a cup of tea?"

"Oh, yes," Scarlet said with fond smile. "She always believed the world would be a better place if everyone sat down and talked over a hot cup of orange pekoe."

"Harper, do you know where Grandma's Madeleine pans are? I used to love Grandma's Madeleines, but I never learned to make them. She died before she could teach me."

A look of profound sadness crossed Maggie's face. Harper reached across the table and took her hand. Being the youngest, Maggie had spent the most time with their grandmother and had been the one most affected by the heart attack that so suddenly ended her life.

"I think they're still somewhere in the kitchen, probably in the back of a cabinet," she said. "I haven't seen them in a long time. Do you want me to find them for you?"

Harper, too, had fond memories of Grandma's Madeleines, the little shell-shaped French cakes that she'd made in both chocolate and lemon flavors and served with tea. They had their own special pans that gave them their unique shape.

"No, that's okay. Someday I'm going to learn how to make Madeleines the way Grandma did, but not today," Maggie said.

"I miss her, and Grampa, too. This place seems so empty without them." Scarlet sipped her hot tea. "Don't you get lonely in this big old place all by yourself, Harper?"

"Sometimes," she confessed. "This place deserves to have people in it. And now that we have an investor, we'll be able to bring it to life again."

"When will we be signing the papers?" Scarlet asked.

"Ethan will be here tomorrow morning."

“Ethan?”

“Ethan James. He’s the representative from Hainstock Investments I told you about.”

Excitement flooded her at the thought of seeing Ethan again. She’d dreamed of the kiss they’d shared, both in her sleep and in her waking hours. She longed to see him, talk to him, hold him.

“You’re smiling,” Scarlet said, her eyebrows raised. “This Ethan must have made quite the impression on you.”

Harper carefully schooled her features into a bland expression. Scarlet had always been very perceptive. But she wasn’t ready to talk about her feelings for Ethan, whatever they were, even with her sisters.

Especially with my sisters.

“He’s very competent and knowledgeable. He’s done his homework and if he says the lodge can be profitable again, I know we’ll be successful.”

“Okay, but what is *he* like? That goofy grin you’re trying to hide says you appreciated much more than his real estate smarts.”

“He’s very nice.”

“Nice?” Scarlet rolled her eyes. “Come on, fess up, Harper.”

“There’s nothing to fess up to.” She decided to change the subject. “I ran into Mike Hunter the other day. He said to say hi.”

Scarlet lowered her gaze. “How’s he doing?”

“He’s good. His oldest daughter is in kindergarten and his wife’s having another baby in a couple of months. Number three.”

"That's nice." Scarlet pushed her tart aside, as if she'd suddenly lost her appetite. "It sounds like he has a lovely family. That was all he ever wanted."

"You did the right thing, Scarlet," Maggie said. "If you'd gone through with the wedding, you wouldn't have been happy."

Scarlet gave her a mocking smile. "And of course my happiness was paramount. Even if it meant dumping Mike at the altar."

"Don't be so hard on yourself. You didn't dump him at the altar. It was two weeks before the wedding."

"Oh, well. It's all right then." Scarlet's sarcastic tone didn't hide her obvious pain.

Harper felt bad for reminding her of her failed engagement. She should have known it would upset her, even after all this time. Judging from her sister's expression, she still experienced guilt for what had happened between her and Mike. They'd both been very young, not long out of high school, and Scarlet hadn't been ready for such a big commitment. But Mike hadn't been the only man she'd jilted after promising to marry him. Scarlet had met Owen in Chicago, but hadn't been able to go through with a marriage to him, either.

She touched Scarlet's arm. "Mike really is happy. He told me so himself." She had to change the subject, again. "How's work going, Maggie?"

Maggie shrugged. "It's fine."

"Do you enjoy working at the restaurant?" She wasn't even sure of the name of the restaurant.

"Yeah. It's good."

Her sister avoided looking her in the eye. Something was going on with Maggie, and it worried her. It hurt to know her sisters had secrets they didn't want to share with her.

But then, she was being just as secretive.

"Quit trying to change the subject," Scarlet said. "I want to know what Ethan James is like."

Harper lifted her teacup to avoid Scarlet's sharp scrutiny. "You'll find out for yourself when you meet him tomorrow."

THE MOMENT HARPER ANSWERED his knock, Ethan knew the feelings he'd experienced during the blizzard were real and not simply a result of their enforced togetherness. And judging from the expression on Harper's face, her welcoming smile and the warmth in her eyes, he knew the feelings were mutual. There was something extraordinary growing between them, something he wanted to explore further.

"It's good to see you again, Ethan," she said, her eyes smiling into his. "Please, come in out of the cold."

He stepped inside and grasped her outstretched hand. "I'm glad to be back."

He wanted to take her in his arms and kiss her, but before he could say or do anything, she let go of his hand and closed the door. "My sisters are here to sign the final papers."

Ethan had been so focused on Harper he hadn't noticed the two young women standing in the foyer. The tall redhead and the petite brunette examined him with open curiosity, the redhead with a hint of suspicion. He stepped toward her and extended his hand. "Hi, I'm Ethan...James."

He cursed himself for his stumble. Unaccustomed to using his middle name, or to lying, he'd almost said his real last name. Fortunately, Harper's sister didn't seem to notice.

She shook his hand briefly, her grip strong and confident. "Hi, I'm Scarlet Lindquist. Harper tells us you believe this place can be profitable again."

"Yes, I believe it can be, given the proper upgrades and marketing."

"I'd be interested in discussing the marketing plans for the lodge with you and Harper."

"Harper said you were a marketing whiz. I'd love to get your input on our ideas."

Scarlet's eyebrows rose at his choice of words. *Our ideas.* He'd already come to see himself and Harper as partners in this endeavor. Harper touched his elbow.

"And this is my sister Maggie. She's a chef in Minneapolis. I'm trying to convince her to help us choose the equipment we're going to need for the new kitchen."

The shape of Maggie Lindquist's face, her fair skin, the contour of her nose, and the small cleft in her chin, echoed the facial features of her sisters, and even though her hair was darker and she was more petite, there was no mistaking their sibling relationship.

"It's nice to meet you, Maggie. The lodge could use your expertise in designing the kitchen."

A blush stained her cheeks, and she looked distinctly embarrassed. *An odd reaction*, Ethan thought. She quickly schooled her expression into a pleasant smile, but avoided his gaze as she shook his hand. "I'll do what I can."

"Why don't we go into the dining room? Lunch is ready," Harper said.

Ethan followed her and sat down at the table she'd already set. Everyone was silent as Harper tossed a green salad and cut a quiche into four even pieces. He sensed the tension simmering between the women and wondered if they were angry Harper had pushed ahead with the deal. She'd said she'd consulted with them, but perhaps they weren't happy with the terms.

Harper took her seat, and though she took some of the food as it was passed to her, he noticed she didn't eat much. She appeared ill at ease and worried. From what she'd told him, she adored her sisters. He looked from one sister to the other, wondering what he could do or say to diffuse some of the strain.

"Harper told me you all grew up here." Ethan hoped that childhood memories were a safe place to begin a conversation.

"Yes, we did," Scarlet said. "After our parents died."

The table went silent again. Not a safe topic after all. He tried again. "The lodge is on a beautiful spot. I'm looking forward to spending the summer here and helping to make it something special again."

Scarlet looked up sharply. "You're planning to spend the summer here? You mean, you're going to live here?"

He caught the worried look in Harper's eyes, and he cursed himself once again. He wanted to be involved with every aspect of the lodge project and to do so, he needed to be on site. He'd told her he wouldn't leave her on her own, but he'd meant to talk to her privately to work out the details of his stay.

And he wanted to convince her they needed to further explore the attraction that had blossomed between them during his storm-stay.

"My, umm, employer," *God, now he was lying to all of them*, "wants to remain in touch with everything going on in this project. He wants me to represent Hainstock Investments' interests here at the lodge during construction."

"Don't you think that's something you should have asked us about before you sprang it at lunch?" Scarlet said, her eyes flashing. "I thought we were supposed to be partners in this project. You can't make decisions like this without consulting us."

"Hainstock Investments is putting a significant amount of money into the lodge. This is going to be a massive undertaking with dozens of different trades and hundreds of workers. It's going to take a lot of coordination and expertise. Mr. Hainstock wants to protect his investment." Did Scarlet object to Hainstock Investment's participation in the project, or was it his presence at the lodge she didn't like?

"Where do you plan to stay while you're here?" she asked.

Harper shot her sister a warning stare. "Scarlet."

"I thought I could stay in one of the cottages or perhaps bring in a motorhome."

"Ethan's right." Harper's fork clattered onto her plate. "I've never dealt with a project of this magnitude before. I'm going to need help."

Scarlet leaned back in her chair and crossed her arms, her blue eyes narrowed at him. “Fine. But from now on, no surprises. As your partners in this venture, we deserve to know your intentions.”

“You’re right. I should have talked to you all about staying at the lodge. I promise in the future to keep all three of you fully informed.” He paused, turning to Harper. “I hope you can chalk it up to over enthusiasm. I'm really excited about the project and can’t wait to get started.”

Harper placed her warm hand in his, her eyes full of trust. Ethan squeezed her hand and then released it before shifting his attention to Scarlet once more. “I want all of you to know that even though a lot of changes are going to happen here, we’re going to make every effort to ensure this building remains the jewel of Solace Lake Lodge. We want to honor what your family accomplished in the past while moving the lodge into the future.”

“I know you will.” Harper’s words were spoken with complete conviction. Ethan was grateful she believed in him. He hoped he could live up to her expectations and trust.

He already had a lot to make up for.

“The architect should have preliminary drawings for the other buildings ready in about a week. Our first step after that is to put our project out to tender and have general contractors bid on it. We’re looking for someone with experience working on projects of this scale.”

Harper nodded. “I’d like a voice in choosing the general contractor.”

"Of course." It didn't surprise him that Harper wanted to be involved. The success of the lodge meant everything to her. "We'll do it together."

She covered his hand with hers. Everything that was in his heart reflected back to him in her beautiful blue eyes. The wonder and excitement of a new relationship, the hope for the future, and a touch of trepidation. He winked, wanting to reassure her that he had the same hopes and fears about their blossoming relationship.

Someone cleared her throat and Ethan blinked. Harper's face flushed as she lowered her gaze and snatched away her hand. He'd been so focused on her he'd forgotten her sisters were watching and listening to their exchange.

"That must have been some meeting you two had." Scarlet's voice dripped with sarcasm. "Do you think my sister is some kind of pushover, Mr. James? Do you think if you sleep with her, your company will get a bigger share of the lodge?"

"Scarlet!"

"I don't think that at all, Ms. Lindquist. In fact, the papers have already been drawn up and signed by Mr. Hainstock. You and your sisters will retain a fifty-one percent share of the lodge."

"Then what's going on between you two? How did you manage to get so chummy over a two-hour meeting?"

Harper blushed once more, but instead of avoiding the question, she straightened her spine and looked directly at her sister. "It wasn't exactly a two-hour meeting."

"What do you mean—"

Maggie placed an arm on Scarlet's shoulder when she would have jumped to her feet. She turned to Harper, her voice calm. "What happened between you and Ethan, Harper?"

He watched Harper's throat work. But to her credit, she faced both her sisters with her head high. "Ethan arrived in the middle of a blizzard and was forced to stay for three nights."

"Well, wasn't that convenient." Scarlet pushed aside Maggie's hand and stood up. "You just happened to arrive during a blizzard and, of course, my compassionate sister wouldn't toss you out in the storm. You saw a woman alone, and lonely, and you took advantage of her, didn't you?"

Harper rose, her chest heaving. "Scarlet, if you're through insulting me, you can sit down and keep quiet."

With a surprised look on her face, Scarlet sat. Ethan had the feeling she wasn't used to Harper asserting herself. He sat back, proud of the way she was standing up for herself.

"Nothing of a sexual nature happened between us while Ethan stayed here. Neither of us wanted any feelings we might have for each other to interfere with our business dealings."

"But something did happen, didn't it?" Maggie asked quietly.

Harper glanced briefly at him before turning her attention back to her sisters. "We got to know one another over those three days. We discovered we had many things in common, and we found we...liked one another."

"So does that mean you're a couple now?" Scarlet's voice held a note of derision.

Color tinted Harper's cheeks once more. "I'm not sure what it means. But one thing I do know. It's none of your business. I count on both of you to respect our privacy, and I also expect you to treat Ethan civilly."

"I don't want anyone to take advantage of you, Harper." Scarlet got to her feet once more, her voice choked with emotion. "What do you really know about this guy?"

Harper turned to him, her eyes clear, and bright, and full of trust. "I know everything I need to know."

Ethan couldn't tear his gaze away from her. She was even stronger than he'd given her credit for. She was a magnificent, beautiful, intelligent woman. He wanted her more than any woman he'd ever known. Not just physically, but emotionally, spiritually, and in every way it was possible to want another human being.

And he'd lied to her. Was still lying to her.

A lump of guilt wedged in his chest. He didn't deserve her. He looked away.

"I don't want you to get hurt."

Harper's voice cracked. "I know you don't, Scarlet. But it's okay. I trust Ethan. He's not going to hurt me."

Scarlet turned to him, her face crumbling in tears. "I swear to God, if you do anything to cause her one moment of pain, you'll have to answer to me. And I'll make you damn sorry."

She didn't wait for an answer. Instead, she hurried from the room. Ethan closed his eyes in misery. It was just as well she hadn't expected an answer, because he had no idea what to say to her. Of course he didn't want to hurt Harper. But it could already be too late to avoid causing her pain.

"Scarlet, wait." Harper started to follow her.

Maggie put a hand on her arm. "I'll talk to her. You know Scarlet. She blows up fast, but she gets over it just as quickly. She'll be okay."

Harper nodded and Maggie left the room. Ethan got to his feet. He wanted to touch her, to take her in his arms and comfort her. But after this blow up with her sister, he wasn't sure if his touch would be welcomed. "I'm sorry, Harper. I've really messed things up for you."

"It's not your fault. I should have told them about us, but it's not easy for me to tell them how I feel, at least not about the important things." She looked away. "That's very presumptuous of me, isn't it? I don't even know if there is an us."

He heard the vulnerability in her voice. He placed two fingers under her chin and gently lifted, urging her to look at him. "Yeah, there's an us."

She gave a small, hiccupping laugh and walked into his arms, holding him tightly. Her voice was muffled against his chest. "That's what I thought. Or at least what I hoped."

"It's what I hoped for, too. I thought about you the whole time we were apart. I couldn't get you out of my head." *Or my heart.*

She leaned back and looked up into his face, her smile hopeful. "Neither could I."

He lowered his lips to hers and his whole body relaxed even as excitement flooded through him. *Yes.* This was what he'd wanted, needed for the last two weeks. Her lips were warm and soft as they pressed against his in innocent invitation. The scent of lilacs filled his senses. She wound her arms around his neck and moulded her body against his. Did she have any idea what she did to him, how much he wanted her?

He parted her lips with his tongue and pushed inside, reveling in the sweetness of her mouth. At first she was hesitant, but then she made a noise deep in her throat and touched her tongue to his, boldly mimicking the act of love with her thrusts. His erection strained at his jeans and he pulled her closer, kneading her buttocks with one hand.

He wanted her. He wanted to be inside her right now.

"Ethan." He heard the plea in Harper's whispered voice, but he was unsure if she was asking for the same thing or begging him to stop.

Guilt suddenly seized him, dousing him like a bucket of cold water dumped over his head. He pulled away from her and stared into her unfocused eyes, her breathing as erratic as his. They were standing in her dining room, with her sisters only steps away. Even if they'd been alone, he knew instinctively she wasn't ready for the next step.

He'd take things slow. Harper was worth the wait.

He kissed the end of her nose and took a step back. "Come on. I'll help you with the dishes."

She nodded and smiled up at him, her eyes full of happiness and trust. The lump of guilt burned in his chest once more. He didn't deserve her trust.

Before things went too far, he had to tell her the truth.

Chapter Nine

ETHAN LAID OUT THE papers on the dining room table and handed Harper a pen. She took the pen from him and glanced at Scarlet.

"Go ahead," Scarlet said. "You sign first."

Harper nodded, relieved that after the earlier upheaval, her sister had calmed down enough to sign the papers. She'd been afraid that Scarlet might be so angry she'd veto the whole project. But even more, she'd been afraid that Scarlet would be disappointed in her for letting her attraction for Ethan get mixed up with the business of the lodge.

Scarlet's opinion meant the world to her. She wanted her to approve of Ethan and of her budding relationship with him, wanted her to say she was doing the right thing by exploring the feelings she had for him. And she wanted Scarlet to say she believed in the project, and in her.

But neither of them had said anything. Scarlet and Maggie had come downstairs after about an hour. Harper had seen the redness in her sister's eyes and knew she'd been crying. She longed to take her in her arms and hold her, the way she'd done when they were kids and she'd tried to protect her. Her heart ached knowing she'd made her unhappy. Though Scarlet showed the world a tough, no-nonsense face, she had a tender heart that bruised easily.

Harper bent over the papers. For the first time she noticed Mr. Hainstock's signature. She looked up at Ethan in surprise. "Mr. Hainstock's first name is Ethan, too?"

He shrugged. "Yeah. Coincidence."

"It is. What are the chances? Ethan isn't that common a name."

"It's more common than you think." He glanced away, just as he'd done earlier during lunch. Harper's stomach tightened in apprehension.

"That's true," Maggie said. "I read somewhere it's one of the top ten names parents in America are giving their baby boys these days."

Harper looked up at Ethan again. He was once again looking down at her with calm assurance and her sudden fears disappeared. A picture of a baby boy popped into her mind's eye. A baby with Ethan's dark hair and eyes.

Their baby.

She swallowed and looked away, her hand shaking slightly as she affixed her name to the document. She was letting her imagination run wild.

When she was done, she handed the pen to Scarlet. She stood over the papers for a moment, the pen poised in her hand. Then, she looked at Harper. "You're sure this is what you really want?"

"Yes. I'm sure."

Scarlet nodded and added her signature beside her typewritten name. Harper let out a relieved breath.

Maggie signed last, then gave the pen back to Ethan. She put her arm around Harper's waist. "I feel like we should open a bottle of champagne and toast our new venture. This is a momentous occasion."

"Sorry, I'm fresh out of champagne. How about sparkling grape juice?" Harper said.

"It'll do."

Harper brought a bottle of chilled juice along with four long stemmed glasses to the dining room. Ethan poured and proposed a toast. "To the Lindquist sisters and the rebirth of Solace Lake Lodge."

Ethan's words touched her. He understood this project was more than business for her. It was home. Family.

Ethan drained his glass and set it on the table, then began gathering the papers. "I've got to take off now, but I'll be in touch. I'll be back in a couple of weeks, and we can begin interviewing contractors."

Harper was relieved she didn't have to make all the decisions about the lodge by herself. Ethan would be there to help her every step of the way. It was comforting to know she wasn't alone.

And the knowledge that he would be close by for the duration of the renovation sent tremors of excitement skating down her spine. They'd have the opportunity to really get to know each other and explore their feelings. She couldn't ask for anything more wonderful. "I'll make sure one of the cottages is ready for you."

She caught the glimmer of excitement in his eyes and her heart quickened its pace in response. He took her hand, lightly running his thumb across her palm.

"I'm looking forward to beginning this adventure with you."

Harper couldn't look away. She desperately wanted to kiss him, but with her sisters watching so closely, she didn't know how to proceed.

But apparently Ethan did. Placing his hand on her hip, he leaned in for a kiss. This kiss didn't have the fireworks of their last one, but it was soft and warm and full of promise, as if Ethan was trying to communicate the depths of his feelings.

Message received.

She walked him to the front door and pulled his coat from the closet. She inhaled the scent of the aftershave lingering on the collar and like the last time she'd seen him off, she wanted to bury her face in it. Instead, she held up the coat and helped him into it. "Have a safe trip back to the city."

He turned to face her, taking her shoulders in his hands. "I will. We'll talk soon, okay?"

"Okay."

"I should go."

"Yeah."

He made no move to leave. Instead, he kneaded her shoulders softly. Breathlessly, she stared into his eyes. He didn't want to go any more than she wanted him to. The knowledge made her heart sing.

At last, he leaned forward to kiss her forehead, then dropped his hands. Nodding at her sisters, he picked up his briefcase and walked out the door. Harper moved to the side window to watch him leave, only letting the curtain drop back into place when his truck was no longer visible. She already missed him.

"I feel like I should smoke a cigarette or something," Scarlet said, breaking the silence. "If there was any more heat between the two of you, your underwear would catch fire."

Harper laughed. "You're being silly."

"Oh, am I?" Scarlet raised an eyebrow, her lips quirking in a smile. "I've never seen you like this before. You really like this guy, don't you?"

Harper wanted to laugh and cry at the same time. She wanted to sing at the top of her lungs and dance in uninhibited joy around the room. She wanted to proclaim her feelings for Ethan to the whole world. She settled for a smile and a whispered declaration. "Yeah, I do."

Maggie grasped her hand. "I'm so happy for you, Harper."

A bubble of laughter escaped her lips. "It's not like we've declared undying love for each other, or anything. We're a long way from that. I don't know where this will go."

"Yes, but I've never known you to be so ga-ga over any other man before."

Neither have I. Her feelings for Ethan were so strong, so *right*, they were almost frightening.

No, not *almost* frightening. This was a road she'd never travelled before, and she couldn't be sure where it led. All she could do was to have faith. And trust.

"I'm happy for you, too," Scarlet said. "As long as he treats you right."

"Yes, you've made that quite clear."

"I'm sorry about earlier." Her brow wrinkled, the corners of her mouth turning down. Harper reached out to touch Scarlet's arm. "It's okay. I understand."

She did understand. None of them could seem to put their feelings for each other into words, but if the chips were really down, Scarlet would be there for her. The same way she'd be there for Scarlet.

Maggie took Scarlet's hand and for a moment they stood united, as close as they'd once been as children. More than anything in the world Harper wanted that feeling of unity again between her and her sisters, knowing they were together no matter what life threw at them.

"I feel like cooking," Maggie suddenly declared. "Let's go see what we can find in the kitchen."

A feeling of total contentment swept over Harper. She wished it could always be like this, safe and happy at home with her family nearby.

"Sounds great," she said. "Let's go."

ETHAN PULLED INTO HIS brother's driveway and cut the engine. When he stepped out of the truck he again heard the sound of a power tool coming from Cam's workshop. He smiled. Cam probably spent more time in his shop than he did in his house. If there'd been a bed in the shop, he'd probably sleep out there.

He opened the side door and entered. His five-year-old niece was the first to notice him.

"Uncle Ethan!"

She ran to him, and he scooped her up into his arms and held her tight for a moment. He inhaled her scent, a combination of baby shampoo and wood chips. He adored Tessa, would do anything for her. He understood perfectly why Cam had pulled up stakes and moved to Minnewasta to be closer to her. If he'd been in his brother's situation, he would have done the same thing.

He closed off that line of thinking immediately. He couldn't let himself think about what might have been.

"What did you bring me?" she asked.

Tessa's question caught him off guard. Cam had warned him he'd been spoiling her with all the things he been indulging her with; toys, clothes, even her own cell phone. Maybe he was right. He didn't want Tessa to like him only for what he could give her. She was already learning that lesson from her mother.

"I didn't bring you anything today. Just me. Isn't that good enough?"

She put her small arm around his shoulders. "Okay. You wanna see what Daddy made for me?"

"Sure."

He set her on her feet. She led him by the hand to a corner of the workshop where Cam had placed a child's table and chairs and some wooden toys, all hand-made. The newest addition to this group was a tall dollhouse.

"Daddy's going to make some furniture for the house." She demonstrated how the front of the house opened to reveal the rooms inside. "He's going to let me help paint it."

"Oh, yeah? What color are you going to paint your house?"

"Purple!"

Ethan ruffled her dark curls. "Of course. Why am I not surprised?"

Tessa's favorite color at the moment was purple in every shade possible. She'd insisted on everything from hair bands to her snowsuit to be that color.

Cam's machine stopped its rumbling and he called over. "Hey! I didn't know you were coming by today. What's up?"

"I was out at the lodge, signing the final papers. Since I was in the neighborhood, I thought I'd drop by and visit my favorite niece. And you, too, of course."

"Of course." Cam scooped Tessa into his arms. "How about we take a milk and cookie break with Uncle Ethan?"

"Okay, Daddy."

Once inside Cam's warm kitchen, Ethan removed his coat and helped Tessa out of her snowsuit while Cam put cookies on a plate and poured a glass of milk for his daughter.

"You want coffee?" he asked.

"Sure."

Cam poured water into the coffeemaker. "So, you've signed the final papers on the lodge renovations? You're really going to go ahead with this?"

"I am. I'm hoping you can help me out. We're going to be putting out tenders and talking to general contractors. This is your area of expertise. I thought you could give me your opinion on the quality of the bids."

"Yeah, I can do that. Do you want me to come to the lodge and meet with you and the owner to go over the bids?"

"Ah, no. Just you and me."

Cam turned and stared at him. "Don't tell me you still haven't told her who you are."

Ethan grabbed a cookie. "No, not yet."

"How do you know she doesn't already know who you really are? How can you be sure she's not playing you?"

"I know. Harper's not like that."

Cam made a sound of disbelief in his throat. "I've heard that before."

He had. Ethan recalled sitting in another kitchen uttering the same words. He believed them then, too, until he'd discovered how horribly wrong he'd been. He thought of Tessa liking him for what he could give her. Was Harper doing the same thing? Even though she didn't know he owned Hainstock Investments, he was responsible for pouring money into her lodge. Money like that had the power to influence feelings, even unintentionally.

No. He wasn't wrong about her. But worry clouded that judgement. After what he'd been through it was hard not to be suspicious of everyone's motives.

Ethan glanced at his niece who stared back at him, her eyes wide. She may not understand what they were talking about, but she could feel the tension in their conversation.

"We'll talk about this later, okay?"

Cam gave a curt nod and went back to making coffee. Ethan finished his chocolate chip cookie and turned his attention to Tessa. "How's school going, pumpkin?"

"Good!" She launched into stories about the exploits of her nursery school friends. "Timmy and me made a snow fort. Timmy says he likes me better than the other girls."

He chuckled at the idea of his five-year-old niece having a little boyfriend. He never imagined Cameron would have to start fighting off boys at this age, but Tessa was a beauty, and he was sure there would be many boys in her future.

"Do you like Timmy, too?" He grabbed another cookie and took a bite.

"Yeah, he's nice. Sometimes he comes to our house with his daddy to visit Mommy and me."

Ethan stopped chewing. Laura had a new boyfriend? He glanced up at his brother, whose jaw was clenched tight. Cameron's relationship with Laura had been tempestuous from the very beginning. She was a piece of work, and Ethan had been relieved when she'd ended their relationship by cheating on Cam. But judging from his brother's reaction, perhaps he still had feelings for her.

Christ, he hoped not.

Tessa didn't seem to notice her father's tension. Between sips of milk she continued to tell Ethan her stories. Cam poured two cups of coffee and then sat beside her.

Ethan was almost finished his coffee when a knock sounded at the door. Before Cam could answer it, Laura stepped inside the house. She ignored her daughter and Cam and focused her attention on him.

"Ethan! I thought that was your truck out there. It's nice to see you again."

Ethan did his best to be polite for Tessa's sake. "How are you, Laura?"

"I'm great!" She slipped off her shoes at the door and slung her coat over one of the kitchen chairs. "I'll have coffee, too, Cam. Two sugars."

Cam didn't get out of his chair. "I thought you had to take Tessa to her music lesson today."

"Why can't you take her?"

"I'm working. We're just taking a coffee break."

Laura waved a dismissive hand. "It's not like you have to punch a clock. You can set your own hours."

"Yes, I can. And I choose to work right now. I'll get Tessa ready and you can take her to her lesson."

"I have to be going, too," Ethan said, getting to his feet. Laura wouldn't leave unless he did. He put on his coat and kissed the top of Tessa's head. "Bye, pumpkin."

Laura made a pretty pout. "Oh, don't go, Ethan. I was hoping we could catch up."

After the way she'd cheated on his brother and continued to use him, he had nothing to say to the woman. He could barely stand to be in the same room with her. He never could figure out what Cam had seen in her. "I need to get back to the city. I'll talk to you later, Cam."

His brother nodded, his eyes clouded with barely repressed anger.

Laura gave a petulant sigh. "In that case, I'll go. Hurry and get your coat, Tessa, or we'll be late."

Ethan didn't wait around. With one last nod at Cam, he left the house and headed to his truck. On the drive back to Minneapolis, he couldn't help comparing Harper to Laura. Harper was hard working where Laura depended on her parents and Cam to pay her way, only working at the local grocery store when it suited her. Harper was loyal to her family. Laura had betrayed Cam.

But as much as Ethan liked and admired Harper, he knew he had to protect himself. Money made people do strange things; Laura was a prime example. Before he'd won the lottery, she'd barely spoken him. But once she'd found out about his win, she'd made a concerted effort to seduce him, even though she'd still been with his brother at the time. Her actions today told him she hadn't entirely given up.

Laura had been easy to resist. He'd seen through her thinly veiled come-on and felt only revulsion for her. But others had been far more clever in their deceit. He'd already made one bitter mistake with a beautiful woman.

He damn sure wouldn't make another.

HARPER CURLED HER FEET under her bottom and sipped her tea. They'd lit a fire in the lounge and, with the added help of a hot drink and a blanket to stave off the cold, she was happy and warm. She was glad that her sisters, both curled under blankets themselves, looked equally content.

"See what you're missing by not living at the lodge anymore?" she said, half-jokingly.

"You mean the freezing cold blowing through the cracks in the logs? Yeah, I've really missed that," Scarlet quipped. "I can hardly wait for my cold shower tomorrow morning."

"Be fair. There's always been plenty of hot water for your showers."

"Yes, but once I step out of the shower, I'll freeze to the floor tiles."

"That's to encourage you to hurry. You always were a bathroom hog."

"Well, all that will be changing," Maggie said. "In the future, the Solace Lake Lodge will no longer be the ice box it is today."

Scarlet frowned. "I hope you know what you're getting into, Harper."

So do I. "I've done my homework, and I believe I've partnered with the right people."

"You mean Ethan, don't you?" Maggie said with a smile. "He seems nice."

"I can see why you're attracted to him. He's certainly good-looking," Scarlet said. "But is it a mistake to mix business with personal feelings?"

She worried about that, too. If the relationship between her and Ethan broke down, the lodge project could be in jeopardy. The thought of that happening, of some kind of problem ruining the trust and rapport they had now, was scary.

"You worry about me too much, Scarlet. I love you for it, but I have faith. It's going to be okay." She chose her next words carefully. "I wish you two were going to be part of this project. I wish you both were going to be here."

"I can't give up everything I've worked for. I have a career in Chicago, Harper. I've got friends, a condo, a life there. You know that," Scarlet said.

"I know. I'm sorry. I shouldn't have said anything."

Scarlet reached over and extended her hand. "Like I said before, I'll do what I can to help. When the time comes,

I'll come up with a marketing plan to help you advertise the lodge."

Harper squeezed her sister's hand. It meant a lot that Scarlet wanted to be part of her project, in spite of her reservations. "That would be wonderful. Thank you."

"And I'm sure Maggie is willing to volunteer her services as well."

"I think I've been volun-told," Maggie said with a smile. "But I'm happy to help you with anything I can."

"I could use your help designing the kitchen and choosing the appliances and equipment. I want to make sure it has everything a professional chef needs."

"I can do that."

"If you decide to come home to work here, my offer is still open." Harper said the words with a laugh, but she was very serious. She couldn't get her earlier conversation with Maggie out of her mind. Something was going on. It was clear she wasn't happy. But Maggie had always been stubborn and determined. She'd sworn when she left home at eighteen that she was never coming back.

"I don't know, Harper," Maggie said. "I'm going to have to think about it."

Maggie's answer surprised her. She'd expected her usual rejection. The fact that she hadn't vetoed the idea outright both delighted and worried her. Something was definitely wrong.

She wanted to ask but if she pushed, Maggie would clam up the way she had since she was a teenager. Instead, she plastered a sunny smile on her face. "You do that and I'll ask you again later." She decided the best thing to do was to change the subject. “I meant to ask if you got a new car. I didn’t recognize the one you and Scarlet pulled up in today.”

Maggie fiddled with the button of her cardigan. “No, that’s Scarlet’s rental. She picked it up at the airport when she flew in from Chicago.”

“Oh, I see. I thought you’d drive up in your red Toyota.”

“I don’t have the Toyota anymore.” Maggie picked up her teacup. “It needed a bunch of repairs, so I decided to get rid of it. I haven’t replaced it yet.”

Another surprise. Harper glanced at Scarlet, who gave a slight shrug that said Maggie hadn’t shared any information with her, either. It was a perfectly good explanation. Getting rid of a car that didn’t work made sense, but Harper suspected there was more to the story. "Oh."

She wished she and her sisters could feel comfortable confiding the truth to each other. They were so intent on shielding one another from pain that no truths were shared, no unpleasantness revealed. Sometimes they acted like complete strangers. Harper wanted to know everything about them, the good and the bad, even the ugly. She wanted to help them in any way she could.

But then, she wasn’t exactly forthcoming either. As the oldest, she’d always believed she had to be strong for them, to protect them. So she’d put on a happy face and buried her hurts and worries.

She sank into the cushions of her armchair. Being the strong one was exhausting.

Chapter Ten

AFTER BREAKFAST THE next morning, Scarlet and Maggie packed their things into the rental car. While the car ran for a few minutes to warm up, Harper gave them each a hug. "It was so wonderful seeing you," she said as she kissed Maggie's cheek.

"It was wonderful to see you, too."

"I'll be in touch about those kitchen appliances. When the time comes, we'll go on a little shopping spree."

"Sounds like fun. Take care, Harper."

Harper kissed her again. "You too, honey. Call me when you get to Minneapolis so I know you got home safely."

"I will."

She turned to Scarlet. "Have a safe trip."

Scarlet hugged her. "I will. And I want you to keep me up to date with the renovations on the lodge."

"I'll be happy to. Call me when you get back to your apartment in Chicago, okay?"

She bent to kiss her cheek. "You worry too much, but I'll call."

A few moments later they got in the car and, with a wave to Harper, they pulled out of the driveway. Harper closed the door against the cold and leaned against it.

Alone again.

She shoved away the wave of loneliness that threatened to swamp her. Having herself a little pity party would only make her feel worse. She'd learned that hard truth in the days after her grandfather's death, when her sisters left and all the neighbors and friends went home to their own lives and families. Suddenly she'd been completely alone, with no one to look after, no real purpose in her life. She'd cried for three days until she became so sick she frightened herself. Finally, she forced herself to eat something, and came to terms with the fact that she was on her own. Completely.

Since then, she'd made a point to keep as busy as possible. She worked as many shifts as they would give her at the restaurant, and she'd expanded her bookkeeping business, picking up several new clients. She volunteered at the library in Minnewasta and in the winter, she helped at the local hockey rink by flipping burgers and serving customers in the concession booth. She even dated a few times, though she gave up after a few unsuccessful attempts. If she kept busy enough, worked hard enough, she almost forgot she was alone.

Almost, but not quite.

Enough. She pushed away from the door and headed up the stairs to strip the beds her sisters had slept in.

The cell phone in the pocket of her sweater began to vibrate. When she checked the call display, she saw Ethan's name. Smiling, she pushed the talk button. "Good morning, Ethan."

"Good morning. Are your sisters still there?"

"They just left. Scarlet's flight back to Chicago leaves this afternoon so they needed to get an early start."

"I hate that you're all by yourself out there."

She was touched that he worried about her and seemed to understand how alone, and lonely, she was sometimes. "I'm fine, really."

He cleared his throat. "I wanted to let you know that the tenders went out today. I'll come out to the lodge in a couple of weeks, and we can go over the bids together. The architect's plans for the other buildings should be ready by then, too. And like I said, I, er, Mr. Hainstock wants me to stay at the lodge from that point on."

Excitement filled her at the thought of Ethan being close by, possibly for months. "Sounds good." She hesitated, unsure how much of her enthusiasm to reveal. "I'm glad you're going to be staying. This is going to be a complex job, and we'll need to stay on top of it every minute. I appreciate your help."

"Are you going to continue working?"

"I have to if I'm going to keep up my truck payments and buy groceries. Besides, I have clients who depend on me, and Miller's has already assigned shifts to me for the whole summer. I don't want to let anyone down."

"You worry more about other people than you do about yourself."

"No, I don't. I'm totally selfish. I've come up with this whole lodge project just so I don't have to move."

Ethan laughed softly, the sound caressing Harper's soul. "Tell it to somebody who doesn't know you as well as I do."

Her throat closed, making it impossible to speak. He didn't know her nearly as well as he thought he did. He didn't know how sexually inexperienced she was. Or the real truth about her parents' deaths.

"Harper? Are you still there?"

She swallowed and cleared her throat. "Yes, I'm here. I was thinking that if our general contractor was from far away, he could stay in the cottage beside yours if he wanted. He could even bring his family. When I need to move out of the lodge, I could borrow my friend's trailer. He already said I could have it if I need it."

If Ethan wondered why she changed the subject so abruptly, he didn't say anything. "I think having a place to live might be an incentive for some contractors. I'll make sure our bidders know about it."

"Good. Thank you." Guilt clogged her throat. More than anything in the world, she wanted a real, honest relationship with Ethan. But how could she have that if she couldn't tell him the truth? All the truth.

"I miss you, Harper."

Her heart heard the longing in his voice. "I miss you, too."

"I'll see you soon. Take care."

"Goodbye."

Harper ended the call, her heart pounding. Emotions swamped her. Exhilaration at the possibility of seeing him again, and guilt for hiding the truth.

She closed her eyes and prayed for courage. If their relationship was ever going to flourish, she'd need to come clean with him.

Chapter Eleven

TWO WEEKS LATER, IT was almost seven p.m. when Ethan pulled into the front yard of the old lodge. As he turned off the ignition, his heart began to pound in anticipation. He'd never experienced anything like this. He'd dreamt of Harper, dreamt of touching her silky skin and making love with her. He'd woken in the middle of the night, sweating and aching with need.

But it wasn't only a physical need. He longed to talk to her, hear her laugh, simply be in her company. Even if all they ever did was hold hands, he wanted to be with her.

He hoped to hell she wanted the same.

Guilt swiftly followed on the heels of that thought. How could he contemplate deepening the relationship between them when she didn't know who he really was? He didn't want to begin their relationship with a lie, but he'd let several weeks go by. If he told her the truth now, he could scuttle things with her before they even had a chance to start.

Ethan ran a hand through his hair as he tried to figure out what to do. He wouldn't push her. If something was to happen between them, he'd let it happen naturally, let Harper take the lead. Then he'd tell her.

His course of action decided, Ethan jumped out of his truck and headed to the front door of the lodge. Harper flung the door wide open before he had a chance to knock. A smile of welcome lit her face. With one hand, she reached out and pulled him inside.

"Ethan."

Only one word, just his name, but she packed a world of emotion in it. He could feel her longing and knew in an instant she understood everything he'd been experiencing because it was the same for her.

He pushed the door closed and gathered her in his arms, burying his face in her hair and inhaling her familiar lilac scent.

"Harper."

He kissed her. She framed his face with both her hands and kissed him back. Her kiss was tender and sweet, with that hint of innocence he'd begun associating with her. However innocent, her touch sent his body up in flames.

Gradually she pulled away, her fingers tracing the lines of his face. His skin tingled under her feather-light touch. He grasped her hand and kissed the palm, his eyes never leaving hers. "God, I've missed you."

Joy radiated in her smile. "I've missed you, too. I'm so happy you're here."

"Me, too."

He kissed her again, shaking with need as he tried to communicate with his body the passion in his heart. She responded ardently at first, then pulled away, as if there was a line she was unwilling, or afraid, to cross. A wave of disappointment washed over him.

Don't push her.

The mantra sang in his head. Reluctantly, he let her go.

She was worth waiting for.

"Did you bring the bids for the renovations with you?"

She was changing the subject. He pointed to the briefcase he'd dropped near the door. "I did, and the preliminary blueprints from the architect, too. We can look them over tomorrow."

"Good. I'm curious to see who bid on the project. Are you hungry? Dinner is ready." She smiled politely, once more turning into the perfect hostess.

"That sounds great."

He followed her into the kitchen where he was greeted by a rich blend of welcoming scents. Harper's kitchen was warm and cozy and comfortable. Like home.

"It smells amazing in here." He pointed to a large pot on the back burner of the stove. "Is that home-made soup?"

"Yes, beef barley, my grandmother's recipe. It used to be my grandfather's favorite. It was the first thing she taught me to make."

"She must have been very proud of you."

Harper shrugged and looked away. "Grandma Dorothy was...difficult. She'd always been the kind of person who demanded perfection, but after my mother died, she was even worse. She ruled this lodge, and the three of us, with an iron fist. No matter what we did, or didn't do, it was never good enough. I don't know if she was proud of me or not."

She turned away, giving the soup a stir with a large wooden spoon. "I added lots of carrots. I hope you like carrots."

From the tense set of her shoulders it was obvious she didn't want to talk about her grandmother any longer. He imagined doing so brought up painful memories of her parents. He wished she could confide in him. He wanted to understand her pain, take some of the burden away.

Don't push her.

He squeezed her shoulders between his hands to let her know he understood, then lightly kissed her hair before stepping away. Her shoulders relaxed, her tension eased.

"I can smell something else, too. Something sweet," he said.

Harper turned to him with a smile. "I have a surprise for you. I told the cook at Miller's how much you enjoyed her pie and she sent another one along. It's baking in the oven."

His nose detected the sweet notes of cinnamon and sugar. "What kind is it? It doesn't smell like apple."

"It's blueberry this time. Martha makes a mean blueberry pie. I've set a table for us in the dining room. Can you help me bring in the food?"

"Sure."

She filled two bowls with the fragrant soup and they each brought one to the dining room table. A loaf of bread and a bowl of butter were already in place.

"Martha also wanted you to sample her bread," she said with a grin. "I think she was as excited as I was that you were coming. She wants to impress the new boss's rep."

He buttered a chunk of bread and bit into it. It melted in his mouth. "I think I'm in love with Martha. Do you think she'd come work for us?"

She shook her head. "No, no way. She's been with the Millers for nearly thirty years, and I believe she's getting ready to retire in a year or two. She's a wonderful cook, but she's not what I have in mind for the lodge."

"You want something more modern."

Ethan watched as she lifted her spoon and blew on the hot soup before sampling it. "Exactly. I want something different. Miller's has already cornered the market on homespun, country cooking around here."

He tasted some of the soup. It was delicious. Harper was no slouch herself when it came to cooking. "It might be difficult to attract that kind of chef to a rural area like this."

"I know. I wish..." She shook her head and lifted her soupspoon once more.

"What?"

She frowned and put down her spoon. "I wish Maggie would see how perfect the job as chef at the lodge is for her. But at least she volunteered to help me shop for all the appliances and equipment a professional kitchen will need."

"That will be very helpful." He took another slice of bread and buttered it.

"Yeah, it will." Her brow wrinkled as she tore a piece of bread into chunks and dropped them onto her plate. She obviously had more on her mind.

"Spill it, Harper. What are you thinking?"

She looked up and blinked. "I didn't know I was so transparent."

"Only to me. What's on your mind?"

"For all that Maggie insists she has a life that she loves in the city, she doesn't seem very happy."

"What's going on with her?"

"I don't know." Harper shook her head. "She doesn't confide in me. It's been that way since our grandmother died. Maggie was fourteen. I came home to look after her and Grandpa, and I sort of took over the role of her mother. I never wanted to be anything except her sister, but she was so young and rebellious that I had to lay down the law for her own good. Fortunately, as she got older, she settled down, and we were able to step away from that adversarial relationship. But she's never trusted me with her thoughts and worries. Not really."

"And that upsets you."

She gave him a sad smile. "Of course it does. I only want to be her sister. I want her to be happy. I would never use anything she tells me against her."

Ethan reached across the table and grasped her hand. She had the softest skin. "I'm sure she knows that."

"I'm not so certain."

"Then maybe you have to tell her."

She surprised him with an amused smile. "Honesty isn't something we're big on in my family."

There was that word again. Hearing her say it sent his heart racing. "Sometimes the people we care about most are the ones it's hardest to be honest with."

Her blue eyes met his. "Yes, that's true."

Ethan had the uncomfortable feeling she saw right through him, past the façade and the fake name to the man beneath. The man who was being less than honest with her.

BY THE TIME THEY FINISHED dinner and cleaned up, it was close to nine, and completely dark. The days were gradually getting longer, but March in Minnesota meant daylight hours were short.

They dressed in warm winter gear and headed for the garage. Once they got there, Harper grasped the handle of the garage's overhead door and pulled as hard as she could. The heavy metal door stubbornly refused to budge. "It must be off the tracks again," she said.

"Can I try?" Ethan asked, stepping closer. She caught a whiff of the citrusy aftershave she liked so much. *God, he smelled good enough to eat.*

She swallowed and stepped aside. "Be my guest."

He gripped the door handle and pulled, but the door didn't move. "Come on, baby," he murmured. "Don't be like that."

He tried once more, his face straining with exertion. The door lifted. The fog of Ethan's warm breath curled around his face in the cold air. "There you go. You just have to whisper a few sweet nothings to her."

Oh, to have him whisper a few sweet nothings in my ear. Harper sighed and stifled a shiver that had nothing to do with the cold. She cleared her throat. "Thanks for muscling it open."

"My pleasure."

She nearly groaned. Did he have to use that particular phrase? Her brain turned everything he said into something sexual.

With an effort, she pushed away all thoughts of pleasure and whispered endearments and did her best to concentrate on the business at hand – getting Ethan to his cottage. The last time Ethan visited, he'd been a passenger on her sled, but this time he'd go solo.

"Have you ever driven a snowmobile?"

"Years ago," he replied. "When I was kid in Wisconsin. My brother and I used to chase each other around the lake near our inn. It was a blast."

"They're a lot of fun, but up here in the woods, they're practical, too. Right now the road up to your cottage is blocked with snow, so this is the only way there, aside from snowshoes."

She'd considered giving him the same room at the lodge he'd stayed in before, at least until construction began, but she knew how cold it could get. With the ancient bathroom a frigid walk down the hall, it wasn't exactly comfortable accommodations. The cottage was new and warm, with a pretty, modern bathroom, a wood burning fireplace and brand-new appliances. It had plenty of space and would afford Ethan as much privacy as he'd like.

Besides, having Ethan under the same roof tempted fate. She wanted him, but she didn't know if she was ready to make love with him, to trust him so intimately. For now, having him stay in the cottage seemed like the safest option.

"I put electric start in these babies, so getting them going is usually pretty easy. I only have to pump the choke a couple of times and turn the switch. Before you start the engine, it's a good idea to depress the throttle a couple of times to make sure it hasn't frozen open, otherwise it could take off without you."

She squeezed the throttle on the handlebar and when she was satisfied it was working properly, opened the choke. Ethan leaned in, watching intently. His close proximity made her forget what she was doing. Her fingers fumbled when she turned the electric start. As the engine roared to life, she released the choke, then handed a helmet to Ethan.

"You start the other one," she shouted over the noise of the sled.

He slipped on the helmet and fastened it under his chin. Mirroring her steps, he started the second snowmobile without any trouble. Harper put on her own helmet and mounted her sled. She drove out of the garage with Ethan following closely behind.

Stopping at his truck in front of the lodge, they picked up Ethan's suitcase. Harper used a couple of bungee cords to secure it on the seat behind him. Then, she remounted her sled and turned in the direction of the cottages.

She'd chosen the cottage closest to the lodge for him. Parking the snowmobiles in front, she led the way up the stairs to the front porch, which she'd cleared of snow. Once inside, they took off their boots. Harper walked to the fridge and opened the door.

"I've stocked the kitchen with a few things I thought you might need. Coffee, juice, bottled water, and some snacks. If you need anything else, let me know."

"I'm sure I'll be fine. Thank you."

"I didn't stock any real food since you'll be eating most of your meals with me at the lodge." She suddenly realized she hadn't asked him if that was what he wanted. "Unless you don't want to."

Ethan took off his gloves and tossed them on the kitchen counter. He grasped her hands and squeezed reassuringly. "I'd much rather have meals with you, spend time with you."

"I'm glad," she said in relief.

"I don't want you to feel you have to cater to me, though. I'll look after cleaning the cottage myself, and I can help you with the cooking. I'm not much of a chef, but I can peel a vegetable."

She loved the warmth in his dark eyes. "Good to know. I'm not going to be around for every meal. I'll be working several lunch and dinner shifts at Miller's, so you'll have to fend for yourself sometimes."

"I'll be away occasionally, too. I'm working on finding new management for Miller's for when we take over in the summer, so I'll have to go back to the city quite often." He lifted her hand to his lips and kissed it. "I'll appreciate the time we have together."

She'd treasure her time with Ethan. She only wished they didn't have so many obligations that kept them apart. "How about breakfast at eight tomorrow morning?"

"Sounds great." He caressed her cheek, his thumb gently stroking the delicate skin below her eye. "Would you like to stay for coffee?"

Her body reacted to his touch with a flash of heat that emanated from her core and spread to her fingertips. She wanted to stay for coffee, but if she did, she might be tempted to stay the night. And though her body might be more than ready to make love with Ethan, her heart and her head weren't there yet.

She couldn't bear the disbelief, and the displeasure, she was sure she'd see on his face when he found out she was a virgin. Or worse, the pity.

Reluctantly, she took a step away from him. "I think it's best if I go now. Good night, Ethan."

Regret flashed briefly across his face. "Good night."

She left the cottage and climbed on her sled for the short trip back to the lodge, wondering when her head was going to catch up with her body. Or if it ever would.

Chapter Twelve

THE NEXT MORNING ETHAN climbed on the snowmobile for the short trip down the hill to the lodge. Remembering the way Harper had started the machine last night, he depressed the throttle a couple of times to ensure it wasn't frozen open. Then he opened the choke and turned the key. To his relief, it started on the first try. He backed off the choke, then squeezed the throttle on the handlebar. With a roar of power the sled took off. Ethan laughed in delight as he shot off the trail Harper had created and steered the sled over the snowbanks. He'd forgotten how exhilarating the freedom of driving a snow machine could be.

The trip to the lodge was too short. Maybe he could convince Harper to take him on another tour around the property. This time he could drive his own sled.

He entered the lodge through the back door, which led to the kitchen. Knocking on the doorframe he called, "You awake, Harper?"

She appeared around a corner wearing a pink apron and carrying a mixing bowl. She gave him a welcoming smile. "I've been awake for hours. Some of us get an early start on the day."

"You do realize it's only seven fifty a.m.? That's practically the crack of dawn in my world."

Her smile disappeared. "I'm sorry. If this was too early for you, I could have made breakfast later."

"I'm kidding, Harper. I'm starved, and I'm dying for a cup of coffee. Is it ready?"

Relief flooded her face. "Of course. Come in and I'll pour you a cup."

After stripping out of his winter gear, he followed her into the kitchen. She pulled two cups from a cupboard and poured coffee into them. "So, this morning we're going to take a look at the bids for the general contracting, right?"

"Right. We've got five bids. I did a little investigation on each of the bidders, some general background stuff. I checked around to see what kind of reputations they had, if there were any negative reviews of their work, or if their business practices had ever come into question. Most seem to be good, solid companies."

"Sounds like we may have a difficult decision to make. Can we take a look after breakfast?"

"Absolutely. But first I want to show you what the architect has come up with. I'd like to get your thoughts."

"I'm excited to see the plans," she said with a smile.

When they finished cleaning up after breakfast, Ethan brought his briefcase and a cardboard tube containing the blueprints to one of the tables in the dining room. He pulled the rolled-up plans from the tube and set them on the table, using a couple of sugar bowls and salt and pepper shakers to hold down the curling edges.

"This first drawing shows how the structures will be situated on the property. It's a bird's eye view from above." He pointed to the lodge. "Here's the lodge with the new guest wing on the south side. To the north, we have the new event center. It's close to the lodge so guests don't have far to go to their rooms. It also shares the parking lot with the lodge."

"Okay." She stepped closer and pointed to a couple of smaller structures near the lake. "What are these?"

When she leaned over the blueprints and tossed her hair over her shoulder, blonde curls tumbled down her back. The scent of lilacs filled his senses. Was it the perfume she used or maybe her shampoo? For the rest of his life he'd think of her whenever he smelled lilacs.

She looked up at him. "Ethan?"

He blinked, struggling to regain his focus. "The first one is the new spa. It has a steam room inside, treatment rooms for massages, and esthetician stations. Outside the spa there's a ten-person hot tub and two outdoor dry saunas. The other building is meant to house recreational equipment, like kayaks, canoes and paddle boards that guests can rent. I see the building as the recreation hub for the lodge, where guests can sign up for bird watching excursions or dog sled rides."

Her blue eyes danced with excitement. "That's a great idea. There's no room for that sort of thing in the lodge itself."

She had the most amazing smile, completely open and full of life and promise. Again, he forced himself to stay focused. "Here's the artist's rendering of the event center."

He heard Harper's quick intake of breath. "It's gorgeous! I love it!"

Ethan let out a relieved breath. He'd suggested the barn-style building to the architect, so he was especially pleased she liked it. "Good. I'm glad."

She touched the roofline of the drawing. "I love that it looks kind of like an old barn. It really fits the vibe we're trying to create."

"All the out buildings are going to be clad with cedar siding that will weather with age. They'll look like they've been here forever."

"That'll be perfect."

"The event center may look old, but it's state of the art. It's got a modern kitchen that can cater a large group, and we're going to equip it with audio-visual equipment so we can host conferences as well as weddings."

"It looks like there's a second-floor balcony. What's that for?"

He flipped through the drawings until he found the detailed rendering of the second floor. "We've got two smaller meeting rooms up there that can turn into one larger room by folding away the dividing wall between them. There's a staircase going upstairs from the main floor of the event center, as well as an elevator. Your owner's apartment is also up there. What do you think?"

She glanced up at him. "Owner's apartment?"

"You're going to need a place to live since we're turning your current living quarters here in the lodge into the kitchen. I figured you'd want something on the property, so I asked the architect to come up with a solution for you."

Harper silently stared at the drawings. Ethan waited, worried he'd overstepped his bounds. Perhaps she'd already made other living arrangements, or maybe she thought this small apartment wouldn't give her enough privacy. He fidgeted with his pen, tapping it against the table.

Finally, he said, "If you don't like it, we can have it removed or changed. These are simply preliminary drawings."

She lifted her head, her eyes bright. "No, don't do that. It's perfect the way it is. Thank you."

Her smile hit him in the solar plexus and robbed him of breath. For long seconds, he could only stare into her eyes.

"I thought I'd have to find some kind of rental in Minnewasta. I've lived here at the lake so long...I wasn't looking forward to that. This is a perfect solution. Thank you for thinking of it, Ethan."

He nodded, his heart thrumming in double time. "You're welcome."

She turned her attention to the drawings once more. "How big is the apartment?"

Ethan forced himself to concentrate on the business at hand and not on his desire to take her in his arms and kiss her senseless. "It's not huge, about eight hundred square feet or so, but it's got two bedrooms, an open-concept kitchen and living area and decent storage space. It's upstairs at the back of the center, and you'll have a private staircase and a private balcony overlooking the lake. We'll make sure it's well insulated so noise from the event center doesn't bother you."

"I didn't expect anything so nice. It's beautiful."

"When the time comes, you can pick out the flooring, and cabinets and all the finishes you'd like."

She touched the drawing reverently. "That'll be fun. I've never had a chance to decorate my own space before."

Something twisted inside his heart. For most of her adult life, she'd been so focused on the needs of her family, even the needs of the lodge, that she rarely thought of herself. It was time someone looked after her.

Someone like me.

They examined the detailed drawings of each structure and Harper made a few suggestions for minor changes, but overall she seemed pleased with the blueprints.

"Are you ready to look at the bids now?" he asked, after rolling up the blueprints and putting them back in the cardboard tube.

"Yes, I'm ready."

Ethan removed the papers from his briefcase and set them on the table for Harper to look at. She read quickly through all the bids and then turned to him. "Except for this one that seems much lower than the rest, the bids for the work are quite similar, aren't they?"

"Yes. Do any of the names sound familiar to you?" He lifted a set of papers. "This contractor's address is in Minnewasta."

She glanced at the papers and nodded. "Reese Hanson. Yes, I know the name, but I don't know him personally. I do know his wife, though, or at least I used to. Abby and my mother were best friends, but I haven't seen her in years. She and Reese married about ten years ago and moved away, to Minneapolis I think. I didn't know they'd moved back to Minnewasta."

"From the checking I've done, it looks like Hanson has been in the construction business for a number of years. His company has tackled some pretty big jobs, some of them even bigger than ours."

"Abby's a pretty good judge of character, and a wonderful, kind person. She wouldn't marry somebody who wasn't honest."

Honesty. It meant everything to her. Ethan set the papers back on the table. "So it looks like Hanson Construction is the front runner at the moment. I'm going to do some more background checking, and I'll let you know what I find out. We should make our decision within the week."

"Don't you have to run your findings past Mr. Hainstock?"

Sometimes minutes went by and he forgot she didn't know he was Mr. Hainstock. He looked into her trusting blue eyes. She valued honesty and integrity and here he was, lying to her. He couldn't continue to deceive her, even if it meant their personal relationship might end. He had to tell her. "Harper—"

A loud crash came from the front of the house followed by muffled curses. A man's slurred voice called, "Harper! Help me!"

She winced. "Oh, God. Not again."

She jumped to her feet and ran out of the room. Ethan followed her, concerned for her safety and unsure whether he should be grateful or annoyed by the interruption to his confession.

When they arrived in the foyer, a middle-aged man lay sprawled on the floor, either injured in some way or drunk. When Ethan got closer, he smelled the combination of body odor and stale booze wafting off the man in sickening waves. *Drunk it was.*

Harper grabbed the man's arm and helped him to his feet, wincing as she did so. "God, Willy, you stink. When was the last time you had a bath?"

He leaned against her, threatening to topple them both. Ethan grabbed his other arm and steadied him. "You know this guy?"

"Sadly, yes. Willy Eklund. He used to work for my grandfather. He and my mother went to school together in Minnewasta."

Willy leaned toward her again, trying to put his arm around her. "I need...need a little drink, Harper. Just one little drink. For an old friend."

Ethan pulled him away. No way was he going to let the drunken bastard hang all over her.

"I don't have any liquor in the lodge and even if I did, I wouldn't give it to you. How did you get here?"

"Drove myself." His words were slurred. Ethan turned away from the stench of his breath.

Ethan followed Harper's gaze out the open door where a beat-up Ford pickup truck was parked, its lights on and the driver's side door still open. Harper shook her head. "God, Willy, how could you? You could have killed yourself, or worse, somebody else." She half pulled, half dragged him a few steps forward. "You're hitting the bathtub, my friend."

"Don't need a bath. I need...need a little drink."

"Here's the deal, Willy. Either you have a good long soak and get yourself clean, or I'm calling the cops right now and telling them you've been driving drunk. Which will it be?"

The drunk shook his head, nearly losing his balance once more. "No, don't do that. Your mother wouldn't call the cops. Miranda was my friend."

A myriad of emotions crossed Harper's face – anger, disgust, sadness, resignation and finally determination. "Too bad. My mother's not here. You're stuck with me. So what's it going to be, a bath followed by black coffee and a sandwich, or the cops, followed by the drunk tank?"

He waved his hand in front of his face. "Okay, okay. I'll take a bath. Don't call the cops."

"Fine. While you're in there, I'm going to wash your disgusting clothes, too." She gave Ethan an apologetic look. "I'm sorry about this. Can you help him to undress and get into the bath?"

Ethan glanced at the old drunk. Seeing him naked was about the last thing he wanted, but there was no way he was going to let Harper handle him alone. "Sure. Where do you want me to take him?"

She thought for a moment. "He'll never make it up the stairs. Let's take him to my bathroom here on the main floor."

He followed her, half-carrying, half-dragging Willy. She led them to a small bathroom next to her bedroom and began running the bath. She added lilac scented bubble bath to the water.

"Maybe it'll help with the smell," she said with a wry smile.

"Couldn't hurt." Ethan leaned Willy against the small vanity. "Let's take off your jacket. It looks like it needs a bath nearly as much as you do."

"Who the hell are you?" Willy demanded.

"He's a friend of mine. His name is Ethan," Harper said. She kept Willy standing upright while Ethan stripped off his winter jacket and then a filthy shirt and undershirt. Together they helped him sit on the edge of the tub and Harper pulled off his boots and thick woolen socks. The smell made Ethan's eyes water.

Harper gathered the dirty clothes. "This is where I leave you. There's a small plastic pail under the sink that you can use to rinse his hair. God knows what's in that tangled mess."

He retrieved the pail, keeping one hand on Willy's shoulder to stop him from falling backwards into the tub. Good thing the bathroom was small.

"Once I get his pants off, do you want me to toss them out into the hall?"

"Yes, please. He can't wear these filthy clothes. I'll find something of my grandfather's until they're dry." She paused, one hand on the doorknob, her blue eyes somber. "Thank you. I appreciate this."

Ethan nodded. In that moment, he realized he'd do just about anything for her. And apparently 'just about anything' included bathing a filthy drunk.

Harper slipped out the door and closed it quietly behind her. Ethan turned to Willy. "Okay, buddy. Time to drop your drawers."

Fortunately, he didn't put up any kind of struggle. He stood on shaky legs and let Ethan strip off his pants and underwear. His emaciated body began to shake, either from the chill of the room or some kind of withdrawal. Willy clung to him as he stepped into the tub.

"Damn, that's hot!"

"Quit complaining. If it was up to me, your ass would be in jail. You're lucky Harper is a hell of lot nicer than I am."

Aside from releasing a hissing breath as Ethan lowered him into the tub, Willy said nothing further. Ethan turned off the water, then gathered the dirty pants and underwear, and tossed them into the hallway. Harper was a damn good friend to be helping someone so obviously down on his luck.

He picked up the plastic pail and stuck it into the bath water. "Get ready, Willy. You're about to get real wet."

WILLY SAT ACROSS THE table from Harper and lifted a coffee cup to his lips with two shaky hands. Her grandfather's robe was at least two sizes too big and gaped at the neck. Willy had shrunken, both physically and emotionally.

His descent into alcoholism broke her heart. His eyes were downcast, as if he were afraid to look at her. Or as if he was ashamed. Now that he was beginning to sober up, bits and pieces of the Willy she used to know, the one who used to take her and Scarlet for boat rides and taught her how to bait a hook, were beginning to re-emerge. And that Willy was embarrassed by what he had become.

Harper glanced at his empty bowl. "Would you like more soup?"

He looked up briefly before dropping his gaze to the table once more. "No, thank you. It was very good, thank you."

"You're welcome. Your clothes should be dry in a few minutes."

He nodded. "Thank you."

"Willy, you can't go on like this. You're killing yourself."

"I can still hold a job," he said, his watery brown eyes flashing with defiance. "I only drink on weekends."

"Where do you work?" Ethan asked. He sat across the table from her, his hands wrapped around his coffee cup. He'd been unbelievably helpful with Willy. She didn't know how she'd ever thank him.

"I clean offices at night."

There was no way any employer would keep him on if they saw him the way they had, filthy and stinking and falling down drunk. Harper laid her hand on Willy's arm. "You have to promise me you'll never drive drunk again. What if you'd hit someone? How would you feel if you caused someone's death?"

Willy shrank from her as if she'd struck him. Tears gathered in his eyes. His mouth trembled as he whispered, "I couldn't take that. I don't want to hurt anyone."

"I know you don't. Please, promise me that if you drink, you'll stay at home."

His Adam's apple worked as he swallowed. "I promise, Harper."

She sagged in relief. "That's good."

He clutched her hand and held it tightly, his eyes bright, almost feverish. "You're like your mother. She was kind, too. She died too young."

"Yes, she did."

He let go of her hand and leaned back against his chair, clearly exhausted. He closed his eyes as he spoke. "Miranda was a good person."

Harper got to her feet, not wanting to reminisce with Willy about her mother. Ethan was listening to everything they said, and she was afraid Willy would reveal too much. She'd have to tell him the truth eventually, but tonight she wasn't ready to talk about it.

Maybe she'd never be.

"Your clothes should be dry now. As soon as you change, I'll take you home."

She didn't wait for him to reply. She hurried to the laundry room and pulled his shabby clothes from the dryer and folded them. At least now they were clean. When she looked up, Ethan was in the doorway.

"You okay?"

She nodded. "I'm fine. Do you think you can help me with one more thing?"

"Of course."

That brought a smile to her lips. "You shouldn't agree too quickly. I may want you to do something you don't want to do."

"After bathing Willy, anything else you want me to do has got to be a piece of cake."

"I'm sorry about that. Thank you for helping."

He waved away her thanks. "What do you need me to do?"

"I want to drive Willy home in his truck. If you follow us, you can bring me back here."

His lips quirked in a grin. "Like I said, piece of cake."

Willy was sober enough now to dress himself, but Harper didn't trust him to drive. Once in his clean clothes, she led him to the passenger side of his truck and buckled him inside. She then slid into the driver's seat and was relieved when she found the keys still in the ignition.

The fifteen-minute drive to Minnewasta was accomplished in complete silence. Willy stared straight ahead the entire time. Harper parked his truck in the driveway of his small one-story house on the outskirts of town. Like Willy, the house looked worse for wear. The paint was worn and chipped, and even with snow covering most of the front yard, she could see that junk was strewn everywhere. It was as if he'd given up.

She turned off the ignition and, taking the keys with her, got out of the truck and walked around to the passenger side. By the time she got there, Willy had already unbuckled his seat belt and opened the door.

"I can manage from here," he said, his eyes not meeting hers.

She walked him to the door. Although the sidewalk was snow packed and slippery, Willy made the short walk without falling. Harper breathed a sigh of relief.

He opened the unlocked door and stood in the doorway facing her. "Thank you, for everything."

She handed him his truck keys. “You’re welcome. Remember what you promised me.”

“I will. I promise I won’t drive when I drink.”

“That’s good. Bye.”

“Bye Harper.”

Ethan was waiting in his truck at the end of the driveway with the motor running. She hopped in the passenger side. As she buckled her seatbelt, exhaustion overtook her. She leaned her head against the rest and closed her eyes. “He wasn’t always like that. He wasn’t always an alcoholic.”

The truck began to move and Ethan asked, “What was he like?”

She turned her head to look at him. “He was kind, and funny, and sweet. If my grandmother was angry at me for something, he used to cover for me. I remember once I stole a cookie from Grandma’s cookie jar after being told I couldn’t have one before dinner. Grandma might never have known about my theft except I dropped the lid and it shattered on the kitchen floor. I knew she was going to be furious, so I ran away. When I told Willy my story, he took the blame for me. He told Grandma he’d broken her cookie jar.”

“Sounds like he was a good friend to you when you were a kid.”

“Yes.” The old memories made her smile and broke her heart at the same time. “I can’t abandon him.”

He gave her a solemn nod. “No, I don’t expect you could.”

“Thanks again for helping. This was the worst I’ve ever seen him.”

"What happened to him? What changed him from the man who shielded you from your grandmother's temper to the person we saw today?"

"I'm not exactly sure. Alcohol, I suppose. He'd worked for my grandfather since he was a teenager and Grampa always said how reliable he was back then. But by the time I was a teenager, he was drinking heavily, and Grampa couldn't trust him to take fishermen out on the lake anymore. By then, business wasn't great and there wasn't enough work to keep him on all year round, so Grampa cut back his hours to a few weeks during the summer. Eventually, Willy got another job in Minnewasta. Like he said, he drinks, but he always manages to hold down a job."

"As long as someone is willing to hire him, he can tell himself he doesn't have a problem with alcohol."

Harper glanced at him again. "You sound like you're familiar with the subject."

He shrugged. "My dad was the same way. As long as the inn was still functioning, he could tell himself, and us, that he didn't have a problem. It didn't matter that he was running the place into the ground and killing my mother."

She heard the bitterness in his voice. "I'm sorry."

He waved his hand. "Ancient history. I'm just saying I understand the situation. Don't let him pull you under with him. Alcoholics have a way of destroying themselves and everyone around them."

Harper said nothing, but continued to watch his profile as he drove. The tense set of his jaw told her the pain from his childhood wasn't quite as ancient as he wanted her to believe.

Chapter Thirteen

AS ETHAN PUSHED OPEN the door to Cam's workshop, his brother looked up from the wood he was sanding. "I haven't seen this much of you since I was twelve."

"Get used to it. I'm staying at the lodge until construction is finished."

Cam narrowed his eyes at him. "You're staying in the lodge? Just you and Harper Lindquist? Are you sure that's such a good idea?"

"Relax. I'm staying in one of the cottages, a quarter of a mile from the main lodge. Besides, Harper and I have a very professional relationship. Neither of us wants to do anything to mess up this deal."

"Glad to hear it." Cam resumed his sanding.

He breathed a sigh of relief when Cam didn't interrogate him further. He only hoped he was telling the truth about not messing things up. Ethan pulled a stool up to Cam's worktable. "So, what are you working on?"

"It's going to be chair, eventually. I found an old wooden chair at an auction sale I really liked, and I'm trying to replicate it."

"Nice." His brother could make wood come to life the way artists could bring energy and soul to a canvass. "I was hoping you could help me out. We got five bids for the general contracting of our project and most of them of are pretty similar. I thought maybe if you knew some of these people, had some clues about their reputations, it would give us insight on which direction to take."

Cam took off his safety glasses and set down his sanding block. "Show me."

Ethan handed him the papers. Cam laid them out side-by-side on his worktable and read through each one. He picked up one bid and set it to the side. "I'd eliminate this one immediately. I don't know this guy, but his bid is significantly lower than the rest, so that makes me think that either he didn't properly cost materials and labour, or he's planning to cut corners. Whatever the reason, I don't think he's the kind of guy you want to work with."

Ethan nodded. "Agreed. One down. What about the rest?"

"I know Jason Cummings. He does good work, but I'm not sure he's done a project this big before. You're talking about totally retrofitting the old timber frame lodge, right?"

"From top to bottom. New plumbing, new electrical, new kitchen, new roof. The whole thing is going to be heated with geo thermal and powered using solar energy with a backup to the electrical grid. We're also adding a new wing of guest rooms and several out buildings."

"Sounds complicated." He pointed to one bid. "I think Reese Hanson is your man. His company has been around for years and they've done a number of larger, complicated jobs like this. I've worked for him from time to time, and he's a good guy. Treats his men right. He's local, too. Lives here in Minnewasta now. I think your project will be safe with him."

It was good to have their first choice confirmed. "Thanks. That helps a lot."

"The only thing with Hanson Construction is that Reese may not be on site for the whole project. I've heard he's been sending his brother to jobs as general contractor the last couple of months because his wife is sick."

"Abby?"

"You know her?"

"No, but Harper does. Abby and her mother were best friends at one time."

"They aren't friends now?"

Ethan shook his head. "Harper's parents both died when she was ten."

"Jeez. That's tough." Cameron ran his hand through his hair, disturbing bits of fine wood shavings through the dark strands.

"How sick is Abby? Do you know what's wrong with her?"

"I don't know. I only know Glenn has had to step in help Reese. But that shouldn't be a problem. Glenn's a good guy and he's been in the business nearly as long as Reese. For all I know, Abby might be better by now. If she wasn't healthy, Reese probably wouldn't have bid on your project."

Cam had a point. Still, Ethan thought Harper would want to know about Abby. From the way she talked, she'd cared very much about her at one time. But he'd have to tell Harper that Abby was ill without revealing anything about Cam. He'd told her he had a brother, but he hadn't told her his first name or that he lived in Minnewasta.

Or that his last name was Hainstock.

Oh, what a tangled web...

"Does this bid encompass the whole lodge project or are the cottages you talked about a separate tender?" Cam asked, breaking into his thoughts.

"No, we kept the cottage project separate. Tenders are going out next week."

"I want to bid on them."

That surprised him. "You do?"

"Yeah, I do. I'd like to work near Minnewasta this summer so I can be close to Tessa. It's a smaller contract that my crew and I can handle. And you know I do good work."

"Yes, of course I know that. But you don't have to work, you know. You could use some of the money I gave you to spend as much time as you want with Tessa." He'd given both Cam and Lydia a portion of the money he'd won, but neither of them had used much of it.

"I like to work, you know that. I need to keep busy. Besides, my crew counts on me."

Ethan nodded, conceding the point. Cam needed to be productive, and if he was busy, there was less chance he'd backslide into drinking. "If it were up to me, I'd give you the contract. But Harper doesn't know you're my brother. She's going to think it's really strange you have the same last name as our mysterious investor."

"For Christ's sake, Ethan." The words exploded from Cam's mouth in a roar of displeasure. "Don't tell me you still haven't told her who you really are. She doesn't know that you and Hainstock Investments are one in the same?"

"No." He wouldn't let him see how guilty lying to Harper made him feel.

Bits of sawdust went flying as Cam ran his hand through his hair once more. "That's the stupidest, most ridiculous thing I've ever heard. This is a small town. If she doesn't know already, she's going to find out soon enough."

"She doesn't know. I'm sure of it."

Cam made a dismissive sound deep in his throat and folded his arms across his broad chest. "If that's true, then she has the right to know who she's dealing with. Why haven't you told her? If you don't trust her, why are you involved in her project?"

"I do trust her. Harper is the most honest woman I've ever known."

"So what's the problem?"

"It's...complicated." Ethan slipped off the stool and went to stand beside Tessa's dollhouse. He picked up a wooden block carved with a T and turned it over and over in his hands.

He had a hard time speaking about what he'd gone through with his ex-girlfriend, Bree. Even Cam, who he trusted more than anyone in the world, didn't know all the details. Bree had betrayed him. She'd cheated him out of the life he should have had. All because of money, either the lack of it, or the overabundance. Every time he thought about telling Harper how much money he'd won in the lottery, fear stopped him cold. The money could change the way she saw him. He cared for Harper, more then he wanted to admit to Cam or even himself. It would kill him if she used sex to reel him in once she found out about the money.

He brought the conversation back to the tenders. "I'll make sure you get the contract. I promise. Can you put together a proposal, maybe some drawings of the cottages you want to build?"

"I can do that. I'd like to see where the cottages are going to be situated. Would it be possible to take a look at the property?"

"Sure. Harper's working at Miller's tomorrow. Come over about ten and I'll show you around. Bring your camera."

Cameron shook his head. "So we have to sneak around behind her back? I don't like it."

"Do you want the work?" Ethan snapped.

"You know I do!"

"Then be at the lodge at ten and quit ragging on me." He busied himself with collecting the papers and stuffing them back into his briefcase.

"Fine. I'll be there."

Cam was right. Harper had the right to know who he really was, for business reasons as well as personal ones. And he was right about Minnewasta being a small town where it was difficult to keep a secret. He had to tell her before someone else did.

ETHAN'S TRUCK PULLED into the yard and a thrill of anticipation pulsed through Harper's blood. He'd been away for four days, and she'd missed him desperately. After she'd come home from her shift at Miller's last week, he'd told her he needed to leave for Minneapolis the next morning. The news disappointed her since he'd only spent three nights at the lodge. She hoped Willy's sudden appearance hadn't put him off. He seemed to understand, and was sympathetic to her desire to help her friend, but then a couple of days later he was gone.

Was he going back to Minneapolis for more than work? Was he going back to a woman?

She wanted to believe Ethan would never lie to her. She wanted to banish the seed of doubt that had suddenly taken root in her thoughts. But now that the thought had been planted, it was difficult to dismiss.

For now, she pushed aside her misgivings and opened the front door for him. When he stepped into the front foyer with a smile and swept her into his arms, she forgot all her doubts. Ethan was here and he was hers.

"I missed you," he whispered against her hair. He stroked her back. "I hate being away from you."

She leaned back to look into his face. "Then don't go away. I miss you, too."

He cupped her face in his hands. "I wish I didn't have to leave, but I've got work responsibilities in the city."

Maybe if she was a different woman, one confidant in her ability to keep a man, she'd ask him not to leave, even demand it. But she wasn't that woman. She had no hold on him, sexual or otherwise.

Especially sexual.

He stroked her cheek. "Hey, don't look so sad. I'm home now."

Home. She wondered if he realized what he'd said, and what the word implied. She made herself smile. "Yes, you are."

She wound her arms around his neck and brought his mouth to hers. In a nanosecond, their kiss changed from sweet and chaste to hot and demanding. Harper pressed herself against him, needing to be closer, needing to feel his desire for her. The hard length of his erection pushed against her stomach, and she reveled in the knowledge that he wanted her. She wanted to give herself to him, body and soul. She wanted him inside her.

Where does he really go when he leaves me? Who does he see?

Icy doubt jolted her eyes open. She ended the kiss abruptly and stepped away. If she gave herself to Ethan and he didn't return her feelings, it would destroy her.

Like it had destroyed her mother.

She'd never shared her thoughts with her sisters, but she believed what had gone wrong with her parents' marriage had been infidelity. Her father had been away from home so often. Perhaps he'd been seeing someone else.

"I'm sorry. I can't." She hated that even though she cared deeply for Ethan, even imagined herself in love with him, she couldn't bring herself to trust him.

Ethan's breathing was erratic, his eyes glassy with desire. "Give me a minute."

He turned away from her and leaned one hand against the front door, still breathing heavily. Harper felt like the worse kind of tease. She'd made a promise with her body that her heart couldn't keep, and now Ethan was paying the price.

"I'm sorry," she said again.

He didn't look at her. Instead, he waved a hand and mumbled, "It's okay. I just need a minute."

Harper left the foyer, feeling embarrassed and stupid. She went to the kitchen to prepare dinner, though all she did was bang some pots together. Perhaps it was acceptable for a teenager to act the way she had, but not a grown woman of thirty-two. She wanted to cry and scream in frustration, her body still thrumming with need. Always thinking too much. Analyzing everything to death. She wished she could tell the stupid, insecure voice in her head to shut the hell up. At this rate, she was going to die a virgin.

She picked up one of the pots and heaved it against the wall. "Damn it all to hell!"

Ethan walked into the kitchen and scooped the pot from the floor. "Was the pot being naughty?"

She couldn't look at him. "It deserved everything it got."

"Did throwing it make you feel better?"

She risked a glance. He looked concerned, but not angry. If she was him, she'd be angry. "Not really. I'm sorry, Ethan."

He put the pot on the counter and gathered her close. "It's okay, sweetheart."

She didn't deserve to take solace in his arms, but it was so good to be held by him. "You're being too nice. At the very least, you should yell at me."

His chuckle rumbled through his chest. "If it'll make you feel better, maybe I can come up with a rant or two. I might even swear."

She tightened her hold around his waist and listened to the steady beat of his heart. "Do your worst. I deserve it."

"No, you don't." He kissed the top of her head. "I know you're not ready, Harper. We both got a little carried away and it took us by surprise. That's all. It's okay."

It's so not okay.

"When the time is right for us, we'll both know it."

Harper didn't reply but held him more tightly. Perhaps the time would never be right. If she was unable to silence her fears, Ethan might get sick and tired of waiting. Her indecision, her fear, her insecurities might not only jeopardize her fledgling relationship with him, it could sink the lodge project.

She couldn't let that happen. Maybe it would be best if they kept their business lives and their private lives completely separate. Harper squeezed her eyes shut, her heart breaking inside her chest.

Whatever the cost, the lodge had to be saved.

AFTER DINNER, ETHAN helped Harper with the dishes before joining her in the lounge with a cup of coffee. She'd been quiet all evening, ever since the explosive kiss that had shaken them both. Thinking about her breasts pressed against his chest, her nipples taut and ready and begging to be sucked, made him hard. He suppressed a groan.

Don't push her.

As he sat in the chair opposite, he repeated the phrase over and over in his head. Maybe if he said it often enough, he'd actually manage to do it.

She wasn't ready to make to love to him and take their relationship to the next stage. They really hadn't known each other all that long and mixing the business of the lodge with their personal relationship was probably a bad idea. He understood her reticence.

That didn't mean he had to like it.

Then there was the whole truth thing, the secret of his true identity. Cam's words played in his head – perhaps someone from town had told her who he was. Maybe that's why she ended their kiss. Guilt kicked him in the gut. If that was true, he had no one but himself to blame.

Today. He'd tell her the truth today.

Harper glanced at him over her coffee cup. "So, did your research conclude that Hanson Construction was the best general contractor for us?"

Ethan pushed aside his troubled thoughts and cleared his throat. "Yes. After speaking to companies Reese Hanson has done work for, and visiting one of his projects in Minneapolis, I believe his company is the best one for the lodge."

"It sounds like you were busy while you were away."

"I was, yeah." He hesitated a moment, unsure how to broach the subject of her mother's friend's illness. "I discovered something during my investigations. Your mother's friend Abby, Reese Hanson's wife, has been ill. Apparently Reese's brother Glenn has had to step into Reese's role as general contractor on a few recent projects because of her illness."

Her fair skin paled. "Abby is sick? With what?"

"I don't know. I wasn't able to find out what's wrong with her or how serious it is. But I thought you should know."

She nodded and her forehead wrinkled with worry. "Yes, thank you. I'll have to find out where she's living and visit her. I hope it's nothing serious."

He hoped so, too. Harper didn't need to lose anyone else she cared about.

For a few moments they sat quietly, though the silence was peaceful rather than uncomfortable. He rested his head against the cushions of the old sofa and listened to the clock on the fireplace mantle tick down the time.

Time. He'd tell her the truth about everything right now. She'd understand his reasons for not coming clean with her from the beginning.

At least, he hoped she would.

"Harper—"

"Ethan, we need to talk."

Something in her voice made him sit up straighter. "About what?"

She lowered her gaze and toyed with her empty coffee cup. "About us not mixing our personal relationship with business."

Her words caused a punch to the gut that was painful and totally unexpected. "Is that really what you want?" Did she know who he was? Had someone told her?

"It's what's best." She looked at him then, and her eyes were clear. Not a trace of regret. "This project is too important to me to let it get entangled in personal feelings."

"Is this because of our kiss earlier? Because if it is, I want you to know I didn't plan for that to happen. It was...spontaneous."

He didn't know how to explain what had come over him when he'd walked into the lodge and saw her. The look of welcome on her face, like he was the one person in the world she wanted to see, like he was something special to her, had caught him off guard. He'd forgotten about the money, the renovation project, the lies. All he wanted was to take

Harper into his arms because *she* was something special to him.

She swallowed. "I know, but we can't let ourselves get carried away like that again. What if we became...involved? What would happen if we had a falling out, and we decided we weren't good as a couple anymore? How could we continue to work together? Would the lodge renovation suffer because we couldn't get along? Every time we disagreed on something to do with the lodge, I'd wonder if we were really disagreeing about business or if you were angry with me."

"We're adults, Harper. We can figure out a way to work together."

"I don't want to have to worry about messing up the biggest deal of my life. I think it's best if we keep our relationship on a completely business level. I think Mr. Hainstock would agree. He probably wouldn't be pleased if he knew..."

She didn't know. *Or is she playing me?* Panic gripped him. "Harper—"

She held up her hand. "I'm not saying forever. Maybe when the construction is done and the place is running smoothly, we can talk. If we're both feeling the same way."

If we're both feeling the same way?

"So that's really what you want? Nothing but business between us?"

She looked him in the eyes. "I think it's best."

Ethan stared at her and, to her credit, she held his gaze. Only a slight tremor in the hand holding her coffee cup betrayed her.

He jumped to his feet, too agitated to sit any longer. "If that's what you want, fine. I'm heading to the cottage."

He strode to the front door and grabbed his parka from the closet, anger dogging his every step. But his anger disappeared when he saw that Harper had followed him, her earlier bravado gone. Her arms were wrapped tightly around her midsection as if she couldn't get warm enough. She looked small and vulnerable, and Ethan had to fight the urge to pull her into his arms.

This wasn't easy for her. She was nothing like Bree.

He had no desire to upset her further. "I'll see you in the morning, at breakfast. Eight am, right?"

Her lovely mouth curled in a half smile. "If it's not too early for you."

"It's not. Goodnight, Harper."

"Goodnight."

He went to the garage and arm-wrestled the door until it opened. He started the snowmobile Harper had assigned to him and drove it out, closing the door behind him. It was late and even though he wasn't dressed warmly enough, he headed out on the lake, needing the freedom and exhilaration the sled could give him. He drove around and around, flying over snowbanks and skidding down steep embankments, until he could barely feel his legs. By the time he got to his cottage, his hands were numb with cold.

But he couldn't forget. Harper's announcement played non-stop in his head like an old cassette on repeat. He couldn't stop thinking of what might have been.

AFTER ASKING AROUND at Miller's, a veritable hot bed of local gossip, Harper discovered that Abby and Reese had purchased Silas Johnson's old house, a modest ranch style home a couple of blocks from Abby's mother's house. Phyllis Carlsson was getting on in years; it made sense that Abby would want to be close by to keep an eye on her. She was Phyllis' only child, after all.

Harper drove to Abby's new address, not certain what she was going to say. She hadn't seen Abby in over eight years, since she'd married Reese and moved away. But even before that, when Abby still lived in Minnewasta, she'd avoided her. Perhaps it had been childish, but she'd been jealous of the close relationship between Abby and Maggie. Abby was the one her sister always turned to, not her. It still hurt.

Harper walked to the front door and steadied herself with a deep breath before ringing the doorbell. At first, there was no answer and she thought no one was home. She tried the bell one more time and as she was about to leave, she heard someone walking to the door. A minute later the door swung open and Abby stood on the other side, a multi-colored scarf in blues and greens and yellows wrapped around her head. She was fifty-six now, the same age as Willy, and the same age her mother would have been, but the lines on Abby's face made her seem much older.

They stared at each other. Finally, Abby smiled and took her hand. "Harper. How beautiful you are. Your mother would be so proud."

Emotion clogged her throat. "Thank you."

Abby tugged on her hand. "Come inside out of the cold and have some tea with me. I want to hear all your news."

Harper followed her through the small living room. Abby picked up some newspapers that were strewn on the sofa and set them on a side table. "Sorry I didn't get to the door sooner. I fell asleep reading the paper."

"I'm sorry to drop by unannounced. I wanted to call first, but I didn't know your number and there was nothing in directory assistance for you."

"We're unlisted. Reese doesn't like getting business calls at home. We try to keep our home and business lives separate. I'll make sure to give you my number before you leave."

"That would be great."

"Come on in the kitchen with me and I'll make some tea."

The kitchen was sunny and warm, though not terribly big. While Abby put the kettle on to boil, Harper took off her jacket and hung it over the back of her chair.

"What made you and Reese decide to come back to Minnewasta?"

Abby placed a couple of teabags into a pot. "It was time to come home. This is where we belong."

Harper blinked at her enigmatic answer. What did 'it was time' mean? Time for what? "How's your mom? I haven't seen her at the hockey rink much this winter. She used to come to all the games."

"She's doing fine. My mother would never let a little thing like age slow her down." She poured boiling water over the teabags. "What about you? Reese tells me you're embarking on a big renovation of the lodge."

"Yes, I am." She launched into her plans for the lodge and the business arrangement she'd made with Hainstock Investments.

"That sounds wonderful, Harper. I think your grandfather would be pleased."

"You think so? If he were alive, he'd probably be fighting me tooth and nail over the changes we're planning to make."

"He'd be pleased you're not letting the lodge die. It's going to be reborn into something new and beautiful. Like a Phoenix."

"I hope you're right."

When she thought of the lodge, she couldn't help thinking of Ethan. In the two days since she announced she wanted to keep their relationship strictly business, he'd been polite but cool. She couldn't blame him since she'd basically told the man she didn't want him.

She was still amazed she'd been able to convince him of the lie.

"And how are your sisters? Where are they living now?"

Abby's question brought her back to the present. "They're great. Scarlet's a marketing exec in Chicago, and Maggie's in Minneapolis working in a five-star restaurant."

"That's wonderful. I know that's what she always wanted to do. Maggie, I mean. She always wanted to be a chef."

Abby poured a little tea in her cup and showed it to Harper. "Strong enough for you?" When Harper nodded, Abby filled both cups. She cautiously sipped the hot tea before speaking again. "Will your sisters be coming out to the lodge anytime soon? I'd love to see them."

"Not that I know of. They were out in February to sign some papers, but they're both so busy with work it's difficult for them to make the trip."

Disappointment swept across Abby's face, surprising Harper. Then, she winced in pain.

"Are you all right? Can I get you anything?"

Abby made an attempt at a smile. "No, I'm fine. Just a spot of indigestion."

"Is everything really all right with you? I'd heard you'd been ill."

"I had an operation a couple of months ago, but everything's fine now."

"I'm glad you're on the mend. I was worried."

"You're a sweet girl, but really, there's nothing for you to worry about." Abby reached across the table to clasp her hand, surprising Harper with her strong grip. "So like your mother. As I said, she'd be proud of you."

"Thank you. I appreciate that."

They finished their tea and chatted about people they both knew, and about Harper's plans for the lodge in the future.

"We're going to add a spa. It's going to be a place where guests can come to commune with nature and get a massage and maybe a mani-pedi at the same time."

Abby chuckled. "Sounds like my kind of place."

"When the lodge is finished, you'll have to visit us. I'd love to treat you to a nice dinner, on the house."

Abby's smile was wistful. "I'd like that a lot. I'll keep your offer in mind."

"Good. I look forward to you and Reese being our first guests."

"That would be wonderful."

Dark circles had formed under Abby's eyes and her skin had a slightly grey pallor. Obviously, she was still recovering from surgery and needed her rest. "I'd better be going."

Harper got to her feet and gathered the teacups. Ignoring Abby's protests, she washed them in the sink and set them in the drain board to dry. She wiped her hands on a towel and reached for her jacket. "Is there anything I can do for you, Abby? You probably don't feel up to cleaning house while you're recovering from your surgery. I could do that for you."

"No, we're fine, but thank you for offering. My mother is helping out, and Reese takes very good care of me."

Abby had married late in life. Harper had heard the story about how, at the age of twenty-seven, she'd met an old friend from high school who was home on leave from the army. Abby shocked everyone in the small town when she announced she was pregnant but wouldn't be marrying her child's father. She'd had a son, Luke, who was a couple of years younger than Scarlet. Abby raised him on her own with the help of her widowed mother and, as far as Harper knew, Luke had had very little contact with his father. The story around town was that she and Reese had reconnected about eleven years ago. They'd known each other before, of course, since they'd both grown up and gone to school in Minnewasta. But this time something must have clicked between them. They'd been together ever since.

"I'm glad to hear it. But seriously, if there's ever anything I can do, like getting groceries, baking cookies, whatever, please call me."

Abby rose slowly to her feet and gave her a hug. When she let her go, she cupped Harper's face with her hand. "I'll keep your lovely offer in mind, but what I'd really like is if you could drop by and say hello when you can."

Harper smiled. "I'd like that. I'll come back as soon as I can."

"Good." She wrote her phone number on a piece of paper and handed it over. "Goodbye, Harper. I'm so glad you came."

"So am I. Bye, Abby."

Harper drove back to the lodge feeling relieved. Though Abby was a little frail from her surgery, she was on the mend and sounded upbeat. Willy was already in bad shape. She couldn't bear the thought of another of her mother's old friends in trouble.

Chapter Fourteen

ON MARCH THIRTIETH, the first shovels went into the ground for the renovation of the lodge. The weather had warmed up enough for Reese and his crew to begin digging below the frost line to pour the piles that would support the new guest wing. Between the piles, the crew put together insulated foam blocks that would create forms into which concrete would be poured for the foundation. When they were done with the foundation for the guest wing, they'd start construction on the new event center.

In a few days, a geo thermal crew would arrive to begin installing the new heating and cooling systems for both buildings. At the same time, a roofing company would repair the roof of the old lodge. Then the forms would go in the ground for the other outbuildings, including the spa and the recreation center. Things were beginning to take shape.

Harper documented the progress with her camera, then sent the pictures to her sisters, hoping to make them feel more involved. She was not a skilled photographer by any stretch, but things were happening so quickly that she wanted to record the stages of development. To see her dream coming true was exciting beyond words.

What wasn't quite so exciting was clearing out the contents of the lodge. Every bed, every table and chair, and all the personal contents accumulated over the seventy plus years of the lodge's existence had to be removed. Aside from a few family heirlooms and mementos, most of the contents of the lodge would be donated to charity. A truck would be coming to make the pickup in a few days.

The furniture was easy. Most of it was older than she was and not of great quality; it held little sentimental value. Going through the kitchen items proved more difficult. So many things, from the collection of salt and pepper shakers to the embroidered tea cozies, reminded her of her grandparents, especially her grandmother. Though she'd had a complicated relationship with her grandmother, she'd still loved her. She could only imagine how hard it had been for Grandma Dorothy to lose her only child. Having to raise three young orphaned children when she was nearly sixty must have been trying, especially since all three of them were headstrong and determined and grieving the loss of their parents.

Harper packed up and labeled all the things in the kitchen she couldn't part with, including the Madeleine pans Maggie had asked about. She would store them in the second cottage where she'd soon be moving. Since Reese lived in Minnewasta now, he didn't need the accommodations. Many of his crew had already moved trailers onto the property to live in during construction.

The home she'd lived in since childhood was going to change so drastically. When she and her sisters had come to live at the lodge, Grampa Bill had added onto their small living quarters on the main floor. The lean-to structure he attached to the lodge became the bedroom she and Scarlet and Maggie had shared. Harper still used that bedroom. Even though it was colder than the rest of the lodge, it was home to her.

Things were changing, but it was a good change. A necessary one. She was excited about the small apartment being built for her on the second floor of the event center, and she could hardly wait to put her own stamp on it. Ethan had been incredibly thoughtful to take her needs into account. But that was the Ethan she'd come to know—a thoughtful, kind and generous man.

If only...

She cut off that line of thinking. It did no good to wish for things that could never be. She had made the right decision.

After finishing in the kitchen, Harper moved on to what would be the hardest part of the lodge go through. In the days following Grandma Dorothy's death, she'd been so busy dealing with Maggie's anguish and Grampa Bill's overwhelming grief she hadn't had time to go through clothes and personal items. Besides, Grampa didn't want anything disturbed, as if he was convinced Grandma was away on a little vacation and would soon arrive home and need her things.

After Grampa died, she'd sorted through his clothes, donating many of them. She'd kept some of them, like the ones she'd loaned to Ethan, in the trunk in her room. Then, she'd simply closed the door of the bedroom her grandparents had shared for so many years and left things the way they were. But now, she needed to go through each item in her grandparents' bedroom and ruthlessly purge. She couldn't put it off any longer.

She dreaded sorting through the old memories. She wished her sisters were here to help, but they were miles away. As usual, she was on her own.

Stop it! Stop feeling sorry for yourself, Harper. Staying at the lodge and renovating had been her idea, her choice. She had to stop blaming her sisters for wanting something different.

She squared her shoulders and reached for the knob.

Opening the door of her grandparents' bedroom was like breaking into a time capsule. She only came into the room occasionally to dust and vacuum, and she hadn't opened the closet or dresser drawers in a long time. Taking a deep breath, she got to work.

The dresser drawers held few surprises. She carefully packaged Grandma Dorothy's jewelry box and a few knickknacks she thought her sisters might want, setting those boxes aside to take to her cottage later. Then, she packed all the clothes from the drawers into garbage bags for donation and did the same with the clothes hanging in the walk-in closet.

When she'd removed all the clothes from the closet, she found several cardboard boxes piled on the floor. A couple were marked 'Christmas Ornaments' in Grandma Dorothy's messy scrawl, and she put those aside to take to her cottage. Others were unmarked and sealed with packing tape. She tried to bring one out into the bedroom, but it was too heavy to lift. She'd have to empty some of the contents before she could shift it.

After finding a box cutter, she sliced through the tape and opened the flaps. The box was filled with photo albums. Harper lifted out the top one and began thumbing through it. Many of the pictures were old black and white shots, probably taken by her grandparents in the fifties and sixties. There were dozens of pictures of her mother as a baby and a little girl, pictures she'd never seen before. Harper quickly turned the pages, fascinated by the recounting of her grandparents' family life in pictures.

She pulled out another album labelled "1974 – 1976". This time, most of the pictures were in color. Her mother was now a teenager, a girl with coltish, long legs, and bright red hair. In a couple of close-ups, the freckles and deep blue eyes Harper remembered so well were clearly visible. Harper lightly ran her finger over her mother's face. Miranda's smile was confident, even a little cocky, as if she had the world by the tail and nothing could stop her.

Except death.

"Hey. What do you have there?"

Harper looked up as Ethan crossed the room. "I found some old albums. See? This is a picture of my mother. She's probably fourteen or fifteen here."

Ethan knelt beside her as he studied the picture and then her. "I can see the family resemblance. The shape of your face and your nose are the same, but your coloring is different."

"I take after my father. He was blonde and fair like me. Scarlet is the only one who got the freckles and red hair." She shook her head. "Why would Grandma hide these pictures? They're just family photos. Why be so secretive about them?"

"You've never seen them before?"

"Never."

Anger bubbled inside her chest. This was part of her heritage. She and her sisters had a right to pictures of her mother. All these years, the only picture they'd had of her was a family picture with her parents, taken when she was fifteen. Grandma Dorothy had no right to lock these away. It made no sense. But then a lot of the things her grandmother had done or said over the years had made no sense to her.

Ethan reached into the box and pulled out another album. "Let's see what's in this one."

He opened the first page to reveal several small colored photos of teenagers, the kind that were taken every year in high school. Excitement replaced Harper's anger. She leaned forward to examine the pictures more closely.

"This must have been my mother's own photo album. These kids must have been her friends."

"Any idea who they are?"

"Maybe. I'm not sure."

This album was the kind with sticky pages. The plastic covering could be lifted and the photos inserted inside, then the plastic covering would be placed back over the pictures, essentially sealing them inside. Miranda may have written names and dates on the backs of the photos, but they'd been entombed inside their sticky homes for so long, Harper couldn't check without the risk of tearing or damaging them in some way. Frustration ate at her. She was on the edge of knowing her mother better but a barrier had been placed in her way.

As she turned the page, her heart lifted a little. She pointed to one of the pictures, a young girl with long dark hair, blue eyes and braces on her teeth. “I think this is Abby. Oh, and this is Willy. I’m positive.” The photo showed a good-looking young man with longish, light brown hair and a sweet smile.

Ethan studied the. “You’re kidding. This is Willy?”

“I’m sure it is. I’d have to check with Abby to confirm, but this is kind of how I remember him.” She touched the picture. “He had so much promise here. It’s heartbreaking what the alcohol has done to him.”

“Yeah, it always is.”

She heard the bitterness in his voice and knew he was thinking of his father. Growing up with an alcoholic parent must have been tough, almost as tough as growing up without any parents at all. Harper wished she could pull him into her arms and offer some kind of solace. Not being able to touch him was like a physical pain, an ache that wouldn’t go away.

Instead, she turned another page. More candid shots, kids playing sports, swimming in the lake in front of the lodge, and generally clowning for the camera. One picture in particular caught her eye. A boy, a young man really, leaning against a tree. The photo was taken at a distance and his ball cap was pulled low, making it hard to get a good look at his face. Though his arms were folded across his chest as if he were impatient with the photographer, his half grin spoke of amusement, and something more. Affection, perhaps?

Harper thumbed quickly through the album before going back to the page with the mysterious young man. “I wonder who he is. There’s no other photos of him.”

"Maybe you'll have to take out the picture to see if there's anything written on the back. Or perhaps you can take this album to Abby. If she was your mother's best friend, I'm sure she wouldn't mind answering a few questions for you."

"Yeah. I'll have to do that."

Heavy footsteps sounded in the hallway before Reese Hanson stuck his head through the door. "You almost finished clearing out this room? We'd like to get a start on the demolition."

Harper got to her feet, taking the photo album with her. "Almost done. I got a little side-tracked looking at some old family albums." She cocked her head to one side. "You went to school with my Mom, didn't you, Reese? Maybe you know some of the people in her album."

"I was a few years older and at least four grades ahead of her. We didn't hang out with the same people."

"It's a small town. You must have seen them around, even if you were older. Humor me and take a quick look. Please?" She held out the album to him.

Reese reluctantly took the album from her and flipped through the pages. He pointed to some of the pictures. "This is Abby, and this is Willy Eklund."

"I thought so. What about some of the others?"

He put names to several of the other pictures, skipping by the one of the young man leaning against the tree. Some of the people he named were familiar to her since they'd remained in Minnewasta, but others were strangers, having left soon after graduation, never to return.

He turned the page to an eight by ten of Miranda wearing her cap and gown at her high school graduation. The corner of his mouth turned up in a half smile. "Your mother was very pretty."

"She was. Did you know her well?"

"I worked for your grandfather at the lodge the summer after I graduated from high school. And like you said, it's a small town."

"Oh. I didn't know you'd worked at the lodge. Grampa never mentioned it."

He closed the album and handed it back to her, signalling the end of their trip down memory lane. "We need to get started on the demolition tomorrow."

Harper blinked. "Tomorrow? I thought I had a few more days."

Reese shook his head. "Change of plan. We finished with the foundation for the new extension ahead of schedule and my crew is available. Time is money."

"I'm going to need help moving the things I want to keep to the cottage where I'll be staying."

"No problem. What about the furniture? Most of it is going, isn't it?"

"Yeah." Harper thought fast. "If you can loan me a truck and a couple of your men, we can take the furniture to the charity in Brainerd today instead of waiting for them to pick it up."

"I can get a few of the guys to help you. You can use my half-ton."

Ethan turned to her. "If we use both of our trucks, we can probably get the lodge cleaned out by the end of the day."

Everything was happening so fast. It would have been nice to have more time to sort through her grandparents' room, but perhaps it was better this way. Better to get this over quickly.

She nodded at Ethan and put the photo album back in the box. "I'll tape these up again. I don't want them to get mixed up with any of the stuff going for donation."

"Write 'Keep' on the boxes and I'll take them to my truck myself and make sure they get stowed in your cottage. What else do you want to hang on to?"

She marked all the boxes in the closet to keep, even though many had no markings to identify what they contained. Then, she helped Ethan move them and the other things she wanted to save to his truck. Reese's crew took apart beds and began moving out the old furniture. They filled her truck with garbage bags full of old clothes and other items meant for donation. By the end of the day, the lodge was completely empty and a few of the interior walls had started coming down.

Later, as she and Ethan walked around the empty lodge, panic gripped her. The memories accumulated within the old wooden beams of the lodge, and her only link to the past, had been boxed up and hauled away. Her heart thrummed in double time. She was overwhelmed by the enormity of what she'd embarked on, and she was terrified she'd made a mistake.

Ethan laid a hand on her shoulder. "You did the right thing. It's going to be okay. You'll see."

His touch was warm and comforting. It took all her self-control not to throw herself into his arms. "How did you know what I was thinking?"

He gave a negligent shrug. "You're not that hard to read."

Only to you.

His calm reassurance eased her fears. Despite everything, there was no one else she'd want beside her on this project.

ETHAN POURED MORE WINE into her glass and Harper raised it to her lips. She'd cooked a simple dinner for them in her cottage, braving the chilly early spring weather to barbecue a couple of steaks out on the deck. She could hardly wait until it was warm enough to eat their dinner on the front porch and watch the sun go down.

"Thanks for bringing the wine. It's really good. Not that I know anything about wine."

"But you know what you like?"

She chuckled at that. "Exactly."

"I thought a small celebration was in order," he said. "The end of three weeks of construction and so far, so good."

She touched her glass to his. "I'll drink to that."

The changes Reese's crew had made in such a short time were remarkable. The interior walls on the second floor of the main lodge had been demolished and the reframing to allow for new bathrooms to be installed had begun. Two bedrooms would have to be sacrificed, leaving only eight upstairs, but it was worth the loss to have an ensuite bathroom for every room. The rough-ins for the new plumbing and electricity were next on the list. The place was a virtual beehive of activity.

This was really happening.

The rich, red wine did a little happy dance on her tongue. She enjoyed wine, but rarely bought any for herself. On the few occasions when she'd bought a bottle, it was usually a modestly priced one that went along with her modest income. This one tasted expensive. She examined the label. Most of the writing was in French, and all she could make out was that it was a Burgundy from France. When she lifted the glass to her nose and inhaled, she could practically see rows and rows of grapevines, feel the sun on her back, and smell the rich, dark earth.

"I've never seen this wine before. Where did you get it?"

"In a wine shop in Minneapolis. There's not a lot of selection in Minnewasta."

He must have picked it up there when he'd gone to the city for work. Or at least that's what he said he was doing.

Stop torturing yourself, Harper.

Harper took another sip of the wine. They'd been working together for several weeks now and, even though their close proximity made her ache with need, she was grateful for the time to get to know him. She liked him a little more every day. She loved his sense of humor, his kindness, and the way he listened to her ideas, took them seriously. That meant a lot to her.

A few months after her grandfather died she'd begun dating Brian, a local she'd gone to high school with who was single after a recent divorce. They'd gone to movies and local events, and she'd been grateful for the company. She'd been desperately lonely and Brian had filled a void in her life, at least for a short while. But when she shared her ideas for renovating the lodge and turning it into an eco-resort, he'd told her she was crazy. A place like that would never take off and besides, no bank would ever loan her the money. What did she know about running a resort?

She'd been crushed and had almost given up the dream. Soon after, they'd gone their separate ways. Brian grew tired of waiting for her to give him sex, and she grew tired of his persistence. Last she heard, he had married a girl from a nearby town.

Ethan believed in her dreams, believed in her, but his frequent trips to the city and his mysterious disappearances worried her. He'd never really explained how he'd found out that Abby had been ill. She hadn't even heard that Abby and Reese had moved back to Minnewasta, and she usually heard all the local gossip at Miller's. Yet, he knew before she did.

The idea of him with another woman, the thought that he'd lied to her by omitting he was already involved, made her slightly queasy.

"I saw that."

Harper blinked. "What?"

"You looked like you'd eaten something sour. What's the matter? I thought you liked the wine."

"I do."

"Then what's wrong? Did you have a tiff with one of your sisters?"

"No." She took a fortifying sip to give her courage. "I was wondering about the wine. You said you got it in Minneapolis?"

"Yeah. In a wine shop on France Street, ironically enough. You don't have to finish it if you don't want to. I'm not going to be offended."

"It's not that. The wine is great. I was just wondering..." She bit her lip, unable to find the words.

"What?" He cocked his head, searching her face. "Come on, Harper, spit it out. You don't usually have any trouble telling me what's on your mind."

She took a deep breath and lifted her gaze to his. He had denied the existence of another woman. But even if there was someone else, it was none of her business. She had insisted that business come before their personal lives. Sure, he'd kissed her, but she had no claim on him. None at all.

So, get over yourself, Harper.

"I was wondering if maybe we could form a partnership with this shop to provide us with wine. This seems like the kind of quality stuff I'd like to serve here." The lie tasted bitter on her tongue.

"That's a great idea. I'll contact them the next time I'm in the city." He took a sip of his wine. "Why were you so reluctant to tell me your idea?"

She swallowed. One lie tended to lead to another. "I was afraid you'd think it was a dumb idea. It's a little early to be thinking about wine when we don't even have a kitchen yet."

"Maybe. But it doesn't hurt to think ahead. In fact, I think we need to start looking for our chef and our resort manager. We'll need experienced people in both positions."

"I'm still trying to convince Maggie to take the position of head chef." She sat up straighter and set her wine glass on the table, glad to focus on something besides her mixed-up emotions.

"Has she held that position in any of the restaurants she's worked at?"

"Not that I know of, but—"

He held up his hand. "We need an experienced person in that position, Harper. We need someone who can come up with signature dishes for the lodge, someone who can supervise a staff and run a kitchen. Someone who knows all about purchasing the correct amounts of quality ingredients."

"Maggie can learn to do all those things."

Ethan set his glass on the table. "I'm all for Maggie working in the kitchen if she chooses, but you know as well as I do that we need to hit the ground running. We don't have the luxury of letting her learn on the job."

Much as she hated to admit it, he had a point. But she wasn't ready to concede. "Maggie is a talented chef, and a very capable person. And she's got as big a stake as any of us in the project. She'll work hard to make the restaurant a success."

"Has she even said she wants the job of head chef?"

"Not in so many words—"

"We need someone who's totally committed."

"She will be. I'm certain of it." Harper crossed her arms and frowned at Ethan. "And what about me? I'm definitely committed to this place. I've been looking after it since I was a teenager. What makes you think I couldn't be resort manager after the renovation?"

"You were fine with a small fishing lodge with ten rooms that were rarely full, but we're talking about triple the rooms, a large staff to supervise, a complex new booking system, and all kinds of new guest activities for you to coordinate.

Running the kind of complex we're creating requires a lot of experience."

Now he was pissing her off. "Are you saying I'm not smart enough to figure it out?"

He raised his hands in surrender. "I'm not saying that at all. I'm only saying that when we first open, we're going to need a manager with experience. Over time, working with a knowledgeable manager, you'll gain that experience, too."

"So in the meantime, I'm supposed to play second fiddle in my own lodge?"

"You want the best staff in place in every position, don't you?"

"Of course."

"Then I know you'll do what's right for the lodge and hire an experienced hotel and restaurant manager who knows what he or she is doing."

She hated that he was right. She didn't have the education or experience to run a world class resort. In truth, she'd been worried about not doing a good job for the lodge as manager. She'd likely have her hands full keeping up with the bookkeeping. But she didn't have to tell him that. "I'm going to soak up every bit of information I can so I can run the place myself in a few years."

He winked, lifting his glass in a toast. "That's my girl."

Ethan watched her raise her glass to his toast. Thankfully, she'd accepted his point of view on both the manager and the chef's positions at the lodge. He wasn't sure she'd be so open-minded about what he had to tell her next. "There's something I need to discuss with you." He cleared his throat. "Mr. Hainstock wants to give the contract to build the new cottages to his brother."

"His brother? You mean he wants to give this guy the contract without getting any other bids?"

"Yes, but—"

Her glass clunked down on the table. "But nothing! In one breath you're telling me I can't give the position of chef to my sister and in the next, I hear Mr. Hainstock wants his relative to build the new cottages? No way!"

"I know Cam Hainstock, and I know his work. He's hardworking and ethical, and he does very good work. We'd likely award him the contract anyway."

"But we don't know that for sure, unless we actually put the job out to tender."

"Mr. Hainstock was adamant on this point, Harper. Cam is to have the contract."

She lifted her chin in defiance. "I want to discuss it with him."

Ethan thought fast. "You can't. He's out of town. In Europe." *More lies.*

"Don't they have phones in Europe?"

"He's on vacation and doesn't want to be disturbed. Can't you trust me on this one, Harper? Cam Hainstock really is the best person for this job." He pulled his phone from his jacket pocket. "I've got pictures of some of his completed jobs. He's worked all over the state."

He found the pictures he wanted to show her and handed her the phone. As she examined them, her mouth curled in a frown. "This is a beautiful building. What is it?"

He leaned over to see the picture she asked about. "It's a law office in Rochester, Minnesota. The client wanted something that would blend in seamlessly with the older existing architecture on the street, and Cam came up with this. It's one of my favorites, too."

She looked at him in surprise. "He designed this building?"

"Yes. He's a very talented draftsman and builder."

She watched him intensely. "You sound like you know him well."

Ethan swallowed hard. "We've worked together on a few projects. I've always been impressed."

Harper scrolled through the rest of the pictures. "Okay, I'll admit these pictures look really good. But how do we know he'll do a good job on *our* project? We don't even know how much he expects to spend on building the cottages."

"Actually, we do." He pulled a file folder from the briefcase he'd brought with him. He had a feeling he'd need to do some convincing this evening. "He's submitted a bid."

Harper accepted the file from him and read through the papers. "This seems...reasonable." She sounded both surprised and reluctant.

"He's also taken the liberty of coming up with some new designs for the exteriors of the cottages. He's proposing to make each cottage slightly different-looking on the outside, but using the same cladding and colors to give a cohesive appearance." He handed her Cam's preliminary sketches.

"This is beautiful."

Ethan blew out a breath, relieved. "I told you Cam was the best man for the job."

She handed him back the drawings. "If you and Mr. Hainstock were so convinced his brother was the best person for the job, why couldn't we put the job up for tender and let him bid? If he was so good, he would have won fair and square."

"Mr. Hainstock wanted to make sure he got the job."

"I don't like being told what to do."

Ethan cringed, his stomach clenching. The lies kept multiplying. He was actively deceiving her at every turn, digging himself deeper and deeper into a pit of falsehoods and fabrications. And, as the pit got bigger, he was having a hard time figuring out how to find his way out. "I'm sorry you feel that way, but this was important to Mr. Hainstock. It was his one demand in the whole project."

"It would have been nice to know that upfront. You didn't need to spring it on me at the last minute."

"You're right. We should have talked to you about this earlier."

She huffed out a breath. "So, when do I get to meet this Cam person?"

"Very soon. The demolition of the old cottages should start in a couple of weeks. He's got a crew ready to go."

"Is he going to need some place to stay while he's here? Are we going to have to bring in a trailer or something?"

"No need. He lives in Minnewasta."

"In Minnewasta? I thought I knew everyone, and I've never heard of Cam Hainstock."

Damn. Maybe he should have lied about where Cam lived. What was one more lie when he'd told so many? "He recently moved here. It's, um, a more central location for his business."

She looked up from the pictures she was scrolling through again. "Really? I would have thought most of the action would be around Minneapolis."

"He does mostly rural and small contracting jobs. He also has a side business building furniture from reclaimed wood." Though the room wasn't overly hot, sweat ran down his back.

"A man of many talents, this Mr. Cam Hainstock."

"Yes, he is."

For the rest of the evening, Ethan steered the conversation away from Cam. He knew she wasn't happy about being forced to accept his brother without any other bids, but it couldn't be helped. Cam needed this work so he could be close to Tessa. If Harper knew the circumstances, he was sure she'd agree.

But she didn't know the circumstances. That was the whole point.

Perhaps she might have forgiven him for withholding the truth, but now he'd outright lied to her. There was no going back.

Chapter Fifteen

HARPER PULLED INTO Abby's driveway and killed the engine of her truck. Gathering her mother's photo album and the container of cookies she'd made, she hopped out of the cab and made her way to the front door. This time she'd phoned ahead and Abby was expecting her.

She knocked on the door and a moment later Abby opened it with a warm smile. "Come in, come in. It's good to see you, sweetheart."

"It's nice to see you, too."

Abby seemed more energetic than she'd been the last time, but she still had dark circles under her eyes that weren't entirely camouflaged by a skillful application of makeup. There was something very delicate about her that Harper didn't remember from years before.

After Harper tossed her coat and the photo album on the sofa, Abby led her into the kitchen and put on the kettle.

"I hope you like tea. I made you drink some the last time you were here, but it occurred to me later that I never asked you if you even like the stuff."

"You're in luck. I love tea."

Abby patted her hand and chuckled. "Well, that's a relief."

"I brought some cookies. Chocolate chip."

"Did you make them?"

Harper laughed. "I did, but don't let that put you off. I'm not as good a cook as Maggie, but I make a decent chocolate chip cookie, if I say so myself."

"I'm sure Reese will love them."

"I hope you'll love them, too. I made them for you."

"I'll try one later. I just had lunch and I'm not very hungry right now." She gave Harper an apologetic smile. "Since my surgery my appetite isn't what it used to be."

"I'm sorry to hear that." That would probably explain why she was thinner than she remembered. "How are you feeling?"

"Better every day." Abby set teacups and spoons on the table. "Do you know what I've been thinking about since the last time I saw you? Chocolate brownies."

"Oh, really? You should have told me. I would have made you some. What made you think of brownies?"

"Maggie used to bring me brownies. I guess talking about your sisters made me think about that." She poured hot water into the teapot to steep. "Has she mentioned anything about coming to Minnewasta since we last spoke?"

That was the second time Abby had asked if Maggie was coming home, and she wondered at the reason. "I'm embarrassed to admit it, but I haven't talked to Maggie since I last visited you. I've been crazy busy with the renovations."

"Don't let yourself get so busy you lose touch with your sisters."

"I won't. I'll make sure to call Maggie tonight. Maybe I'll even get her to give me her brownie recipe."

"That would be awesome. Tell her I said hi, would you?"

"Of course." Abby was so anxious to see Maggie. Perhaps she missed her. They had been close at one time, after all.

Still, if she missed Maggie, why hadn't she contacted her in the last ten years? She was sure Maggie would have told her if she had.

Harper picked up her delicate china cup and sipped at the hot tea, struggling to come up with another topic of conversation. "How is Luke? I haven't heard any news about him for a long time. Is he still in California?"

Abby smiled proudly. "He is. He's doing great. He's the hotel manager of a resort in the Napa Valley. He's become something of an expert in California wines."

"He sounds like the kind of guy we're going to need at the lodge when we reopen." She told Abby how Ethan wanted someone with more experience than she had to manage the new lodge.

"I think he's wrong. I'm sure you could do the job. You've always been so strong and determined, ready to take on anything."

Abby's faith in her was gratifying. "I appreciate the vote of confidence, but much as I hate to admit it, I think Ethan is right. Managing the resort is too important a job to leave to an amateur."

"It would be my fondest fantasy to have Luke come home," she said with a sigh. "But I don't think that will ever happen. He made it pretty clear when he left that he was never coming back."

He sounded like Scarlet and Maggie, so determined to stay away. But a small rural area like Minnewasta, as beautiful as it was in her eyes, was no match for the stunning vistas and opportunities to be found in the Napa Valley.

"Oh! I almost forgot. When I was cleaning out the lodge, I found my mother's photo albums. I was hoping you could help me identify some people."

"Sure. Let's take a look."

Harper jumped to her feet and retrieved the album from the sofa in the living room. Pulling up a chair to sit next to Abby, she set the album on the table in front of her.

"I was hoping you could tell me who some of these people are. Reese identified several for me, but there are still some question marks."

"You showed this to Reese?" She sounded surprised.

"He was there when I found it." She pointed to the pictures of Abby and Willy. "You guys look so young."

"That's because we *were* young," she said with a laugh. "We couldn't be more than fifteen or sixteen in these pictures." Abby ran her index finger over Willy's picture. "Poor Willy. He was such a sweet guy. It's a shame what the alcohol has done to him."

"I know. It's kind of scary, too." Harper told her about how Ethan had ended up bathing Willy and his promise not drive drunk again.

"Is that a promise you think he'll keep?" Abby asked.

"I hope so, for his sake. And for everyone else on the road."

Abby turned another page of the photo album. "You know, Willy had the biggest crush on your mother back in high school."

"Really? I didn't know that."

"I don't think he ever told her. I only found out because I snooped through his desk and found some poetry he'd written for her. He swore me to secrecy." She gave Harper a wry smile. "Oops. Seems I broke my promise. You're the only person I've ever told."

"He never told my mother he cared about her?"

"I don't think so. Miranda cared for him, too, but she thought of him more as a friend."

"Do you think that's why he never married? Because he was holding a torch for my mother?"

"I think Willy's marital status has more to do with his drinking than holding any torches."

Abby was probably right. What woman would knowingly marry an alcoholic? Even if someone had been willing, by the time he was in his twenties or thirties, there probably hadn't been a lot of eligible, unmarried woman in the community to choose from. Just like there weren't many eligible men now.

Abby flipped the page to the picture of the young man in the ball cap. Harper pointed at it. "Do you know who this is?"

"You said Reese saw this photo album?"

"Yeah. Why do you ask?"

Abby's lips quirked in amusement. "Because apparently he couldn't identify himself. This is Reese. He'd be about eighteen or nineteen here, I'd guess."

Harper squinted at the picture. "He said he worked at the lodge the summer after he graduated high school."

"Yeah, he did."

She still found it unusual that her grandfather had never mentioned it. But then it had been years before she'd been born. Ancient history.

Abby identified several other people in the photo album that Reese hadn't known. She told Harper stories about her and her mother and some of the crazy things they'd done as teenagers. The Dynamic Duo they'd been called. Harper wished she'd talked to Abby years ago. Her stories helped to bring Miranda to life.

They laughed and talked for over an hour, until Harper noticed Abby was looking tired. "I should go and let you get some rest. Are you sure there isn't something I can do for you? Some housework, or maybe some gardening when the weather gets warmer?"

"No, we've got it covered, but thanks for asking." She cupped Harper's face. "Miranda would be so proud of her girls."

"I wish she was here."

"I know you do, sweetheart. So do I."

The lump in Harper's throat prevented her from responding with more than a nod. She didn't often let herself go down the 'what if' road, but talking about the past with Abby had brought back those old childhood longings she'd neatly packed away years ago. How different her life, and the lives of her sisters, would have been if their parents had lived.

If they'd lived, it was possible she wouldn't be here now, renovating her grandfather's old fishing lodge. She wondered if the lodge would mean as much to her if she'd grown up in Minneapolis with her parents. Maybe she and her sisters would have been closer if she hadn't had to take on a parental role. If her parents had lived...

She gave Abby's hand a squeeze and got to her feet. "I should go. It's been fun playing hooky with you, but I've got a client I need to meet with this afternoon."

"It was wonderful seeing you again, Harper. I hope you come again."

"I will. Maybe next time I'll even have some brownies with me."

"Maggie's brownies. That would be wonderful."

"I'll make sure to tell her you asked about her."

"Thanks. Take care, Harper."

As she climbed into her truck and headed to her client's business, an overwhelming desire to talk to both of her sisters assailed her. She desperately wanted a new relationship with them, one in which they were simply sisters and friends.

WHEN HARPER GOT BACK to her cottage, the first thing she did was phone Maggie. Even though she was likely at the restaurant, Harper gave it a shot. Nothing ventured, and all that.

She was surprised when Maggie picked up on the second ring. "Harper. What's up?"

Her voice was crisp, even a little impatient sounding, as if she'd been taken away from something important. Or maybe seeing Harper's name on her cell phone set her off.

"Nothing really. I wanted to hear your voice, that's all. I'm sorry if I'm catching you at a bad time."

"No, not at all." Maggie's voice softened, relaxed. "I'm just hanging around my apartment."

"I was afraid I was going to catch you at work."

"Not today." The same crisp edge crept into her voice. "Is something going on? You usually only call me if there's some kind of problem."

"Really?" She hadn't realized she'd done that. "Well, today all I want to do is talk. I miss you."

There was silence on the other end of the line for a couple of heartbeats. Then Harper heard her sister's whispered reply. "I miss you, too."

Harper swallowed the lump in her throat and launched into a play by play of the renovations and the new construction on the lodge that had taken place so far.

"Did I tell you that Reese Hanson is our general contractor, and that he and Abby have moved back to Minnewasta?"

"No, you didn't. Have you talked to her?"

"Yes, I was at her house this afternoon. She asked about you and said she wanted to see you. She remembered the chocolate brownies you used to make for her."

"The chocolate brownies? Oh!"

Maggie was silent for a moment. All Harper could hear was her erratic breathing, as if she was trying to hold back a sob. "Honey, are you all right?"

"Yeah, yeah, I am. I haven't thought about those brownies in a long time. When I was upset with you or Grampa, I used to bake. Many times I brought something to Abby and she'd listen patiently to all my complaints and my heartaches. Then, she'd gently tell me I should go home and talk to you."

"But you never did. Why not?"

"Because you were so bossy!"

Harper winced at her sister's rebuke. "Yeah, I guess I was. I was the oldest, so I thought I had to look out for you and Scarlet. I thought I had to be the parent, especially after Grandma died. You were so upset after she died, and I was afraid..."

"What were you afraid of?"

"Of losing you, too."

It was the first time she'd admitted her fears to Maggie, to anyone. Maggie turned fifteen a few months after Grandma Dorothy died and for some time after their grandmother's sudden death, she seemed to lose control. Harper had been afraid that in her grief she'd turn to drugs, or sex, or something else that would ruin her life. Her biggest fear was that she'd run away and be lost to them forever. So she'd kept a close eye on her, monitored all her activities, and strictly controlled whom she could see and when she could go out. Maggie had hated her for it, but at least she'd been safe.

"I'm sorry I was such a brat, Harper. It was a bad time. I had a lot of trouble coping."

"I wish you would have talked to me back then, told me what you were feeling."

"I didn't think you'd understand." Maggie's voice was barely a whisper.

"Oh, honey!" Harper pushed back her own tears. "I'm sorry you felt that way. I'm sorry I was such a hard ass with you."

"I know I wasn't fair to you. You were in an awful position. Abby tried to tell me that, over and over, but I wouldn't listen. If it wasn't for you and Abby, I might have done something stupid. I'm sorry, Harper."

She swiped at her eyes. "It's in the past. Can we go forward now? All I want is to be your sister and your friend. I want you to know that you can come to me with any problems, and I'll listen and not judge. At least, I'll try not to judge."

Maggie gave a hiccupping laugh. "I'd like to see that. It would be a first."

Harper gave a half-laugh, but her sister's words made her think. Had she judged Maggie all these years? She hadn't meant to question her choices, especially as an adult, but she'd always worried about her. Much more than Scarlet, and she worried plenty about Scarlet. Perhaps if she started treating Maggie like an adult instead of a recalcitrant teenager, she'd start behaving like one. "Be gentle with me. I'm new to this non-judgemental stuff, so I might backslide from time to time. You'll have to cut me some slack."

Maggie chuckled. "I'll keep that in mind."

They said nothing for a few moments, but Harper welcomed the silence. A window had been opened in their relationship. They hadn't yet said everything that needed to be said, but it was a start.

"When I was cleaning out the lodge, I found a photo album that belonged to Mom. Grandma had them boxed up and hidden in the back of her closet."

"What was in the album?"

"Mostly school photos of her friends and some lovely pictures of Mom I'd never seen before. There were pictures of Willy and Abby, and even Reese. Abby told me the names of the people I couldn't identify."

"I wonder why Grandma hid them away from us. It doesn't sound like there were any racy pictures in the album."

"No, not at all. I didn't always understand the things Grandma did."

"No, me either."

"I haven't had a chance to go through all the boxes I found in Grandma's closet. Maybe sometime you can come out here and we can go through them together."

"Yeah, maybe."

"Abby asked when you might be coming home for a visit. I got the impression she really wants to see you."

"I'm...I'm not sure when I'll be able to come home. My schedule is kind of hectic."

Harper tamped down her disappointment. "I understand. Maybe I'll come to you then. I'm going to need to shop for kitchen supplies and appliances soon, and you promised to help, remember?"

"I remember, but isn't it a little premature to buy supplies when you don't have a kitchen yet?"

Harper laughed. "Maybe a little, but you know me. Ms. Type A Personality."

"Oh, yes. I know you well." The amusement in Maggie's voice was a welcome sound, but it quickly faded. "So Abby says she wants to see me?"

"Yes, she does. Very much."

"How is she?"

"She's okay. She had some surgery a couple of months ago that she's still recovering from, but she seems to be in good spirits. She tires easily, though."

"What kind of surgery?" There was a note of alarm in Maggie's voice.

"I'm not sure. She didn't volunteer the information, and it seemed too personal a question to ask."

"But she's okay?"

"Yes, I think so. In a lot of ways, she's the same old Abby. She still has the same sense of humor."

"That's good." Maggie sounded relieved. "I'll definitely go shopping with you for supplies. And I'll try to come out to the lodge, Harper. I really will."

"That would be wonderful, honey! Just name the date." Harper checked her watch. "I've got to go. I'm working the dinner shift at Miller's tonight, and I'm running a little late."

"You work too hard."

"No harder than you."

"Yeah, well, I don't know about that. It was good talking to you. We'll talk again soon, okay?"

"Yes, absolutely. Take care, Maggie."

"You, too."

Harper disconnected the call. The conversation with Maggie had been good. Maybe being more open with each other was what they needed to set their relationship on a more adult footing. Perhaps it would help them become closer. She prayed that would happen because she needed her sister, now more than ever.

She picked at the frayed edge of her shirt cuff. Perhaps if she'd been more open with Ethan they could have had a relationship, too.

Chapter Sixteen

ETHAN KNOCKED ON THE door just as Harper removed the lasagne from the oven, the cheese still bubbling. She tossed a smile over her shoulder. "Talk about perfect timing. I'll let this cool for a few minutes and we can eat."

He sniffed the air. "Lasagne? It smells fantastic, and I'm starved. I worked up an appetite today."

"Oh, yeah? Doing what?" She threw the olive oil and lemon juice dressing she'd prepared earlier over the greens and began tossing the salad.

"Working with the guys on the lodge. Reese has me doing mostly grunt labor since I don't have any carpentry or trade skills, but it feels good to get in there and get my hands dirty."

Harper stopped tossing and turned to stare at him. "Seriously? I thought you were more of a numbers guy. I didn't know you had any interest in the actual work."

"There's a lot of things you don't know about me." Ethan broke eye contact and moved to the sink to wash his hands.

Harper resumed tossing the salad. He was right. There were a lot of things she didn't know about him. If she looked closer, learned more, what would she find? If they were more open, maybe she'd find him even more desirable.

It was hard to imagine she could be any more attracted to him.

She conjured up a smile. "I guess there is. I'm glad you're enjoying yourself. I'm just surprised. I didn't think laborer was part of your job description."

Ethan moved to the table and sat in his usual place. "It's not, but it gives me a good perspective on what's going on with the build. I can see the effort and the care that's going into the renovation first hand. I think Reese and the crew respects me a little more because they see I'm willing to work."

"I have to admit I'm impressed, too." Harper cut the lasagne into several pieces and placed the pan on a trivet on the table. Oregano scented steam rose from the pan. "I appreciate you going above and beyond for this project."

"It means a lot to me."

She waited for him to elaborate, but instead he reached for the spatula she'd set next to the lasagne pan and helped himself to a piece. Harper passed him the salad and then dished herself a portion of lasagne. For a time, he was too busy eating to make more conversation. Why would this project mean more to him than other projects Hainstock Investments was involved with? She wanted to believe it had something to do with her, but she knew thoughts like that were ridiculous.

He was halfway through his second helping when Harper's cell phone rang. She retrieved it from the kitchen counter and checked the call display. Her heart sank. "It's Willy."

She hit the talk button. "Hi, Willy. What's going on?"

"I'm trying to be good, Harper, trying to do what you told me."

His words were slurred and she could hear bar room music in the background. She closed her eyes and bowed her head. *Drunk again*. "What are you talking about?"

"You said I shouldn't drive after I've been drinking. I don't want to hurt anyone, but I've got to work tonight. Can you come get me, Harper?"

She should have known the order she'd given Willy would come back to bite her in the ass. "Fine. Where are you?"

"At Murphy's in St. Cloud."

"St. Cloud? What are you doing there?" The town was at least an hour and a half away.

"Came here for an auction sale today."

"And of course, you had to stop at Murphy's. Honestly, Willy, this is too much."

"It's 'sokay," he slurred. "You don't have to come. I'll take the backroads home. No one will know." He made a shushing sound.

No one but me. She couldn't in good conscious let Willy get behind the wheel when she knew he'd been drinking. "I'll be there as soon as I can. Don't leave Murphy's, okay?"

"Okay. Thanks Harper."

"Don't thank me yet. You and I are going to have a little talk when I see you."

She disconnected the call with a furious jab and pulled her jacket from a peg near the door. "I've got to run. Willy's drunk and I have to pick him up before he drives again. Can you put the food in the fridge?"

"I'm coming with you."

As she shoved her arms into her jacket, she said, "You don't have to do that."

"Don't argue with me, Harper. I'm not letting you go alone."

Harper stared at him as he grabbed the lasagne pan and the salad bowl and stuffed them into the fridge. A minute later he was at the door, putting on his jacket.

"Since when do you get to boss me around?"

"Since you appointed yourself Willy's chauffeur. He's a drunk, Harper. That means he's manipulative and unpredictable, and I'm not going to leave you alone with him."

"That's ridiculous. I've known Willy all my life."

"Are we going to stand around arguing about this, or are we going to pick him up before he decides to drive himself home?"

She threw up her hands. "Fine. Let's go."

"We'll take my truck."

Harper considered arguing but decided that if he wanted to use his gas, it was fine with her. She followed him out of the cottage.

A short time later they were flying down the Interstate toward St. Cloud. They were silent for several miles until Ethan finally started talking, his eyes on the road ahead. "If you get into the habit of picking Willy up and driving him home, he's going to get into the habit of calling you every time he's drunk."

That possibility had occurred to her. "So, am I supposed to let him drive drunk?"

"No, but if you keep bailing him out, you're enabling his drinking and his bad behavior. You're allowing him to keep doing what he's doing without any consequences."

She hadn't thought of it that way. All she wanted was to keep Willy off the roads, but she could see his point. Harper turned toward him, hoping she wouldn't overstep her bounds with her next question. "Are you speaking from personal experience?"

He gave her a quick glance before returning his attention to the road. "Yes. My mother tried her best to cover up the fact that my father drank. She did his work for him, she lied for him, she picked him up when he was too drunk to drive. She did everything she possibly could to deny he was an alcoholic. But everything she did made it easier for him to drink. She might as well have held the whiskey to his lips and poured it down his throat."

"And you think I'm doing the same with Willy?"

"You're on the verge. I don't want you to get sucked into his mess. I know your intentions are good, but things never work out the way an enabler wants them to. My mother enabled my father's drinking until she was too sick with cancer to do it anymore. Without her, everything fell apart and we had no choice but to sell. In the end, my brother, sister and I were left with nothing, not even a family. We each went our own way to try to scratch out a living."

"Despite all that, you've done well for yourself."

"Have I?" He shook his head. "Alcoholism leaves all kinds of scars, some you can't see."

She hadn't seen the scars. Until now. "He must have been a difficult person to live with."

"He was difficult until the day he died. He got sick with liver disease a couple of years after mom died. My sister had a husband and kids by then, but she took him in and looked after him. My brother and I sent money to help her when we could. I stayed with him a few times to give her a rest, but my brother wouldn't have anything to do with him. He blamed him for Mom's death, but I think he saw too much of himself in the old man and it scared him." There was anger evident in his voice and in the whitened knuckles gripping the steering wheel.

"I'm sorry."

He glanced at her again, his dark eyes flashing. "I didn't tell you this story to make you feel sorry for me. I told you to help you realize you're not doing Willy any favors by being his enabler. Willy is an addict, and he'll do whatever he has to do to get his next drink, including using you. If you let him, he'll drag you down with him."

"So what am I supposed to do, Ethan? Am I supposed to abandon him? I've known him since childhood. He was someone I went to as a kid when things got tough. He helped me through some rough patches. How can I turn against him now?"

"All I know is that if you continue to play chauffeur for him, make excuses for him, he'll keep telling himself he doesn't have a problem. At least, that's the way it worked in my family."

Harper remained silent. The best thing she could do for Willy would be to convince him to get some help. The thought of cutting off her ties to him until he did so made her feel disloyal and ungrateful.

Within the hour they arrived at Murphy's, a bar on the outskirts of St. Cloud. She'd never been inside, but with its fading paintjob and the burnt-out light in the Y of its sign, it looked tired and seedy. Of course, any bar that had Willy as part of its clientele wouldn't be posh.

"I see Willy's truck over there." She pointed to the old green Ford half-ton parked close to the front door. "I'll find Willy and drag him out of the bar."

Ethan narrowed his eyes at her as he reached for his door handle. "As if I'm going to let you go into that place alone."

Harper pursed her lips to keep a sharp retort from escaping. However annoyed she might be by his caveman attitude, she had to admit she was uneasy going into Murphy's alone. "Suit yourself."

They entered the bar. Once her eyes adjusted to the dim light, she spotted Willy sitting alone at a table in the back, a drink in his hand. After getting Ethan's attention, she led the way through the crowded room. The country music of a three-piece band set up in the corner of the bar blasted through the speakers, making conversation difficult. The place smelled of stale booze and unwashed bodies, and she couldn't get out fast enough.

When they reached Willy's table, Harper touched his arm and leaned forward to speak to him over the music. "Come on. Let's go."

He lifted his glass to his lips with a shaky hand. "Have to finish my drink first."

"No, you don't. If you want a ride home, get your ass out of your chair. Now."

He blinked at her, surprised. She was pretty surprised herself. She rarely lost her temper with Willy, and she never swore at him, but he was pushing all her buttons tonight. He knew she was coming for him, yet he'd casually ordered another drink, and then expected her to wait while he drank it.

Willy downed his whiskey in one gulp and rose unsteadily to his feet.

A waitress hustled over to his table. "You've got to settle your tab, Willy."

He fumbled in his pockets for some money and handed it to the waitress. She counted it and shook her head. "You're five dollars short."

Willy went through his pockets again. "Don't have no more." He turned to Harper. "Can you lend me a five?"

"Why did you let him run a tab?" Harper asked the waitress.

Before she could say anything, Ethan answered. "So he could drink more. He probably lost track of how much he drank or how much it cost."

"That's disgusting." Harper dug in her purse and handed a five to the waitress. She didn't know who she was angrier with; Willy, for drinking away all his money, or the bar for knowingly over-serving him. "Let's get out of here."

Willy leaned on her as they left the bar. After getting the keys from him, she helped him into the passenger seat of his truck and buckled him in. As she went to open the driver's door, Ethan laid his hand on hers.

"I'll be right behind you all the way. If he gives you any trouble, pull over."

"He's not going to give me any trouble."

Even in the dim illumination from the light over the bar's front door, she could see the intensity in his face and the flicker of anger in his eyes. "Damn it, Harper. Quit trying to handle everything on your own. Willy's had a lot to drink and no matter how well you think you know him, he could be violent. Drunks are unpredictable."

Had his father been violent? "I'm pretty sure Willy will sleep all the way home, but if anything happens, I'll pull over."

He nodded, then headed for his truck. Harper took a deep breath before opening the truck door and sliding behind the wheel.

As she predicted, Willy slept the entire drive back to Minnewasta. When she pulled in front of the office building he cleaned every night, she shook his arm. "Willy, we're here."

He groggily looked around. "This isn't my house."

"No, you said you had to work tonight. I brought you to the office building."

Leaning against the headrest, he closed his eyes. "Too tired. Take me home."

Harper stared at him. He *was* using her, sucking her into his downward spiral. They'd both crash and burn if she didn't do something to stop the progress right now.

With her heart racing, she turned off the motor and pulled Willy's keys from the ignition. As she opened her door and walked around the hood of the truck to the passenger side, she heard the door of Ethan's truck slam shut.

She wrenched open the passenger door and leaned over Willy to unbuckle his seat belt. "Get out. Now!"

Willy blinked at her. "I'm too tired, Harper."

"Too drunk, you mean. Get out and do your job."

"I can't. I'm too sick to work tonight."

She stood next to the open door. Ethan stood a few feet away, his presence giving her added courage. "If you don't work tonight, you're admitting you're too drunk to hold down a job. Is that what you want? To lose your job and admit you're an alcoholic?"

"I'm not an alcoholic!" Willy swung his legs out of the truck and lowered himself to the ground. "I like to have a drink now and then, but I'm not an alcoholic."

"Prove it. Get out of this truck and go do your job."

She held her breath as he pushed himself to his feet. "I thought you were kind, like Miranda, but you're a mean bitch. Not like my Miranda at all."

His words cut deep into her heart, but she schooled her features to show no reaction. "I'm sorry you feel that way. When you're ready to admit you have a problem with alcohol, I'll get you some help."

"I don't need your help," Willy spat. "I don't need you at all. Leave me alone, bitch."

Ethan stepped forward. "Watch your mouth, Willy, or I'll plaster your face to the sidewalk."

Harper put her hand on Ethan's chest to stop his advance. "Don't, please."

He said nothing but continued to stare at Willy, as if ready to pound him into the dirt if he stepped out of line again. Harper took the truck key off the ring and handed the rest to Willy.

"I'm going to drive your truck home and park it in your driveway. I'll leave the key in the glove compartment."

He glared at her. "How am I supposed to get home?"

"You can walk. It's only about a half-mile. Maybe the fresh air will sober you up." She took a deep, calming breath. "When you're ready to get some help, let me know. But until then, don't call me or come to my place. If you call me looking for a ride again, I'll phone the police and tell them you plan to drive drunk."

"Go to hell, Harper. You're no friend of mine."

He turned unsteadily and headed to the office building. She watched as he fumbled with the keys, finally finding the right one and opening the door.

She closed her eyes and let the pain wash over her. Ethan touched her arm.

"You okay?"

She stared at him. Sometimes life was so hard, and she was so alone. Maybe, for once, she could forget about her worries and fears and go after what she wanted. She wanted Ethan so much...

Where does he go when he leaves you, Harper? Who does he go to?

"I'll be fine."

His expression softened. "I know you will. You ready to go?"

She swallowed her tears. "Yeah. Let's take this truck to Willy's place so we can get home."

He nodded. "I'll follow you."

A few minutes later she pulled the truck into Willy's driveway and stuck the key into the glove compartment the way she told him she would. Then, she made her way to Ethan's truck and climbed inside the cab, grateful for the warmth.

"Are you okay?"

She buckled her seat belt, avoiding his eyes. "You keep asking me that. My answer hasn't changed from the last time. I'm fine."

Ethan put his truck into gear. They drove through town, and at the lights turned toward the lodge. Neither of them said anything until they were about a mile from home.

Ethan cleared his throat. "I know that wasn't easy for you, but it was the right thing to do. For you and for Willy. I'm proud of you."

She couldn't hold back the tears any longer. "What if the next time he drinks he doesn't call me because he knows I'll call the cops? What if he drives anyway, even if he's drunk? What if he kills someone, or kills himself? How am I supposed to live with that?"

Ethan pulled over to the side of the road and stopped the truck. In a matter of seconds, he'd unfastened her seatbelt and she was in his arms. She clung to him as he gently kissed her hair.

"I don't have any answers for you. All I know is that you did the right thing."

"I hope you're right."

His arms tightened around her, but he said nothing. As she listened to the steady beat of his heart, her tears subsided. It would be so easy to take comfort in his arms, to lose herself in them. It would be easy to lean on him, use him, like an addict uses his drug of choice. But what happened to her when he walked away, when her drug was taken away? The fear of that happening, of knowing it was inevitable, sent shivers down her spine.

A memory played through her head, the sound of voices raised in anger making her want to cover her ears, even after all these years. Her parents' argument had woken her and she'd crept out of her room to the banister that overlooked the first floor. Between the spindles she saw them, sensed the fury in the room. Suddenly, her mother raised her hand and slapped her father. Hard. They'd stared at each other in shock, neither of them saying or doing anything, until finally her mother spoke. Her words had burned themselves into Harper's memory.

"I'll never forget what you just said. I loved you once, but there's nothing left."

The next day, her father left. Would any relationship she had end up like theirs, with unhappiness and infidelity? With death?

Harper pushed herself out of Ethan's arms and gave him what she hoped was a composed smile. "I'm okay now."

He brushed away an errant tear from her cheek with the pad of his thumb. "You're sure?"

No, I'm not sure about anything! "Yeah, I'm sure."

He nodded, and while she moved back into her seat and buckled her belt, he put the truck into gear. In a short time, they were back at the lodge. Ethan took the road to their cottages. Driving past his cottage, he pulled into the driveway in front of hers, keeping the motor running.

She unbuckled her seatbelt slowly. "Are you coming inside? Do you want to finish your dinner?"

"No, I'm good. Unless you want me to stay with you for a while?"

As he quietly watched her, a war between fear and longing raged within. How she wished she could be the kind of person who embraced life and everything it had to offer, instead of being crippled by fear and 'what-ifs'. "I think I'm going to have an early night. I have an appointment with one of my clients at seven in the morning."

If he was disappointed, he didn't let it show. "Okay. I'll see you tomorrow then."

She opened the door of the truck. "Yes, tomorrow. Thank you for everything. Goodnight."

"Goodnight."

Harper hopped out of the truck and walked up to her front porch. She watched Ethan's truck until it disappeared behind a wall of trees. Longing for him assailed her, but she pushed it away.

Chapter Seventeen

"DO YOU WANT THE BAD news first, or the very bad news?" Reese asked.

"Are those our only options?" Harper murmured.

Ethan wasn't sure he wanted to hear what their general contractor had to say either, but they didn't have much choice. "What's going on?"

"Come with me," Reese said. "I need you to see a couple of things."

He led them around to the west side of the lodge, the side facing the lake. He stopped near some scaffolding and pointed to the crumbling chinking between the massive logs.

"On our first inspection, we thought we'd only need to replace the chinking on the north side of the lodge. But when we took a closer look, we discovered areas on all sides where the chinking has crumbled."

"That might explain why the lodge has been so cold the last few years," Harper said.

Reese nodded. "Probably. I've consulted with a log home specialist and, aside from the chinking, he says we need to do quite a bit of maintenance on the logs, especially on the exterior. Some areas need sanding and cleaning to get rid of mold and mildew, and the whole thing needs to be stained, inside and outside, to protect it from water damage, UV light, and insects. We've only partly budgeted to have this work done. The entire job will eat up the contingency we built into the budget."

"It's not a big surprise. Maintenance was deferred on the lodge for a lot longer than it should have." Harper exhaled. "So is this the really bad news?"

"Not even close."

She gave Ethan a worried look, and he tried to reassure her with a quick grin, but he was concerned, too. From Reese's demeanor, he could tell something was very, very wrong.

They followed him to a corner of the building where the dirt and sand had been pulled away from the foundation. Ethan immediately saw the problem. "The foundation is crumbling."

"Yes." Reese climbed down a ladder into the hole the crew had dug next to the foundation and ran his hands over the stones. Bits of mortar fell to the ground. "It's the same all around the lodge. There's no point putting thousands of dollars into upgrading the lodge if you don't take care of the foundation."

"What needs to be done?" Ethan asked.

"We'll need to jack up the house and lift it. While it's raised, we'll build a new, solid foundation. We could even put in a basement if you want. Once the concrete has cured, we lower the lodge back onto the new foundation. It'll be solid as a rock."

"So, you've done this before?" Ethan asked.

"Yes. The lodge is a little bigger than other structures I've lifted before, but I'm confident we can do the work without any issues."

"This sounds very expensive," Harper said. "What do you think it's going to cost?"

When Reese named a figure, her face went white. "This could be the end of the lodge. Everything I've dreamed of, gone."

Would she ever care about him as much as she cared for the lodge? He doubted that was possible. "We'll get the additional money from Hainstock Investments. Mr. Hainstock knows we're committed at this point. We can't stop now. I'll talk to him and explain the situation."

She frowned. "I thought he was in Europe on vacation."

Another lie coming back to haunt him. "This is an emergency. I'll find a way to talk to him."

Reese took off his ball cap and ran his hand through his thick, dark hair. "You'd better talk fast. We can't sit around waiting for a decision. We'll need to fix the foundation before any other work on the lodge can be done. While the lodge is hoisted, it's too dangerous to have people working inside. We'll have to reschedule some of the trades."

"How long will building the new foundation take?"

"This is a significant delay. It will take at least a couple of weeks to hoist the building and then pour the footers and foundation walls. Then, we have to let the concrete cure for a minimum of twenty-eight days before we lower the lodge back onto the foundation. Any sooner and the concrete might not be strong enough to handle the weight."

Ethan made a quick decision. "Go ahead and make arrangements for the new foundation. And while we're at it, let's dig a new basement. We need storage and this seems like the best solution. I'll make sure the money is made available."

Harper touched his arm. "Do you have that authority, Ethan? Maybe he'll think he's already put in too much cash. What if he shuts down the whole project?"

She was scared. She'd made it clear the lodge meant more to her than anything.

Including him.

"He's not going to do that. We're too far in to turn back now." He'd have to convince his sister and brother-in-law, who guarded his money like pit bulls, but in the end, it was his money. And he wanted this project to succeed.

"I'll get everything in place to start the process," Reese said. "One last thing. If we're digging a basement now, we'll need stairway access from the inside the lodge. When it was simply a crawl space, no stairway was required. We'll have to talk to the architect and have him make adjustments to the plans."

Harper shook her head. "More expense."

Ethan squeezed her arm. "Think of this as making lemonade from lemons. A full concrete basement is going to provide valuable storage space for the lodge that we wouldn't otherwise have. We'll also have a better spot for all the mechanicals like the furnaces and water heaters."

"I suppose," she conceded. But she still looked worried.

"I'll talk to the boss and we'll figure this out. Don't worry." He wanted her to trust him, to have full confidence he could get her lodge built.

"And what if the boss says no?"

"Then, I'll have to charm the money out of him."

That made her smile. "You're full of it."

"Probably. But seriously, I don't want you to worry. This is just a minor hiccup. I'll take care of it."

She took a deep breath, let it out. "Okay. I trust you to get this done."

"Good."

Though he was sure Harper didn't realize he was THE Mr. Hainstock, he wondered what kind of relationship they'd have if he didn't represent the accomplishment of her most cherished dreams. If he was still an ordinary working stiff, living from paycheck to paycheck, would she have the time of day for him? He couldn't help feeling used, like he was nothing to her without the money.

Yet, her happiness meant everything to him. If rebuilding the lodge and turning it into a viable business again would make her happy, then that's what he'd do.

More fool him.

He hated lying to her, but he was so deep into this lie he couldn't find his way out. He couldn't hide his true identity from her forever. Eventually, she'd figure it out. Or someone would tell her.

Cold fear twisted his gut. When she discovered the truth, would she be angry at him for lying and want him out of her life? Or would she throw herself at him, tossing aside her former concern about mixing business with a personal relationship?

Ethan didn't know which scenario he feared most.

ETHAN WALKED TO HIS cottage and closed the door firmly behind him. He needed to talk to his sister about the extra money they needed, and he didn't want anyone overhearing him. Least of all Harper.

Another pang of guilt jabbed him in the gut. He pushed it aside and dialed Lydia's number in Minneapolis. She answered immediately.

"Hey, little brother. I haven't heard from you in a while. How's it going?"

"It's going great. The place is really starting to take shape. We've run into a bit of a problem though." He told her about the crumbling foundation and how much fixing it was going to cost. He heard her groan.

"Seriously? This is getting out of hand. Maybe it would be cheaper to tear the place down and start over."

"There's no way we're doing that. You can't get logs that size anymore and even if we could, this lodge has a lot of history that we want to preserve. It means a lot to Harper."

"You're getting in very deep here, Ethan. You've got a lot of money on the line. What if the eco-lodge concept doesn't catch on with the public? What if you've got a spectacular flop on your hands?"

"That's not going to happen. I believe in this project more than ever."

"Cam thinks you're only doing this because of Harper Lindquist. He says she has some kind of hold on you."

"That's ridiculous." He'd never admit to his sister he had the same concerns.

"Is it? Are you sleeping with her? Is that why you're so willing to give her all this money?"

He clutched his phone to keep from throwing it against the wall "First of all, I've done my research. I've talked to a lot of people whose opinions I respect, and they all tell me this project is viable. And secondly, whether or not I'm sleeping with Harper isn't any of your damn business. Harper is the most loyal, hardworking, honest person I've ever known. She doesn't play games. You and Cam need to stay the hell out of my personal business and stop treating me like your doofus little brother. If you can't do that, maybe I should start looking for someone else to look after my finances."

Lydia was silent for several beats, giving Ethan's heartbeat a chance to slow down.

She cleared her throat. "I've never heard you talk about a woman that way before. She must be something really special."

"Yeah, she is."

She is. He realized in that moment that he wanted her in his life. Forever. But that couldn't happen as long as there were lies between them.

"I think I'd like to meet this girl. When are you going to let me come up there and check out the lodge?"

Not anytime soon. "I'll let you know."

"We don't have a lot of cash readily available since most of it is tied up in investments. But I can liquidate a couple of accounts, move some money around. It might mean getting hit with penalties for pulling out of an investment early."

"Do what you have to."

"I should be able to have the money available in about a week. I'll let you know."

Relief flooded him. "Okay, thanks."

"And for the record," Lydia said, a laugh in her voice, "you'll always be my doofus little brother."

Ethan chuckled and shook his head. "Good to know."

WHEN HARPER ARRIVED home late that afternoon, she found a sticky note pasted to the door of her cottage.

My turn to cook. Come over to my cottage when you get home. E.

It was sweet of him to want to make a meal for her. She didn't know he could cook.

There were a lot of things she didn't know about him.

Pushing the thought aside, she walked the hundred feet or so down the road to Ethan's cottage. She climbed the front steps to the porch and knocked on the door.

"Come in!" Ethan called from inside.

When Harper opened the door, the pleasant aroma of garlic and chili and an assortment of spices greeted her. "Mmmm. Something smells good."

Ethan chuckled. "You sound surprised."

She took off her jacket and tossed it on the sofa. "I wasn't sure what to expect. You never mentioned your cooking skills."

"I'm no expert, but I have a few dishes in my repertoire that I don't screw up too badly. I hope you like chili."

"Love it."

He turned back to the stove. "Good. I think I made enough to last a week."

"Maybe I don't love it that much."

He laughed. "I'll freeze whatever we don't eat tonight. Would you like a glass of wine?"

"I'd love one."

"How was your day?" he asked.

She slid onto a stool at the island and watched as he took two wine glasses from the cupboard and poured red wine. "Busy. I visited four different clients and reconciled their month end accounts. I had to get everything done today because I'm leaving first thing in the morning for Minneapolis. Maggie and I are going to order kitchen equipment."

"Oh, right. You mentioned you were doing that with her."

He handed one of the glasses to her and she accepted it with a smile. "I think I could get used to being waited on. It's been a long day."

"You deserve a bit of pampering." He touched his glass to hers in a toast. "To good food, I hope, good wine, and very good company. And to good news. The extra money we need for the foundation will be available in about a week."

"Oh, Ethan! I will definitely drink to that. What a relief!"

"Did you seriously doubt I wasn't going to come through for you?"

His choice of words hit her. Not 'for the project'. *For you*. Warmth filled her soul. "I have to admit I was worried. I guess I should have more faith in you."

Their gazes met, held. The air between them was charged with electricity and emotion. "I guess you should."

Ethan had come through for her every step of the way. And not only on the lodge project. He'd helped her with Willy, too. Without his support, she wouldn't have been able to do the right thing for Willy – make him take responsibility for his drinking. The jury was still out on that one, but she knew letting him lean on her was killing him.

As she stared into his dark eyes she realized how much she trusted him, and relied on him. That was something rare for her. The only people she trusted as much were her sisters.

I'm in love with him.

The thought blasted through her brain with the force of a tsunami. The tension of the last few weeks, the insecurity, the mistrust, the fear, slipped easily from her shoulders. For the first time, her mind was clear. She was in love with Ethan and she didn't want to wait anymore. She wanted him. She wanted him to be her first, her last.

Finding courage she didn't know she possessed, Harper slid off the stool and walked around the island. She plucked the wine glass from his hand and set it on the counter, then placed his hand on her breast. "Make love with me, Ethan."

A fire lit in his eyes, telling her he wanted her, too. But there was a question there, a hesitation. "Are you sure?"

She'd never been more sure of anything in her life. "Yes."

"Harper—"

"Shhh. Let's not talk anymore." She placed one finger over his lips, then stood on her tiptoes and kissed him.

Ethan's reaction was lightning swift. He wrapped his arms around her and brought her close, his mouth descending on hers in a wild, warm kiss. Their tongues tangled, slid over each other. She'd missed his touch, his taste. She moaned, and in the sound she heard thirty-two years of longing.

For this. *For him.*

He led her to the bedroom and began to undress her, first unbuttoning her flannel shirt, then pulling her T-shirt over her head. As she stood in front of him in only her bra, doubt struck her. What if he didn't like what he saw? She crossed her arms over her chest and avoided his eyes.

"Look at me, Harper," he said.

She slowly dragged her gaze to his. He smiled reassuringly, then gently pulled her arms away from her breasts. "You're beautiful."

All traces of self-consciousness fled. This was Ethan, and she trusted him.

"So are you," she whispered.

He touched the lacy edge of her bra, tracing his finger over the swell of her breast. "I didn't figure you for the sexy, lace bra type."

"It's my one concession to girlieness. I like pretty underwear."

He pulled the elastic from her ponytail, and her hair cascaded around her shoulders. He ran his fingers through the strands, brushing it away from her face. She closed her eyes and revelled in his gentle, sensuous touch.

"I don't know," he said in a husky tone. "You look pretty girlie to me."

She chuckled at that. With surprising boldness, she pulled his head down to hers for a kiss, then whispered in his ear. "I'm wearing the matching panties. Wanna see?"

"Hell, yeah."

He unzipped her jeans and pushed them down her legs with a speed that astounded her. Laughing, she stepped out of her jeans, but stopped when she saw the stupefied look on his face. She crossed her arms over her chest once more. "What's wrong?"

He shook his head. "I knew you were beautiful, but I didn't expect..." He took a ragged breath and reached for her hand. "Trust me when I tell you you're very girlie."

She smiled, relieved that everything was fine, that she hadn't disappointed him. She unbuttoned his shirt. "I may have to trade in my flannel shirts for silk camisoles."

"I wouldn't have a problem with that."

He helped her strip off his clothes and then stood before her completely naked. She drank in his broad shoulders, the smattering of dark hair on his chest, his flat stomach. Her gaze fell to the part of him that told her he wanted her and was more than ready. She swallowed. He was so *big*. Biologically speaking, she knew men and women were designed to fit together, but how that was supposed to happen between them frightened her a little.

No. She wasn't going to give in to worry. With an effort, she pushed away her fears. This was Ethan, and she loved him. It would all work out. And if she was lucky, he wouldn't notice she'd never done this before.

In one deft move, Ethan unfastened her bra and let it fall to the floor. Then he picked her up and carried her to the bed, laying her gently on top of the comforter. He stretched out beside her, one hand propping his head, the other exploring her body, lazily tracing a path from her thigh to her chest. When he reached her breast and gently rolled her nipple between his thumb and forefinger, a shaft of desire rushed straight from her breast to her core. She arched her back, pushing against his hand. She wanted to get closer to him. She wanted...more.

When he replaced his hand with his mouth, she thought she might die of the pleasure. His tongue swirled around the nipple, gently sucking and pulling. She moaned in response and dampness pooled between her legs. Why had she waited so long!

After giving equal attention to her other breast, Ethan moved his exploration lower, licking and kissing his way down her torso and across her stomach. When he reached her lower abdomen, he pulled down her panties far enough to reveal the dark hair between her legs. He licked the lace edge of the leg opening, then looked up at her with a wolfish grin. "I think we need to get rid of these, don't you?"

"Yes," she said breathlessly.

He pulled them down her legs and tossed them to the floor in one swift motion. Then, he positioned himself between her legs. "Spread your legs for me, baby."

She did as he asked, excitement and trepidation building inside her as he lowered his head. She'd read about oral sex, and had wondered how something that seemed kind of gross – really, putting his mouth *there?* – could be considered sexy. But from all accounts, people of both sexes found it pleasurable. She hoped she didn't hate it. If worse came to worse, she hoped she could fake her way through it. Nerves got the better of her and she tensed. She clutched the comforter as he hovered over her.

And then, Ethan raked his tongue over her most private parts and her mind stopped operating completely. All she could do was feel, and the feelings were exquisite. When he found the knot of nerves deep inside her and gently sucked, she nearly rocketed off the bed. She moaned and thrashed, reaching for something so close yet so elusive. He pushed one finger inside her, and it felt as if he was touching that knot of nerves from both the inside and the outside.

Her climax came without warning. She screamed at both the surprise and the strength as it spread over her body, starting from her core and radiating out. *So they were right*, she thought vaguely. *It does feel like crashing waves.* The waves crashed again and again, and when she thought it was all over, Ethan doubled his efforts, licking and sucking, his finger seemingly massaging her from the inside. To her amazement, she came twice more.

Finally, the waves subsided, and Harper sank against her pillow, completely spent. Ethan raised his head, one eyebrow cocked.

"I didn't think you'd be a screamer."

Neither did I. "Good thing we're alone in the woods."

He chuckled as he reached into the nightstand and pulled out a condom. "Yeah. I wouldn't want anyone to think I was murdering you in here."

She pushed herself up on her elbows. "Was I that loud? I'm sorry, I didn't mean to be."

"I'm teasing, Harper." He rolled the condom over his engorged penis. Harper couldn't take her eyes from it. The sight was both delicious and scary.

A thought momentarily derailed her. Did he always keep condoms in his room? Was he expecting this? Or had he used them with someone else?

No. She pushed the doubts away. This was Ethan.

Straddling her, he pushed her gently onto her back and kissed her, his penis nudging the opening to her body. "You can be as loud as you like. In fact, I encourage screaming."

"You do?"

"Yeah. I want to hear you scream my name."

He nudged his way inside her, and Harper willed herself to relax. She read that being tense made sex more uncomfortable for a woman. She concentrated on Ethan's kisses. He was such a good kisser. The way his tongue silkily stroked hers made her forget that other business down below. She put her arms around him and ran her hands over his back, loving the satin smooth skin stretched over hard muscle. He was nearly completely inside her now, having slowly inched his way in. It really hadn't been so bad. Quite pleasant actually. This was going to be okay. He'd never know.

And then, without warning, he thrust deep inside her, hard and fast. A thousand knives sliced her insides. She screamed her agony.

There was no faking this.

Ethan withdrew immediately and took her into his arms. "God, Harper, what happened? Did I hurt you? What's wrong?"

Tears gathered in her eyes, not from the pain, which had dissipated, but from humiliation. He didn't deserve this. He'd expected someone else, someone who wasn't an inexperienced and, as it turned out, tender virgin.

"I'm so sorry," she began.

He ran his hands over her face, drying her tears with the pad of his thumb. "I'm the one who's sorry. I hurt you. Has it been like this for you before?"

"No."

He winced. "Dammit. I'm sorry. I was too rough."

She couldn't let him blame himself. "No, it's not your fault. It hasn't been like this before because I've never done this before." Her face heated in embarrassment.

"What do you mean?" His eyes clouded with confusion.

God, he was going to make her spell it out. She pushed back her humiliation. "I've never been with anyone before." She took a deep breath and looked into his eyes as she pulled the comforter over her breasts. "I'm a virgin."

He stared at her. "How is that possible?"

"It's possible because you're the first man I've wanted to have sex with." She swallowed and turned away. He deserved the truth. "The first man I trusted enough to have sex with."

He grasped her chin and gently forced her to look at him. "You should have told me. I would have done things differently, been more careful."

"I didn't want you to do things differently! I didn't want to have this conversation at all. I just wanted to make love with you. Is that so wrong?"

He smoothed her hair from her forehead. "No, of course not. I'm deeply honored, Harper. That you would choose me to be your first is a gift. I'm sorry it didn't work out the way you planned."

She touched his face, falling a little more in love with him. He was the kindest man she'd ever known. "There's no one else I'd rather be with. Please, do you think we can try again?"

"I don't want to hurt you. When you cried out..." He shook his head.

"It was okay until that last push. Maybe if we go slow."

"I don't know..."

"Please, Ethan. I still want you, and I think you wanted me too, until I ruined everything."

"Of course I wanted you," he said fiercely. "I've wanted you for a long time. And you didn't ruin anything."

"I've wanted you for a long time, too, but I was scared. I'm not scared any more. Not with you." As she spoke, she stroked his shoulders, then ran her hands down his chest. The skin over his stomach was smooth and hot to the touch.

"All right." He caressed her face. "You tell me if I'm hurting you and I'll stop right away, okay?"

Relief nearly swamped her, knowing he still wanted her. "Okay."

He kissed her closed eyes, her cheeks, her lips. She let her hands drift downward. When she touched his penis with her finger, he inhaled sharply, then gently grasped her hand. "We'll take it real slow, right from the beginning."

She breathed in his scent, loving his kisses, loving him. "Yes."

He pushed her onto her back once more. He hovered over her, bracing his weight on his arms, not quite touching her. She wanted to feel his weight on her, wanted everything he had to give. But he was determined to go slow, and though impatient with need, she realized she needed that. She focused on relaxing and satisfied herself with touching him everywhere she could reach, from his broad shoulders to his taut buttocks.

Gently, he nudged her legs apart and settled himself between her bent knees. His erection pushed at the opening to her body and excitement built inside her, quickening her breath.

He watched her face intently. “I’m going to enter you very slowly, a little bit at a time. If it starts to hurt, tell me and I’ll stop.”

She nodded. She prayed it wouldn’t hurt this time. She’d read that some women’s first time could be uncomfortable to start, but gradually became more pleasurable. She hoped that was the case with her. She so wanted to give him pleasure, make it good for him, too.

Perhaps if I do, he won’t leave.

Ethan pushed inside her with excruciating slowness. There was no pain, and the excitement that she’d experienced when he sucked her began to slowly build once more. She writhed beneath him, wanting more of him, wanting all of him, her hands moving restlessly over his back. Her breath came out in little pants, but she kept her gaze focused on his face.

“Ethan.”

Sweat dotted his forehead, his expression intent, as if every bit of his concentration was focused on the joining of their bodies, and she realized what it cost him to go slow for her. That he would forego his own pleasure to help her only made her love him more. She lifted her hips and her movement pulled him deeper inside, short-circuiting his careful progression.

There was a sting of pain. Something must have shown on her face because Ethan stopped moving immediately. "It hurts, doesn't it?"

"Just a twinge. Not like before. Don't stop."

She lifted her hips again, testing. There was a ping of tenderness, but more muted this time. She moved again, and then ... nothing. No pain, no discomfort.

Nothing but the pleasure of having Ethan inside her. Her whole body relaxed.

She squeezed his buttock. "It feels good. It feels really good."

Excitement flared in his eyes. "Yeah?"

She moved with him. "Don't hold back. Please."

"You're sure?"

"Yes. Yes! Do you want me to beg?"

One corner of his mouth turned up in amusement. "I don't think that will be necessary."

He set up a rhythm, pulling back almost to the point of withdrawal, then thrusting inside, a little deeper each time. But she could feel the restraint in him. He was still holding back.

But she didn't care. That something, that wave that had rushed over her earlier, was beginning to build once more. So good, so close. *Almost there, almost there...*

Her climax began in the tips of her toes and radiated through her whole body, tossing her in a turbulent sea of desire. All she could do was to hold on to him and ride the waves. Her heart sang with satisfaction when a moment later he cried out his own release.

Harper held him close. He'd waited for her. She'd been so lucky to find such a generous lover for her first time.

After a few moments, he rolled off and left the bed to go to the bathroom. She heard the water running, and he returned a moment later with a washcloth.

"Lie back, sweetheart. I think this might help with some of the discomfort."

Without a word, she rolled onto her back. He sat on the edge of the bed, moved her legs apart, then carefully washed her vaginal area with the cloth. The warm moisture soothed her. She looked into his face. He was intent on his mission to bring her comfort.

She'd never been so intimate like this with anyone before. She'd never trusted anyone like this before. But with Ethan, it felt right.

He used a small towel to pat her dry. "Better?"

"Yes. Thank you."

His eyes were warm. "You're welcome." He took her hand and laced his fingers with hers. "How did it happen that you never lost your virginity? Was it a conscious decision to wait?"

"No, not really. Part of it was living here and being so busy running the lodge, looking after Maggie after Grandma died, and then caring for Grampa when he was sick. I didn't have much time for dating and even when I did, the pickings were slim around Minnewasta."

He smiled faintly at that. "But what about before, when you were off at college. There must have been young men who interested you. I'm sure they were interested in you. What stopped you from having sex then?"

She wanted to be honest. "I certainly thought about it. I even got close a couple of times. But I couldn't go through with it. I was afraid."

"Were you afraid it would hurt, like it did tonight?"

"No, not that. Every time I thought about giving myself to some boy I was attracted to, I thought about my parents, about how they'd once loved each other, but it had all gone wrong. And then they were gone. Maybe some part of me was afraid to let myself feel that much for a man. Because I was scared I'd lose him, lose his love, the way my parents lost the love between them." She'd never given voice to her fears before. It was a relief to confess them now, and somewhat surprising.

He squeezed her fingers. "And yet tonight, you were willing to take that chance."

"Yes." *With you.*

They stared into each other's eyes, neither of them speaking. Then, Ethan let go of her hand and took the washcloth and towel back to the bathroom. He returned a moment later, shut off the lamp next to the bed, and slid onto the bed beside her. Pulling her close with her back against his chest, he spread the covers over her.

"Sleep well, sweetheart."

Harper settled into the cocoon of warmth provided by his arms. She exhaled and closed her eyes, relaxing completely. She'd never been more in tune with another human being, or so completely happy.

Smiling, she drifted off to sleep.

Chapter Eighteen

HARPER WALKED ALONG the shoreline of Solace Lake, picking up stones and tossing them into the calm water. It was a beautiful summer day with just enough breeze to make the heat bearable.

In the distance, she heard voices raised in anger. When she looked out over the lake, she saw her parents several yards offshore in a yellow canoe. Her heart lifted. They were alive! But then, her father suddenly lifted his paddle and struck her mother. She fell into the water with a loud splash and thrashed around, screaming for him to help her. Harper breathed a sigh of relief when he dove into the water. But instead of saving her, he held her head under the water until she quit struggling.

"No! No, don't!"

"Harper! Wake up. It's okay. I'm right here."

She woke with a start. It took a moment to realize where she was. She was in Ethan's cottage, in his bed. She reached for him, and he enfolded her in his arms.

"I'm so sorry," she said, her voice muffled against his broad chest.

"Shh. Don't worry. Did you have a bad dream?"

"I saw them. My parents."

He stroked her hair and held her a little tighter. "It was only a dream."

After what they'd shared tonight, she had to tell him the truth. If she kept this from him, there would always be something between them. Secrets had a way of bubbling to the surface, no matter how deep one tried to bury them. She leaned back to look into his face.

"My parents ... they died on the lake like I told you. But that's not the whole story."

He brushed the hair from her forehead. "What happened?"

"They were found floating on the water, their canoe overturned. When they pulled her out, the police discovered a huge gash on my mother's forehead. She'd been struck hard with a paddle. The police speculated that my parents got into an argument and my father became so enraged he hit my mother as hard as he could with his paddle. She fell backwards into the water and since she was likely unconscious, she drowned. She was an expert swimmer, had even been a lifeguard during her teen years and through university. If she hadn't been so badly incapacitated, she could have saved herself."

"What about your dad?"

"He wasn't a strong swimmer. In fact, he couldn't do much more than dog paddle. Some believed that either the canoe overturned when he struck my mother, or he jumped in after her and tried to save her. Others speculated he held her head under the water until she drowned. The police decided it was a murder/suicide he'd either planned in advance or happened spontaneously in a fit of passion. They believed that when he realized what he'd done, he couldn't live with the shame, and he drowned himself."

"Christ."

"No matter which theory you subscribe to, it doesn't make them any less dead. And it still means my father murdered my mother." Tears rolled down her cheeks. Though so many years had passed, the impact of their deaths hit hard. It still felt like yesterday.

"It makes a big difference, especially to you. I choose to believe he tried to save her, that he hadn't meant to hurt her."

Harper looked up into his face. He didn't look shocked or appalled by what she'd told him. She had to know the answer to her next question, but she couldn't quite look him in the eye, so she stared at his bare chest. "If you change your mind about the project, about this," she said, indicating the rumpled sheets they'd slept in, "I understand."

"Why the hell would I want to change my mind about anything?" He sounded almost angry at her for suggesting it.

"Because I wasn't honest with you. People around here have been gossiping about Solace Lake Lodge for twenty-two years. There's a stigma attached to this place. Maybe no one will want to come to an inn where a murder took place. I didn't tell you about things in the lodge's past that could affect its future. I'm sorry, and I understand if you want to back out of the project."

"I knew what happened here."

She sucked in a breath and brought her gaze back up to stare at him. "What?"

"After you told me your parents drowned in the lake, I wanted to know what happened. I read newspaper accounts from the time, so I knew it wasn't an accident. But that's in the past and I don't believe it has any bearing on what we're doing here now."

Harper sat up, rubbed the tears from her face. "But you didn't say anything."

"I figured you'd tell me in your own time. And if you didn't, I understood why. It's a painful part of your history."

"And what about us? Do you want a personal relationship with a murderer's daughter?" Even though she'd conquered her fear about making love with him, she could still lose him.

He cupped her face with a warm hand. "What happened in the past has nothing to do with you, or with us. Besides, I don't believe he meant to kill her."

She squeezed her eyes shut. "He was a good man, a good father. But I don't get to remember him that way."

He sat up and leaned against the headboard before pulling her into his arms. "I hate that this has caused you so much pain."

"Not only me." She burrowed closer to him. "My sisters grew up without parents, too. Maggie doesn't even have memories of our parents, only the gossip that surrounds their death. Our grandparents suffered. My paternal grandfather was a judge, a good, honest, ethical man. He couldn't accept what his only son had done. It was too much for him. He had a heart attack and died a few months later. My maternal grandparents, the ones who raised us, were never the same after they lost their only child. Grandma Dorothy had always been strict with a million rules we all had to follow. But after my mother died, she became bitter and angry. Part of the reason I left to go to college was to get away from her. I left Maggie and Grampa to fend for themselves."

Guilt brought fresh tears to her eyes. "The angrier Grandma become, the quieter Grampa got. After she died, he didn't care about anything anymore. They both died sooner than they should have."

Ethan stroked her hair. "I'm sorry, Harper."

She laid quietly in his arms, his gentle strokes soothing her. She closed her eyes, but she doubted she could sleep again. The scene from her dream kept replaying in her head. Over and over she saw her father hold her mother's face under the water. Had her father intentionally murdered her mother, or had it been a spur of the moment lashing out, one that he immediately regretted, the way Ethan believed?

Ethan. He knew, and still recommended that Mr. Hainstock invest in the lodge. She touched his bicep, loving his physical strength and his strength of character.

How she loved this man.

She turned in his arms, bringing her bare breasts against his chest. His chest hair teased her sensitized nipples into hard buds, awakening an arousal she'd thought sated. She wound her arms around his neck.

"I can't sleep." She kissed his chin, his stubble rasping against her lips.

He kissed her mouth and the passion in his kiss told her they were on the same wavelength. "What do you want me to do about it?"

"Make love with me again. No holding back this time." Her hand drifted down his body and found him hard and ready. She encircled him with her hand, a bold move she would never have thought herself capable of even yesterday. "You know you want to."

He made a deep growling sound in his throat. "Dammit, Harper. You've been through a lot tonight. I'm trying to do the right thing here, but it's damn difficult with your hand around my cock."

She ignored his hesitation. Instead, she climbed on his lap and faced him. His penis was poised at the entrance to her body and the thought of him inside her again, of his mouth on her, made her wet with desire. She took his hand and placed it on her mound. "I want you. See how wet I am for you?"

Ethan's mouth crushed hers in a deep, drugging kiss. At the same time, he inserted two fingers inside her, expertly finding her most sensitive spot. She came with a shattering force that thrilled her.

This is what I need. To feel alive.

When her climax subsided, she barely had time to recover before he removed his fingers and reached for another condom. He slipped it on, then repositioned her so she could impale herself on his hard shaft. She lowered herself slowly, taking him inch by inch. He filled her, stretched her. This angle was so different from before, the sensation an exquisite agony that set her blood on fire.

He let her set the pace while he gave his full attention to her breasts. He cupped them in his hands, rolled the nipples between his thumbs and forefingers until she wanted to explode. She leaned toward him.

"Oh, God, I'm coming again."

He continued to fondle her while she climaxed, making the ecstasy last even longer than before. Her inner muscles clenched around him.

When the waves of pleasure finally ended, he lifted her once again and lay her flat on her back. Then he was on top of her, inside her once more.

"Tell me if this is too much for you. Promise me, Harper." His eyes were glazed with desire and she understood he was on the edge of control.

"I promise," she said. She'd have to be split in half before she stopped him.

His first thrust made her eyes roll back in her head. Instinctively, she lifted her hips and arched her back to meet the next one. Over and over, deeper and deeper. He felt so good inside her, like he belonged there.

She wanted to be like this with him always.

He came with a shout and collapsed on top of her. She wrapped her arms and legs around him and held him tightly while his breathing slowed. She loved this closeness between them, this moment of connection.

She loved him. She wanted to tell him, wanted to shout it from the rooftops of Minnewasta, but the feeling was too new, too fragile. And she had no idea how Ethan felt.

WHEN ETHAN WOKE THE next morning, the sun was beginning to lighten the bedroom. He rolled onto his side to check the time, being careful not to wake Harper. It was almost eight. In a short time, he'd have to wake her so she could get ready for her trip to Minneapolis. But for right now, he wanted to watch her sleep.

She was beautiful, his little blonde angel. He didn't think there was anything she wouldn't take on, whether it was a huge renovation project, a snowmobile motor, or a newborn's tiny knitted hat. Harper was the strongest, most amazing woman he'd ever met.

Last night had been a revelation, to say the least. At first, when he'd told her he'd acquired the extra money for the renovations and she'd offered her body, he was sure he was being played. But he wanted her so much he was willing to take anything she offered, despite his doubts. Then he discovered she'd never been with a man before. All his doubts were blasted away. She wouldn't offer up her virginity simply because of the money.

That she trusted him to be her first humbled him. He hoped her first sexual experience had been wonderful for her, so wonderful that she'd want to repeat it often.

With him. *Only with him,* a possessive voice inside him added.

She'd trusted him with her secrets and the truth about her parents' deaths, too. Trust didn't come any easier for her than it did for him. She'd gifted him with her body and her heart, and it was a gift he could never repay. All he could do was treasure it.

It was his turn. He had to tell her the truth. Today. Now. She'd trusted him and now it was time for him to trust her.

And he did trust her. She'd never betray him or play games. She was good and honest down to her marrow.

I love her.

The thought caused his throat to close with emotion. He loved her. He never thought he'd feel this way about a woman again, never thought he'd find someone like Harper.

His body stirred. He wanted her again with a ferocity that almost scared him. No, that wasn't quite true. He needed her. Somehow, she'd become the missing piece of his life that he hadn't even realized he was lacking.

He stroked her blonde head. He'd tell her truth this morning. But right now he needed her.

Ethan kissed her forehead, her eyes, her hair as he ran his hand over the smooth skin of her back and hip. The intoxicating scent of warm, fragrant woman surrounded him, making him crazy with need. He willed his hands to be gentle as they caressed her. He'd never known a woman with softer, more silky skin. It invited him to touch, and he couldn't get enough. When he cupped one perfect, small breast in his hand, she moaned sleepily, her eyes still closed.

"Ethan."

She kneaded his shoulder with her hand, a smile on her face. God, how he wanted to always keep that smile on her face. He needed her smile like he needed air to breathe.

He needed her.

Harper's hand drifted down his chest, gently caressing while at the same time burning a trail of fire along his skin. When she touched his erection with one tentative finger, tracing a path from the base to the tip, he nearly lost control. He pulled her against him and groaned, his eyes closing. All he wanted to do was feel.

"You like that?"

He could barely speak. "You know I do."

"Tell me what else you like. Tell me what you want me to do."

With anyone else, he would have dismissed the words as simple pillow talk, an attempt to be sexy. But because of Harper's inexperience and innocence, her request was genuine. She wanted to please him.

Love for her expanded in his chest. It filled his whole body, heart, mind and soul.

He opened his eyes and looked into her expectant blue ones. Did she know her heart was in her eyes when she looked at him like that? Like he was the only man in the world, in her world?

"I like when you touch me. Wrap your hand around my cock, Harper."

She did as he asked, holding him gently as if he were made of glass. But even her lightest touch nearly sent him over the edge.

"Like this?" she asked.

He took a breath and dug deep for control, wanting to let her explore and become comfortable with his body. But it was killing him not to lay her on her back and plunge inside her, feel her sweetness surround him.

"You can hold me tighter." Sweat broke out on his forehead. "Move your hand up and down."

When she did, it nearly undid him. His control was stretched to the limit but he hung on, needing to please her as much as she wanted to please him.

"I want to kiss you," she whispered against his ear. "Like the way you kissed me. Intimately. Down there. Would you like that?"

Hell yeah. "Are you sure? You don't have to do that if you don't want to."

When she leaned back to look at him, her eyes were clear and determined. "I want to. Would you like me to?"

"Yeah." His mouth was so dry he could barely get the word out.

Her eyes lit with excitement. "Good."

She pushed him onto his back, then kissed her way down his body, stopping to lick and tease along the way. Her long hair brushed against his sensitized skin, making him grip the sheets.

The first lick of her tongue over his cock nearly knocked him off the bed. And when she took him in her hand and guided him into her warm mouth, his whole focus narrowed to what she was doing. He lifted his hips in a silent plea to take him deeper. She understood what he needed. Her tongue worked over his cock even as she took all of him into her mouth. Such exquisite torture.

But if she continued, he couldn't hang on a moment longer. He reached down to touch her face. "Baby, stop."

She let him go. When she looked up at him, worry lines furrowed her brow. "Am I doing something wrong? Am I hurting you?"

"You're killing me, baby. In the best possible way. But I can't wait any longer."

In one quick move, he flipped her onto her back and laid beside her. He found the opening to her body and inserted a finger, grateful to find her slick and wet and ready for him. He couldn't wait much longer.

He reached for the box of condoms on the night table and with shaking hands, sheathed himself. Nudging Harper's knees apart, he positioned himself over her, supporting his weight with his arms, his cock touching her mound.

"I need to be inside you," he whispered, shocked by the desperation he heard in his voice.

She wrapped her legs around his waist, her hands clutching his shoulders. "Yes. I need that, too. Hurry, darling."

It was all the invitation he needed. He slid inside her, her moist heat enveloping him. For a second, he simply reveled in the sensation. Then he withdrew as far as he dared and plunged deep inside her. She moaned his name. "Ethan."

The sound of his name on her lips snapped the last shred of his restraint. He thrust inside her over and over, harder and deeper. She stayed with him, lifting her hips to meet him every time. He was so damn close. But he wanted her to come with him.

The next time he withdrew, he replaced his cock with his finger, curling his knuckle to stroke her from the inside. Her eyes flew open.

"Ethan! Oh, my God!"

Her body shook with her orgasm. He slid inside her once more and his own orgasm was immediate. Wave after wave swept through him, over and over, until he thought he would die right there on the bed from an overdose of pleasure. But eventually the spasms eased and he fell on top of her, too exhausted to even roll over.

"I'm too heavy," he mumbled against her neck.

"I can take it." He heard the amusement in her voice. "You're a featherweight."

He mustered the energy for a chuckle. "Yeah, right."

"I've got you exactly where I want you."

Her hands ran up and down his back, gently kneading and caressing. Ethan exhaled in pleasure and completely relaxed against her. He'd never experienced this intimacy with a woman before. He wanted this closeness, this completeness, every day. With Harper.

After a few moments, he summoned the energy to roll off her and onto his side. He pulled her to him, not ready to let her go.

She snuggled against him. "I can't say I've ever been woken with more... enthusiasm before."

He nuzzled her sweet-smelling neck. "Consider me your new alarm clock."

Harper laughed and reached over to caress his face. "I look forward to it. Starting tomorrow morning?"

"You bet."

She yawned and stretched. "Speaking of alarms, what time is it?"

Ethan leaned over her to look at the clock. "Eight thirty-five."

"Eight thirty-five? Oh, my God!"

Harper jumped out of bed. "I should have been on the road a half-hour ago. I told Maggie I'd be in the city by ten."

Ethan slid out of the bed and disposed of the condom in the bathroom. When he came back to the bedroom, Harper was frantically searching for her clothes, tossing blankets and sheets in the process. He found his jeans in the corner where he'd tossed them in his rush to make love to her last night and pulled them on.

"Take it easy, sweetheart. So you're a little late. You deserve a break now and then."

She slipped on her bra and panties. "We have a lot to do today. We've got all the appliances, kitchen equipment and dishes for the dining room to pick out. I was going to stay at Maggie's for the night and come home tomorrow, but now I want to get home to you."

"That's good." Ethan's mind was in turmoil. He couldn't let her go before she knew the truth. "Before you go, can we talk for a few minutes?"

She pulled her T-shirt over her head. "Can you make it quick? I've got to run back to my cottage to shower and change."

He couldn't explain the reason he'd held back the truth for so long in a few minutes. He needed time.

He gave her a quick, hard kiss. "For now, I want to tell you that last night was the most amazing experience of my life."

"Ethan." Her smile was tender. She clasped his face between her hands and kissed him. "I feel exactly the same way."

"There's lots more I need to tell you, but it will have to wait until you get home tonight and we have more time."

"Okay. I'll get back as soon as I can. There are things I want to say to you, too."

Ethan's heart lifted at her words. He kissed her again. "I look forward to it."

"Me, too. But right now, can you help me find my pants?"

The wayward pants were soon located and with one last kiss, she was off. Ethan walked out onto his porch to watch her run down the road to her cottage. She rounded a bend and was soon hidden from his view by the thick forest.

Despite the loving way they'd parted, fear lingered at the back of his mind. He couldn't predict Harper's reaction to his confession. She valued honesty. He wasn't sure she'd understand his reasons for hiding his identity. And he was afraid he'd carried out the charade too long to deserve her forgiveness. He ran his hand through his hair, worry replacing the contentment he had so recently found in her arms.

Chapter Nineteen

HARPER DROVE HARD, making it to the city in record time. She pulled up to Maggie's apartment building at ten-fifty a.m., nearly an hour late. But she couldn't regret her tardiness, not when she remembered why she was late. Waking up with Ethan, making love with him again this morning, had been incredible. A shudder of desire coursed through her body as she thought about his hands and his mouth on her. She couldn't wait to finish her business in the city so she could rush home and make love with him again.

Was he going to tell her he loved her? Was that what he wanted to talk to her about tonight? She prayed that's what he wanted to say, because she desperately wanted to tell him she loved him, too.

Humming, she locked her truck, ran up the steps and pushed the intercom button. Maggie answered immediately, as if she'd been waiting for her.

"Hi, I'm here," Harper said. "Sorry I'm late. Why don't you come down and we can start our shopping right away?"

"Can you come up?" Maggie asked. "I'll buzz you in."

The buzzer rang. It seemed she didn't have a choice in the matter. Harper pulled open the door, trying not to be annoyed. After all, she was the one who was late. She hurried to Maggie's second floor apartment.

The door was partially open when she arrived. She pushed it open.

"Are you almost ready? I'd like to get going—"

The words died on her lips when she saw Scarlet standing in the middle of Maggie's living room. Harper went to her immediately and enveloped her in a hug. "Scarlet, what a wonderful surprise! I didn't expect to see you. Are you here to help us with the shopping?"

Scarlet's face was pale and anxious. "No, I need to talk to you. That's why I came to Minneapolis."

Harper's gut twisted. Scarlet wouldn't leave work in Chicago in the middle of the week unless something was very, very wrong. "Scarlet, you're scaring me. Are you all right? Are you sick?"

Scarlet took her hands and squeezed. "No, nothing like that. I'm fine. I ... I have something I need to tell you."

"What is it?"

Scarlet swallowed and glanced at Maggie before turning back to her with a look of resigned determination on her face. "Let's sit down."

Harper's heart picked up pace as she followed Scarlet to the sofa and sat beside her. Maggie sat across from them in an armchair, wearing an anxious expression identical to Scarlet's. Something was definitely wrong.

"Do you know what's going on, Maggie?"

She nodded reluctantly. "Yes. Scarlet just told me."

Harper turned back to Scarlet. "Whatever it is, spit it out. The suspense is killing me."

"Okay, but I want to tell you I take no joy in giving you this news." She reached for a tablet and booted it up. "I did some digging. It seemed very odd to me that you'd never met Mr. Hainstock. From what you told me, he was always unavailable. I wondered if he had something to hide."

"Hainstock Investments and the Hainstock Foundation are totally legit. I checked them out myself. I had our lawyer investigate the worth of the company before we signed anything. I'm not an idiot, Scarlet."

"Of course, you're not. But you didn't expect someone to deliberately deceive you either."

A sick feeling began to build in her stomach. "What are you talking about?"

Harper watched as Scarlet opened some websites on the tablet. "I did a search online for Ethan James, but I couldn't find anything. No Facebook page, no Twitter or LinkedIn account. Nothing. Most people normally have some kind of online presence."

Harper didn't like the direction the conversation was taking. Ethan had been completely honest with her regarding his association with Hainstock Investments. "So what? I don't have any of those things either."

Scarlet gave her a quick grin. "I said normal people." The grin disappeared. "So then I started to search for something personal about Mr. Hainstock, not just about the company. And I found this."

She handed Harper the tablet. The headline on the Minneapolis *Star Tribune* screamed out the news in bold type. "Duluth resident wins largest lottery in Minnesota history". The article was dated five years previously.

With trembling fingers, she scrolled a little further down, afraid of what she might find. When a picture of Ethan rolled into view, her worst fears were confirmed.

He lied to me.

"He isn't Mr. Hainstock's representative. He's Ethan James Hainstock, multi-millionaire businessman and philanthropist, thanks to a hundred and seventy-five-million-dollar lottery win a few years ago," Scarlet said. "I don't know what kind of game he's playing with you, but I thought you needed to know the truth. I'm sorry, Harper."

Harper nodded absently, her attention still on the newspaper article. The story talked about how Ethan was three days away from being unemployed when he won the lottery. The pulp and paper mill he'd worked at in northern Minnesota was going out of business.

Harper was sick to her stomach. The worst thing that could possibly happen had happened. For a moment, she was ten years old again on that terrible day when Grampa Bill told her that mom and daddy were dead. Ethan had lied to her, and he was going to abandon her just as her parents had.

Was that what he'd planned to tell her tonight? That he was leaving her?

She wouldn't let it happen again.

She handed the tablet back to Scarlet and stood. "I need to go home. I need to talk to Ethan."

"We'll go with you," Scarlet said. "You've had a shock. You shouldn't be alone."

She shook her head as she headed to the door. "No, I need to do this on my own."

Maggie followed her. "What about our shopping? We need to order the appliances and equipment so we have them in time for the lodge's reopening."

"It doesn't matter anymore."

"What are you talking about? Of course it matters. You've been working on getting the lodge in shape for weeks. You've been planning this for months, years even."

She stared at her little sister's incredulous face. Didn't she understand that nothing mattered anymore? Renovating the lodge wasn't going to bring their parents or grandparents back. She'd been delusional all this time, but the scales had finally fallen from her eyes.

They were totally alone in the world, and they needed to get used to it.

"I have to go."

Maggie stood in front of her, blocking her path. "Harper, don't go. Not like this."

Scarlet put her hand on Maggie's arm. "Let her go. We have to let her work this out for herself."

"We should have driven out to the lodge, told you our news there." Maggie said. Tears filled her eyes and spilled onto her cheeks. "At least you wouldn't have to face this drive."

"It doesn't matter," Harper repeated. She was numb and dead inside. Ethan had made love to her, listened to her confession of being an virgin, her retelling of her parents' deaths and throughout it all, he was lying. Playing her for a fool.

"I'm sorry, Harper. This is the last thing we wanted to have to tell you." Maggie wrapped her arms around her.

Harper felt stiff and awkward in her embrace, as if her body had turned to stone.

Like my heart.

"I have to go," she repeated.

Maggie let her go and Scarlet gave her a fierce hug. "Call us as soon as you get home. Let us know you arrived safely, okay?"

Harper nodded, then left Maggie's apartment.

The drive back to the lodge passed in a blur. Pieces of conversation kept playing in her head. She'd actually thought he was as excited about this project as she'd been. Worse, she'd actually thought he'd been interested in her. How stupid she'd been, how gullible. It had all been nothing but a business deal for him.

When she got back to the lodge, workmen were everywhere. As she drove past the lodge on her way to her cottage, Ethan waved to her, but she kept on driving. When she confronted him, she wanted to do it in private.

She didn't have to wait long for that confrontation. A few minutes after she arrived, Ethan knocked on her door, then came inside. He walked toward her as if to touch her, but Harper evaded him by stepping behind the island.

Worry lines creased his brow. "Harper, what's going on? Are you okay? I thought you and Maggie would be shopping all day."

There was no point beating around the bush. "Why didn't you tell me about the lottery?"

He stood completely still in the middle of the living room and stared at her. She held his gaze, praying he would tell her it was all a terrible misunderstanding, even though she'd seen the evidence with her own eyes. But when he turned away, his face a mask of guilt, she couldn't pretend any longer.

"How did you find out?"

"It doesn't matter. It's not like you can hide the truth about that much money forever."

He turned back to face her. "I'm sorry, Harper. I should have told you."

"Yes, you should have."

"I wanted to, a hundred times. But every time I thought about telling you who I really was, I got scared. People change when they know you have that much money. I've had some bad experiences."

"So you didn't trust me. Is that what you're saying?" Anger burned in her chest.

"No! Once I got to know you, I knew you were the most trustworthy person I'd ever met. But the longer I kept my secret, the harder it was to tell the truth. I was going to tell you tonight, I swear."

"I told you everything! Do you know how hard it was to tell you my father murdered my mother? I was so afraid that once you found out you'd walk away. But I told you because I thought you deserved to know. I wish you could have given me the same honesty."

He came around the island and lifted his hand to touch her, but when she backed away, he let it drop to his side. "I'm sorry, Harper. I never meant to hurt you. What I've done is about me, not you."

"How am I supposed to believe that now?" She choked back her tears, not wanting to cry in front of him. "Tell me the truth. Why did you come here? Why did you bother with the lodge?"

"Because it reminded me of the inn where I grew up. Small, intimate, and off the beaten path. Everything I told you about my family, my parents, was true. I was honest about that part of my life." He closed his eyes and ran his hand over his brow. "Maybe I wanted to right some wrongs from the past. I couldn't save my family's inn, but maybe I could save this one."

He opened his eyes to look at her. "And I wanted a project. I wanted something I could get involved with, something I could build. For the past couple of years, I've had people running the foundation and the investment firm. I don't have to do a thing, and I'm bored out of my mind. I needed this.

"And then I met you. You were so passionate about the lodge, and you had so many dreams. I wanted to make all of them come true for you. I still do. I believe in you. I believe in us." He stepped closer and took one of her hands. "Last night, that was the truth. Everything we said to each other, everything we did was the truth. That was the real Ethan."

She shook her head. Pulling her hand from his grasp, she gave a bitter laugh. "So did you think that if you slept with the poor, pathetic virgin she'd be so grateful she'd give you a bigger share of the lodge's ownership? Does money mean so much to you?"

He stepped back as if she'd struck him. "No! Harper, you know none of that is true. I want to bring all your ideas for the lodge to completion. I want to have a life with you. I love you."

Yesterday, she would have given everything to hear him say those words. But today, they sounded hollow and empty.

She shook her head again. "It doesn't matter anymore. The dream is over and I've finally woken up. Thinking I could make the lodge into something special was as stupid as believing we had something together."

"You don't mean that. I know how important the lodge is to you. Last night... I thought I meant something to you, too."

Despite all the lies, she still loved him. But she couldn't trust him. She stepped out from behind the island, needing to put some distance between them. "I think you should go back to Minneapolis."

"No, no way. I still have work to do here. I'm not going anywhere until the lodge is finished."

"What if I don't want you here anymore?" She crossed her arms over her chest, struggling to keep from falling apart.

"We signed a binding contract and I intend to live up to my end. The lodge is going to be rebuilt." He paused to take a breath, his head downcast. When he looked at her again, she saw the resignation on his face. "I can't tell you how sorry I am for deceiving you. But I won't abandon this project. I know what it means to you. And, maybe you don't want to hear it right now, but I won't abandon you either."

Harper stared at him, too angry to believe a word he said. It had been about the money all along. He must believe the lodge so valuable it was worth sleeping with her to secure it.

The idea made her sick to her stomach. The logical part of her brain told her she was the one who made the first move last night, and that the Ethan she knew wasn't capable of such deception. But the frightened ten-year-old inside her was hurt and questioned everything he'd ever said. She wrapped her arms around herself to stem the pain.

She shrugged, feigning indifference. "Do whatever you want. I don't care."

He stepped forward, reaching out his hand to touch her. "Harper—"

She moved out of his reach, afraid that if he touched her she'd be lost. She couldn't trust him, but her traitorous body still wanted him. "I think you should go."

He lowered his hand. "I'm sorry. I never wanted to hurt you. I love you, Harper."

He turned and left the cottage, closing the door quietly behind him. Harper stood in the middle of the kitchen, tremors racing through her body. The protective numbness that had allowed her to confront Ethan was rapidly crumbling.

Sinking to the floor, she let waves of grief and tears wash over her.

ETHAN PACED BACK AND forth on Harper's front porch. It had been three days since she'd discovered who he really was, and he hadn't heard a word from her. He'd tried to call her numerous times, had sent dozens of text messages, but she hadn't responded. His only alternative was to confront her in person. He had to make her understand why he'd done the things he'd done.

So there he was, camped out on her front porch, waiting. Where the hell was she? It was getting late, nearly nine p.m. If she was working the dinner shift at Miller's Resort, she should be home by now.

Was she out with another man?

The thought made his gut twist. He leaned against the porch railing and took a deep breath. Had she moved on so quickly?

No. He couldn't believe it. But still, the idea of some other man kissing her, touching her, made him want to punch his fist against the solid wood door of the cottage.

Finally, headlights made their way up the hill to the cottage and he drew a relieved breath. A moment later, Harper pulled up to the front porch. She got out of the truck cab, then came to a complete stop when she saw him.

"What are you doing here?" she asked.

She didn't sound happy to see him. Ethan swallowed. "I had to talk to you. You wouldn't take my calls, so this was the only way."

"There's nothing you can say that can make up for lying to me."

"I know that." He walked down the front steps. "But I need to tell you why I felt I had to hold back the truth."

"Don't bother. I think you should go."

"Harper, please. Hear me out. Don't I at least deserve that much?"

She hesitated. In the dim glow of the front porch light he couldn't see her eyes clearly, couldn't read her emotions. Had she thought about him the last three days? Had she missed him the way he'd missed her? His body was an open wound, his heart ripped from his chest.

"All right. You said that people treat you differently when they find out you have a lot of money."

"Yes. I've had people I've known all my life suddenly treat me like some sort of celebrity. When I first won the money, people I hadn't seen since grade school suddenly showed up asking for money. Others figured I was putting on airs, thought I was too good to hang out with them anymore. I didn't change, but the way people treated me certainly did."

"So when we met, you assumed I'd be the same, that I'd be blinded by the money."

He answered cautiously, feeling like he'd entered a minefield. "I didn't know what to expect when I met you."

"Did you pretend to be Mr. Hainstock's representative with anyone else?"

"Well, no, but—"

"So you made up Ethan James just for me?" She gave a bitter sounding laugh. "Maybe I should feel honored that I got my own custom lie."

"It was a way to protect myself, that's all."

"In case I wanted more money? Or in case I came on to you? Oh wait, I did that. And you were only the guy who worked for the millionaire. Imagine what I would have done if I'd known you had money."

"I should have told you, I know. But the longer I hesitated, the harder it was to tell the truth. I never had a conscious plan to deceive you."

"I can understand that you've had bad experiences in the past, and I can even understand why you made up your Ethan James persona when you first came here. But to carry the lie so far, to the point where we slept together and you still didn't tell me, I can't forgive that. If you'd confided in me, I would have kept your secret. I wouldn't have told anyone about the money, not even my sisters. But you didn't trust me."

She brushed past him and climbed the stairs. Ethan followed her. "Harper, wait. Let's talk some more."

"There's nothing to talk about. I needed honesty from you, but you couldn't give that to me." She fumbled with her keys before finding the right one and inserting it in the lock. "If you were dishonest in our personal relationship, how can I trust you in our business relationship? When the renovations are finished, I'm going to recommend to my sisters that we sell. You can buy it, or someone else can. I don't care."

He grasped her shoulders and turned her to face him. "You don't mean that! I know what this place means to you. Your great-grandfather built it. Your family has lived here for three generations. You can't walk away."

"I finally realized this place is simply a pile of logs, nothing more."

Shocked by her words, he let her go and staggered back a step. "You would sell this place just so you don't have to see me or deal with me anymore?"

He saw uncertainty flicker in her eyes, but she didn't waver. "Yes. I have to."

She opened the door of the cottage and stepped inside, closing it firmly behind her. For a few minutes, Ethan stood immobile, too shocked to move. She really hated him that much.

No amount of explanation was ever going to make Harper feel the way she once did. It was over.

Chapter Twenty

WHEN ABBY OPENED HER front door, Harper was momentarily taken aback by the grayness of her complexion. It had been over three months since her surgery. She should be back to good health by now. Maybe her surgery had been a bigger deal than she'd let on.

"Harper, come in! It's good to see you."

She stepped over the threshold. "Thanks. How have you been feeling?"

Abby waved her hand in dismissal. "Oh, I'm fine."

"You look tired." Harper didn't want to dwell on a subject Abby wanted to avoid, but she was concerned.

"I have trouble sleeping," Abby admitted. "My doctor is giving me something for it. That should help."

"That's good. I hope you get a good night's sleep soon."

"Me, too. But enough about me. How are you? Reese tells me the reno is going well. You must be excited."

The sob escaped without warning. She covered her mouth with her hand, trying to get herself under control. Embarrassment and despair swirled in her head.

"I'm sorry," she managed.

Abby put her arm around her shoulders. "Honey, what's wrong?"

"Everything's so messed up."

"Come with me to the kitchen. We'll have a cup of tea."

She led Harper to the kitchen table and pulled out a chair for her before setting a box of tissues in front of her. "Don't try to be brave for my sake. Maybe a good cry will make you feel better."

Harper blew her nose and wiped her eyes. "I've done plenty of crying the last couple of weeks. It hasn't helped any."

"I've been told I'm a very good listener. Would it help to talk?"

"I don't know."

"You haven't spoken to your sisters about whatever's bothering you?"

"No, but they already know part of the problem." She couldn't bring herself to tell them how stupid she'd been, how naïve. Fresh humiliation swamped her.

Abby filled the kettle with water and set it on the stove to boil. When she took a seat at the table, she reached for Harper's hand and waited.

"Everything's a mess."

"Why do you think that?" Abby asked kindly.

"I fell in love with Ethan, and he's not who I thought he was at all."

Everything started pouring out of her, from her first meeting with Ethan and the time they'd spent together, to finding out he'd lied to her. She still couldn't get her mind around the fact that he hadn't even told her his real name. Abby listened patiently, only letting go of her hand when the kettle whistled.

"Have you confronted him?"

"Yes."

"What did he say?"

"That he was sorry he lied to me, but he'd found that people did strange things when they discovered he had a lot of money. I think that's what hurts the most, that he didn't trust me."

"It hurts when someone we love lies to us."

"Yes." More than she'd ever thought possible.

"Does he love you, too?" Abby set two teacups on the table and sat down.

Harper hesitated. "He said he does."

"But you don't believe him."

"How can I believe him after the lies he's told me? How can I believe anything he said, that anything we shared, meant as much to him as it did to me?"

"Were you intimate with him?"

Harper closed her eyes in agony, tears threatening to fall again. She was so tired of crying. "Yes." She wrapped her hands around her warm teacup. "It was my first time. I gave my virginity to Ethan."

"Oh!" Abby sounded surprised.

"I know. Ridiculous to be a virgin at my age, isn't it? I didn't mean to wait so long."

"I'm hardly in any position to judge. My first sexual encounter was at twenty-seven, and Luke was the result."

"Oh!"

Abby lifted her shoulder in a shrug. "Yeah, I was surprised, too. Jerry Fields was someone I'd gone to high school with, but we'd never been particularly close. When he came home on leave from the army, something clicked between us, and one thing led to another..."

Her smile held an edge of sadness. "I think we needed each other. His mother had just died and I, well, I guess I was tired of waiting. When I found out I was pregnant, Jerry offered to marry me, but I knew he was going through the motions, trying to do the right thing. He didn't have any deep feelings for me, and I didn't love him either. So I told him no."

"Did you ever regret not marrying him?"

She shook her head. "No, I don't regret anything. There were some tough times, but I had Luke. And eventually Reese and I found each other. I'm very lucky to have those two men in my life."

"I'm happy for you, Abby. Reese is a good man." Harper's thoughts returned to her own problems. "Is it stupid for me to still love Ethan after what he's done?"

"Of course it's not stupid. We can't turn off our feelings as easily as we turn off a faucet. Has he tried to contact you, to explain his actions?"

"Yes, numerous times. He says he's sorry for hurting me, and he's asked me to come back to the project."

"Come back to the project? What do you mean?"

She carefully sipped her hot tea. "The lodge renovation doesn't mean anything to me anymore. Everything I thought was important to me, simply doesn't matter." Harper took a deep breath. "When I found out Ethan wasn't who I thought he was, I felt cheated, angry, abandoned, all those feelings I had as a child when my parents died. I know it sounds crazy, but I felt the same way I did when I lost them."

"It's not crazy at all. It sounds like he's very important to you."

She swallowed, then nodded. "Yes."

"Perhaps you need to talk to him."

"I can't do that, at least not yet." She was afraid if she saw him again, touched him, she'd end up in bed with him. But nothing would have changed. She still wouldn't be able to trust him and without trust, there could be no relationship.

"He must have had a very good reason for creating a secret identity for himself."

"He says it was because people treated him differently when they found out about the money. But once he got to know me, why couldn't he have told me the truth? If he couldn't trust me then, how am I supposed to trust him now?"

Once trust was lost, could it ever be restored?

ETHAN JABBED HIS SHOVEL into the ground as far as he could and heaved out another load of dirt, not an easy task when the trench he was in was eight feet deep. He pushed himself to finish digging the short trench between the old lodge and the new wing of rooms. The trench would connect the plumbing between the two buildings, but because the space was tight up against the lodge, the excavator hadn't been able to get close enough. The trench had to be below the frost line so it wouldn't freeze in the winter. Reese had told him he could get someone else to dig the trench, but Ethan volunteered. The same way he'd volunteered for every other dirty, physically demanding job he could find the last two weeks.

Better to be working than to be sitting around thinking about what a mess he'd made of his life, and Harper's. Not that he'd actually stopped thinking about it.

He'd only seen her from a distance since the night he met her on her front porch. Every day she drove by the worksite on her way to one of her jobs. She stopped occasionally to talk to Reese if he flagged her down but according to him, she didn't ask about progress on the lodge. It was as if she'd given up.

That was the worst. His deception had taken away all her enthusiasm for the project, all her joy and hope for the future. He'd never forgive himself for that.

"Ethan, where are you?"

He recognized his brother's voice. "Down here, in the trench."

Cameron peered over the edge of the trench and chuckled. "I thought you hired people to do your dirty work for you."

Ethan hefted another shovelful of dirt and mud over the top of the trench. He wasn't in the mood to be the butt of his brother's jokes. "What do you want, Cam?"

"I came to talk to Reese. I'll be starting on the new cottages as soon as my crew and I finish another project. I wanted to coordinate with him so we don't get in each other's way."

"Did you work things out with him?"

"Yeah."

He hoped Harper would like Cam's work. If she was still there when the cottages were finished. He worried that his lies had not only pushed her away from him but pushed her to the point of leaving her home. Had her disinterest in the lodge extended that far?

What the hell have I done?

He stabbed viciously at the hard earth with his shovel. "Good. Then you can be on your way."

"What the hell is wrong with you?" Cameron demanded. "Reese says when you're not sniping at him and everyone else, you're killing yourself with work."

"I'm fine." He didn't bother to look at Cam, but he heard his scoff.

"He says Harper hasn't been on the work site for at least a couple of weeks. He was surprised since the lodge is her baby. What's going on with her?"

"She's busy." He didn't want to talk to his brother about this.

"Did you have some sort of falling out with her? Don't tell me you still haven't told her who you really are?"

He flinched at Cameron's words. "It's none of your business."

"It is if this project is in some kind of trouble and I'm not going to be working here his summer."

"The project's not in trouble."

"Then what the hell's going on?"

Ethan shoved his shovel into the ground and glared up at his brother. "Dammit, Cam, I don't want to talk about it, okay? Leave me the hell alone!"

Cameron folded his arms across his chest and stood on the edge of the trench with an 'I'm not going anywhere' expression on his face. "I remember having a conversation very similar to this one three years ago, except I was the one in the trench. Or more accurately, the gutter."

Ethan turned away and resumed his work. "It's not the same thing."

"Close enough. You wouldn't give up on me then, and I'm not giving up on you now."

"That was different. You were killing yourself with your drinking. I had to step in."

"You know I'm grateful. Which is why I'm not going to leave here until you tell me what's going on."

Ethan groaned, stuck his shovel in the dirt again and leaned on it. Knowing Cameron's legendary stubbornness, he had no doubt he meant what he said. Might as well save them both a lot of time and aggravation. "Turns out you were right. Harper found out about the lottery win. She was angry I didn't tell her myself, that I lied to her about who I really was." He shook his head, remembering. "Actually, that's putting it mildly. She's beyond angry."

"What do you mean?"

"She's given up on this place, even though she was the one who fought so hard to save it. Says she's going to sell it." He turned away. "I hurt her that much."

"Have you talked to her, told her why you did what you did?"

"I tried. She didn't want to hear it."

"Did you tell her about Bree?"

"No." He should have realized that Harper was nothing like Bree. He should have trusted her with the truth from the beginning.

"Maybe if you told her, she'd understand."

"She isn't taking my calls, and she sure as hell doesn't want to talk to me face to face." He kicked a clump of dirt with his boot. "I really blew it."

"If she can't be bothered to listen to your side of the story, she isn't worth the aggravation."

A red haze of anger clouded Ethan's vision. "You don't know what you're talking about. Harper is the kindest woman I've ever met. I'm the one who lied. She was nothing but honest with me, so shut the hell up!"

Cameron took a step back, hands up in surrender. "I stand corrected. Sorry."

Ethan turned away, his hands fisted at his sides and his chest heaving. Cam was his best friend in the world. He didn't want to fight with him.

He couldn't afford to lose anyone else he loved. He took a deep breath to ease his anger. "I'm sorry, too."

"This woman means a lot to you, doesn't she?"

"Yes." She meant more than he could possibly make Cam understand.

"Come on. Let's get out of here and have some lunch. I brought enough sandwiches for both of us."

Ethan stared up at his brother. "What kind of sandwiches?"

"Ham and cheese for me, roast beef for you."

Cam would never say it, but Ethan knew he was worried about him. When the chips were down, his brother would be there for him. Just as he'd been there for Cam. Too bad there was nothing Cam could do.

He climbed up the ladder leaning against the side of the trench. When he reached the top, he grasped his brother's outstretched hand and let him pull him over the top. He brushed the dirt from his clothes. "Thanks."

"You're welcome. Hungry?"

"Yeah."

Harper didn't want him in her life. Somehow, he had to find a way to live with that.

ETHAN WORKED UNTIL long after the rest of the crew had gone home for the day, only quitting when it got too dark to work safely. The muscles of his back and arms and shoulders groaned in relief when he put down his tools and walked the quarter mile back to his cottage.

Once there, he pulled a beer from the fridge and sat at the island to drink it. He thought about food but aside from the beer, he didn't have anything in the fridge. It didn't matter. He didn't have much of an appetite anyway. Maybe he'd soak in the hot tub before trying to sleep.

His phone rang. Ethan groaned when he saw Lydia's number. He loved his sister but wasn't in the mood for a heart to heart. Or a tongue lashing. Reluctantly, he hit the talk button. "Hi."

"Hi, yourself. Cam tells me you and Harper Lindquist had a falling out."

Typical Lydia. Straight to the point. It was a character trait both his siblings shared. “Cam should have kept his mouth shut.”

“He was worried about you. So am I.”

“I’m fine.”

Lydia snorted. “Right. I can hear how fine you are. What’s going on, really? Cam said something about Harper finding out about your secret identity and flipping out over it. He said you gave her a false name. Is that true?”

“Yeah. Stupid, huh?”

“You were trying to protect yourself.”

His sister knew him well. His voice cracked. “Yeah.”

“Honey, why don’t you come to Minneapolis this weekend and stay with us? Cam is bringing Tessa for a visit. It’ll be nice to have the whole family together. Besides, it’ll give me a chance to cook all my baby brother’s favorite meals. You know how I like to spoil my family.”

“Yeah, I know.” The idea of being surrounded by people who cared about him sounded good right now. "I’ll be there.”

“That’s great. We’ll see you on Friday for dinner?”

“Sure. I’ll see you then.”

They ended their call and Ethan moved to the dining room table where he’d set up his laptop. As it booted up, he drank the last of the beer. He hadn’t wanted to mention to Lydia that he already had an appointment in the city on Friday.

He opened the document his lawyer had drawn up for him to sign on Friday and read it carefully one more time. Everything seemed to be in order. Lydia and Graham wouldn’t like it, but this was something he needed to do.

Once it was done, he would leave. There was nothing left for him at Solace Lake.

Chapter Twenty-One

HARPER WIPED TABLES and gathered dirty dishes in the dining room of Miller's Golf Resort, glad the lunch hour rush was over. She didn't have the energy to serve another customer, and she couldn't manage one more polite smile. Sleep had been elusive the last couple of weeks and the lack of it was taking a heavy toll. She could barely keep up in the dining room, and she found herself making stupid mistakes in her clients' bookkeeping. But every time she closed her eyes she remembered lying next to Ethan, his arms around her, holding her as if he'd never let her go.

But he'd lied to her. Now, she had to let him go or go mad.

After hauling the last tray of dirty dishes to the kitchen, she returned to the dining room to set the tables for dinner. When she saw a tall, dark haired woman standing near the entrance, she suppressed a groan. She took a deep breath, grabbed a menu and headed toward her. She made herself smile, even though it was the last thing she wanted to do. "Good afternoon. Would you like a table for one or are you meeting someone?"

The woman didn't return her smile. "Are you Harper Lindquist?"

The question surprised her. "Yes, I am. Who are you?"

"Lydia Hainstock Barnes. I'm Ethan's sister."

Ethan had spoken fondly of his sister. When Harper looked more closely, she could see the family resemblance. The dark, wavy hair, the chocolate brown eyes, even the shape of her mouth. "Why are you here?"

"I'd like to talk to you."

Harper waved her hand, indicating the tables. "I have work to do."

"I need a few minutes of your time. It's important."

She clutched the menu to her chest. "Did Ethan send you?" She barely got the words out of her parched throat.

To her surprise, Lydia laughed. The smile transformed her face, making her look even more like Ethan. Harper's heart lurched in pain.

"No, he doesn't know I'm here. If he did, he'd probably be very unhappy with me."

"Then why did you come?"

The smile disappeared. "Because I want to set the record straight. There are some things I think you should know. I came all the way from Minneapolis to talk to you, and I don't intend to leave until I do."

Judging from the stubborn set of her jaw, Harper believed her. Best to let her have her say and get her out of the restaurant quickly before she caused some kind of scene. The humiliation of having her co-workers know what a fool she'd been would be too much.

The deck beyond the French doors would give them privacy. Plastic chairs and tables had already been set out after being in storage all winter, but the late April chill made it too cold to sit outside, so the deck was deserted. "Wait for me out on the deck. I'll grab my jacket and tell my boss I'm taking a break."

Harper pushed her arms through the sleeves of her jacket as she opened the French doors and stepped onto the deck. Lydia stood at the railing with her back to her. As the older woman turned to look at her, Harper did her best to school her features into a neutral expression. "So, I'm here. What did you want to say to me?"

"You're being totally unfair to Ethan."

"I'm being unfair? He lied to me. He didn't even tell me his real name."

"He had a reason for doing that."

"Really? If he did, I haven't heard a good one, which leads me to believe he was playing me."

Lydia's expression darkened. "My brother doesn't 'play' people. You don't know anything about him."

"No, I don't, because he wouldn't tell me anything. Not really." She remembered the stories he told her about growing up in Wisconsin with an alcoholic father. He said the stories he'd told her about his family had been real, but now she couldn't help doubting everything he'd said.

"Everyone thinks winning big in a lottery would mean all their troubles would be over. But after what happened to Ethan, I can tell you it's only the beginning of trouble."

"What do you mean?" Harper asked, curious in spite of herself.

"It started the day he won the lottery. The pulp mill where he was working was about to close. He and all his co-workers were going to be out of jobs. Three days before the scheduled closure, Ethan won the lottery. Once the congratulations died down, he started to get requests from his buddies for money. Everybody was desperate. Some wanted him to buy the company so they could all keep their jobs, but that made no sense since the place was hemorrhaging money. Ethan actually looked into it, but even with the huge amount of money he'd won, it wouldn't be enough to save that place. When he said he couldn't buy the company, a lot of people were angry. They told him he was being selfish and didn't care about anyone but himself.

"That really hurt him. For a while, he passed out money right and left to anyone with a sob story, but it was never enough. He decided not to give one co-worker money because he knew the man was struggling with drug addiction, and he was afraid anything he gave him would be smoked or snorted away. The guy came after Ethan, robbed him at gunpoint and threatened to kidnap a member of his family if he didn't give him what he wanted." Lydia paused, closing her eyes for a moment before resuming. "He talked about taking one of my children. He and Ethan had been friends. He knew where we lived."

Harper pulled her jacket closed, shocked to hear this. "Oh, my God!"

"Fortunately, he ran away after stealing a few hundred dollars and Ethan wasn't hurt. The police arrested the guy and he spent some time in jail. It was pretty scary, for all of us."

Harper shook her head, shocked at what Ethan had been through, what his whole family had been through. He should have told her.

"The incident served as a wakeup call. Ethan realized he had to be more cautious about his personal safety and the safety of the whole family. He moved to Minneapolis from Duluth to gain more anonymity. My husband and I sold our house and moved our kids to a private school with more security. Our brother Cameron changed the daycare his daughter was going to."

"Wait. Cameron Hainstock is your brother? Ethan's brother?"

"Yes. Have you met?"

"No." At least he'd been truthful about Cameron Hainstock being 'Mr. Hainstock's' brother. If only Ethan had told her the story Lydia was telling her now.

Lydia paced the deck. "Ethan also realized he had to be a lot smarter about what he did with the remaining money. My husband Graham and I have been in the financial services industry for years, so he turned to us for help. Together, we established the Hainstock Foundation so that any requests for money had to come through a board of directors. Every request is judged on its merits. The foundation has given away millions to all kinds of charities – children's hospitals, medical research facilities, environmental groups – you name it. Ethan could have blown the money on fancy houses and fast cars, but he decided to do something good with it instead."

Harper had read about the charities the Hainstock Foundation had supported but at the time, it had been a big, anonymous company, not a person she cared about. She should have known Ethan was the type of person who would think of the needs of others before his own.

"Getting held up at gunpoint was bad, but it wasn't the worst that happened to him."

Harper shook her head. "How could it possibly get any worse than that?"

"What I'm going to tell you next gets to the heart of Ethan's actions with you. All I ask is that you listen and try to understand. Okay?"

Harper nodded her assent. Ethan's sister nodded back then began to pace the deck once more.

"Ethan's girlfriend Bree broke up with him a couple of weeks before his company was scheduled to close. She didn't see any future with a guy who had no job and no prospects. When he won the money a short time later, she turned up again, saying she was pregnant."

"Oh." Harper's heart fell, the pain nearly unbearable. One more deceit. "So he lied. He told me he didn't have any children."

"He doesn't."

"I don't understand."

"When he found out he was going to have a baby, Ethan wanted to do the right thing, so he proposed to Bree. My husband and I were suspicious. How very convenient for her to find out she was pregnant just when Ethan became a millionaire. We hired an investigator to check her out, and he discovered she'd had an abortion six months previously. Her sister spilled the whole story."

Harper clutched the back of one of the plastic chairs. "You mean, she aborted Ethan's child?"

Lydia nodded, her jaw tense with anger. "Ethan was devastated. Bree's plan was to quickly get pregnant again so she could hide her lie. Once she had her hooks into him, she'd be set up for life."

Harper's legs trembled and threatened to buckle. She plopped down into the chair.

"Do you understand now why he was reluctant to tell you the whole truth?"

"I understand he had to be cautious when he first met me. But once he got to know me, he should have told me the truth. I would have understood."

"People Ethan knew all his life completely changed toward him after he won the money. He didn't know what kind of reaction he was going to get from you. Would you be the kind who threw yourself at him, or would you treat him with disdain and jealousy because he was so rich? He's had both."

"I don't give a damn about the money! All I ever cared about was him!"

"Are you sure about that? If Ethan hadn't shown up, you would have lost your lodge, wouldn't you? As far as Ethan knew, that was all you cared about."

She stared at Lydia, stunned. Is that what Ethan thought? That he was only a means to an end for her? That she only liked him because he provided the money to fix the lodge? "It's not like that, not at all."

Lydia shrugged and looked out over the lake. "If you say so."

"Why are you telling me all this?"

"Because someone has to set you straight."

"He really doesn't know you're here?"

"No."

Harper's head was spinning. "What do you want me to do with this information?"

She shrugged again, but Harper sensed the tension beneath her apparent indifference. "Ethan blames himself for what happened between you. From what I can see, so do you. Before you dismiss him as a liar and a cheat, I thought you needed to know the truth. Ethan deserves that much."

Without another word, she turned and left through the French doors. Harper stared out at the lake, trying to make sense of everything Lydia had told her. Ethan couldn't possibly think that the only thing she cared about was the lodge. She closed her eyes in misery. She'd given him plenty of reasons to believe that was true. In fact, until Ethan, she'd thought saving the lodge was the most important thing in her life. But she'd been wrong.

ETHAN'S HEART RACED as he dialed the number. While the phone rang, he wiped his sweaty palm on his jeans.

"Scarlet Lindquist."

He cleared his throat. "Scarlet, it's Ethan. We met when you and your sisters signed the contract with Hainstock Investments."

"Oh." She managed to pack a big load of disdain into one small word. "How did you get my work number?"

"Harper mentioned where you worked." Harper had only told him she worked at a marketing firm in Chicago. He'd scoured the internet to discover the rest.

"Wait. Is something wrong? Is Harper all right? Has she been hurt?"

"No, she's not hurt. Not physically anyway."

"What the hell does that mean?"

He took a deep breath. "It means I hurt her. I made a big mistake."

"Yeah, I'd say you did. You lied to her. You misrepresented yourself to her. If she's kicked you to the curb, you deserve it."

"So you know who I am."

"Of course I do, *Mr. Hainstock.* I don't know what your game is, but I've got to get back to work."

"Wait! Don't hang up! I'm giving the lodge to Harper."

There was a moment of silence before Scarlet asked, "What are you talking about?"

At least that got her attention. He told her Harper's plan to sell the lodge.

"It's my fault. I can't let her do this." When his voice cracked, he had to pause for a moment to regain composure. "If she sells, she'll lose the lodge forever. So, once the renovations on the lodge are finished, I'm going to hand over ownership to her, free and clear. She'll have no debt, and she can operate the lodge as she sees fit."

"How do I know you're telling the truth?" Scarlet asked. Ethan didn't miss the cynicism in her voice.

"My lawyer has drawn up the transfer papers. I'll have him email you a preliminary copy so you can look it over and see if there's anything you think I should change. I'll send a copy to Maggie, too."

"Have you told Harper any of this?"

"No." She didn't want to hear from him. "After you look over the papers and I make any changes you want, I'll send the final copy to her."

"Why are you telling me this? Are you hoping I'm going to intercede on your behalf with my sister?"

"No. It's too late for that. I'm telling you because you and Maggie are co-owners and this affects you as much as it does Harper. But mostly I'm telling you because I'm hoping you can help Harper run this place. It's going to be too much for one person alone. She'll need help from people she can trust. From you and Maggie."

"Have you talked to Maggie?"

"She's my next call."

Scarlet was silent for several long seconds and if he hadn't heard her soft sigh, he might have thought the line had gone dead.

At last she spoke. "Why are you doing this, really? Handing over the lodge has to cost you thousands, maybe millions. Why would you take such a financial loss?"

"If I've learned anything in the five years since I won the lottery, it's that the money doesn't mean anything without the people I love. It's not important without them." He swallowed and closed his eyes, tamping down the emotion that threatened to swamp him. "Will you consider coming home to help Harper?"

"The lodge is her dream, not mine."

"Please, Scarlet. She's your sister and she needs you. Even if it's not forever, could you give her your support?"

There was another moment of silence. "I'll see what I can do."

"That's all I ask. Thank you."

"When can I expect those papers?"

"My lawyer will email them to you by end of business today."

"Right. So you're going to call Maggie now?"

"Yes. Thank you for taking my call. I'll let you get back to work."

"You really love her, don't you?"

"Yeah." He managed that one word before his throat closed with emotion.

Scarlet's sigh echoed over the phone lines. "I have to go. Goodbye Ethan."

He hit the off button and set his phone on the kitchen counter. He needed to talk to Maggie, but he had to compose himself first. Talking to Scarlet had been much more difficult than he'd imagined.

Telling her of his plans made them feel so real, so *final.* Once he handed over his share of the lodge to Harper, it would be over. He'd never see her again.

He let the pain of that thought wash over him.

When he'd recovered sufficiently, he made his call to Maggie. She was less confrontational then than Scarlet, but no less surprised by what he was proposing. When he asked her to come home to help Harper, she said she'd seriously consider it.

Tomorrow, he'd speak to Reese and let him know he'd be heading back to Minneapolis immediately, and that if he had any questions or problems he could contact him there.

And then he'd pack up and leave. Because of him, Harper had been avoiding the lodge, and working far more hours at Miller's than was good for her. He didn't want to inflict his presence on her any longer than he had to.

Chapter Twenty-Two

IT WAS NEARLY NINE p.m. when Harper pulled into the driveway leading to the lodge. The worksite was dark and quiet, the workers having left hours ago. She drove past Ethan's cottage. His truck was gone and the cottage was dark.

When she rounded the curve that led to her own cottage, she was surprised to find all the lights on and an unfamiliar car parked in the front yard. As soon as she pulled up to the cottage, the door opened and her sisters stepped onto the porch.

Harper sprang from the truck and hurried up the steps to hug them, so happy to see their familiar faces. "This is a lovely surprise. What are you two doing here?"

"We had to talk to you. Why don't we go inside?" Scarlet said.

She followed them into the cottage and hung her jacket on a peg near the door. "When did you get here?"

"About five. We had a chance to talk to Reese before the crew wrapped up for the day. He said the renovations are on schedule."

A few weeks ago she would have been thrilled they were finally taking an interest in the project. But now... "That's good."

"He said he hasn't seen much of you lately," Maggie said.

Harper looked away and then headed for the fridge. "I've been busy, with work. Have you eaten? I'm starved. I didn't have time to grab anything at Miller's."

Scarlet followed her into the kitchen and put her hand on her arm. "Harper, Reese told us that Ethan left."

Her heart dropped into her stomach. She opened the fridge door and stared inside. "So? He often goes back to the city. He has other responsibilities there. He'll be back."

"Not this time. He told Reese to contact him if he has any questions about the lodge, but that he wouldn't be back. He's gone, Harper."

She clutched the handle of the fridge. She'd chased him away. Lydia had been right. She'd refused to listen to him or to try to understand what he'd done.

And now he was gone.

Scarlet gently pried her fingers from the handle and closed the door of the fridge. "There's more. Come sit down."

She let Scarlet lead her over to the sofa and sat down. Maggie sat beside her and took her hand while Scarlet rummaged in her handbag. She pulled out a sheaf of papers and handed them to Harper.

"I think you should read this."

Harper stared unseeing at the papers. "What is it?"

"It's a legal document that Ethan had his lawyer draw up. It states that Hainstock Investments is relinquishing its forty-nine percent share of ownership of the lodge and giving it to you."

Harper stared at her, not sure she'd heard correctly. "What do you mean, he's giving it to me? That's not possible. He's put hundreds of thousands of dollars into the lodge."

Scarlet nodded. "I know, but that's what he's doing. I had a lawyer from my company take a look at this document. It's a totally legit and legal contract. All we have to do is sign it and it becomes binding. You'll own sixty-five percent of the lodge free and clear, and Maggie and I will own the rest."

"Free and clear?"

Maggie squeezed her hand. "Ethan didn't want you to sell the lodge."

Scarlet sat next to her. "But the contract doesn't go into effect until the renovations are complete. He's going to honor the original contract to finish what you two started."

Harper looked from Scarlet to Maggie and then down at the papers. "I don't understand. Why is he doing this?"

"Because he loves you." Scarlet put her arm around her shoulders. "I was sceptical of his motives at first, but after going over this contract with my lawyer friend, and now speaking to Reese, I realize it's true. Reese says Ethan instructed him to continue to send his invoices to Hainstock Investments for payment until the project is completed. Nothing has changed."

"I knew he loved you as soon as he told me he wanted to do this for you," Maggie said. "You can't fake something like that."

"Sure you can," Scarlet countered. "But not in this case."

Harper turned to Maggie. "When did you talk to him?"

"A couple of days ago. He called both of us to tell us what he planned to do, and then he sent Scarlet a copy of the contract he'd had drawn up. The originals are going to be mailed to you." She paused and squeezed Harper's hand once more, her dark eyes shining. "He asked us to come home to help you with the lodge."

Harper bowed her head. It was too much. Her fondest wish was to have her sisters come home. Ethan knew and he'd tried to make it happen for her.

"I've arranged a five month leave of absence from work, beginning June first," Scarlet said. "That gives me time to put together a marketing campaign. We'll have to sit down and figure out the direction we want to take and who we'll be aiming our marketing toward. But we can talk about that once I get here."

Harper lifted her gaze to her sister. "Wait. Are you saying you're going to stay here at the lodge for five months?"

"Yes." Scarlet looked down at their joined hands. "When Ethan told me you planned to sell the lodge, I suddenly realized I didn't want to lose it. I always thought it would be here, you know? I guess I'm more attached to the old place than I thought." She shook off the sentimentality with a flip of her hair, all business once more. "I've already rented my condo to a co-worker for the duration. It's important for the three of us to work together closely and get this right."

"The three of us?" Harper turned to Maggie. "Does that mean you're coming home, too?"

Maggie nodded. "I want to be part of this crazy plan of yours."

"But what about your job, your apartment?"

A shadow briefly crossed Maggie's face, but she covered it with a smile. "I never liked that place anyway. I gave my notice at work and the lease on my apartment is up at the end of May. If you still want me, I'll be arriving with Scarlet at the beginning of June. There's nothing holding me in Minneapolis."

"Of course I still want you!" She turned to Scarlet. "Thank you, both of you. You don't know what this means to me."

"I think Ethan knew," Maggie said softly. "He really loves you, Harper."

"Maggie's right," Scarlet said. "I still don't understand why kept his identity a secret from you, but I think he's really trying to make it up to you."

"He had good reasons. I should have listened—"

She put her hands over her face to cover the sudden sob. She'd been so hard on him, but after what Lydia told her, she now understood why he'd lied.

It didn't matter anymore. Her reasons for being angry had more to do with her past and her fears than with anything Ethan had done. But she was afraid it was too late to undo the damage she'd caused.

"I love him, too," she whispered. "I can't sign those papers. If I do, he'll be gone from my life forever. He'll think the money is more important to me than he is."

Scarlet stroked her hair. "What do you want to do?"

"I'm not sure. All I know is that I can't lose him."

"What happens if you don't sign the new contract?" Maggie asked.

"My lawyer friend said the original contract is still in force in that case," Scarlet said.

"So Ethan would still own a forty-nine percent share in the lodge, right?"

"Right."

Harper remembered the argument she'd had with him about the share structure. She'd been so adamant about retaining a majority share for her and her sisters that she nearly walked away from the deal. It all seemed so meaningless now.

She suddenly knew what she had to do. "I have an idea, but I'll need your help."

Scarlet didn't hesitate. "Tell us what you need."

ETHAN WANDERED AROUND his spacious condo, too restless to land in one spot for long. Since leaving the lodge, he was at loose ends. He had nothing to do and all day to do it.

The only thing left to occupy his time were thoughts of Harper and the mess he'd made of their relationship.

He'd spent the weekend with his family at Lydia's house and, as comforting as it had been to be with people who loved him, he hadn't wanted to stay any longer. They'd treated him with kid gloves, as if they were afraid he might break. Though no one mentioned her name, Harper seemed to be on everyone's mind.

Especially his.

He stared out the living room window at the panoramic view of the night-time Minneapolis skyline. He'd go crazy if he hung around this place much longer. Maybe he should take off. He'd always liked Playa del Carmen in Mexico, and he'd been meaning to visit Italy. Perhaps now was the time.

But he couldn't get excited about going anywhere. The idea of travelling alone left him cold.

What he needed was a project, something to occupy his time and his mind. He could buy another small inn or hotel and fix it up. He could do whatever he wanted with it.

But his heart wasn't really in it. Without Harper, everything was meaningless.

A knock sounded at his door, surprising him. Visitors needed to be buzzed in, and he didn't know many of his neighbors, so it was unlikely one of them was looking to borrow a cup of sugar. But he was glad for the distraction, even if it was someone trying to sell him something.

When he opened the door and saw Harper standing on the other side, he could only stare, his powers of speech deserting him. Her long blonde hair was unbound, the way he liked it best, the silky length of it nearly reaching her trim waist. She wore a bright red jacket and a short denim skirt that showed off her lovely legs. It was the first time he'd seen her in a skirt, and she couldn't have looked more beautiful. He ached with love for her.

"Hi. One of your neighbors let me into the building. I guess he figured I didn't look too threatening. I'm sorry to barge in unannounced."

"It's okay."

She swallowed, appearing uncomfortable. "Do you think I could come in? There's something I need to talk to you about."

He stepped aside, embarrassed by his lack of manners. "I'm sorry. Please, come in."

For the first time, he noticed she carried a large brown envelope in her hands. "Can I get you anything, coffee, tea?"

She shook her head, her smile tense. "No, thank you. I'm fine. I brought some papers with me. My sisters and I have already signed, so we just need your signature."

Disappointment hit hard. *Of course.* The new contract he'd had drawn up. Scarlet must have given her the preliminary copy he'd sent. He wasn't sure why Harper was delivering it in person, but at least it gave him one last chance to see her.

"Why don't you come into the living room?"

She set her envelope on the coffee table and walked over to the windows. "This is an incredible view of the city, Ethan."

"Yeah, it's okay." He'd take the view of the lake from her lodge over his cityscape any day.

Harper looked around the room. "You have a beautiful home."

Not a home, simply a place to hang his hat. No place was home without her.

"Thank you."

He clenched his fists at his sides to keep from reaching for her. It killed him to have her so close and not be able to touch her. The familiar scent of lilac filled his senses, inviting him to bury his face in her neck and drink her in. He wanted to sink his hands into her hair and feel its softness flow through his fingers, the way he'd done when he'd made love to her.

Don't go there.

"I'll find a pen and sign the papers. I'm sure you're anxious to be on your way."

She reached into her handbag and pulled out a pen. "Here. You can use this."

He took it from her and walked to the coffee table where she'd left the envelope. With a heavy heart, he sat on the sofa and removed the papers from the envelope. Shuffling to the last page, he saw the other signatures and the spot where he was supposed to sign. For a moment, he held the pen poised over the signature line. When he signed this, it would be over. He'd never see her again.

"Aren't you going to read through the contract before you sign it?" Harper asked.

He looked up at her, surprised. "I know what's in it. I told the lawyer what to write."

She bit her lip, her face pale and tense. "Would you read it, Ethan? Please?"

What was going on? "All right, if you want me to."

She looked relieved. "I do."

He turned back to the first page and began to read. After the first few lines, he realized this wasn't the same document he'd had his lawyer draw up. "Harper, what is this?"

"Please. Read the whole thing and then we can talk."

He nodded, confused, but he did as she asked and continued reading. The contract, as it was now worded, divided ownership of the lodge equally between him and Harper and her sisters. Fifty percent for him, fifty percent split between Harper, Scarlet and Maggie.

Dear God. Instead of taking his offer to own the lodge outright, she was giving him an equal share.

He looked up at her. "I don't understand."

She sat next to him on the sofa and grasped his hand. "I couldn't sign that first contract. I couldn't let you believe that all I wanted from you was your money. And I couldn't lose you. I'm sorry, Ethan. For not listening to you, and not trusting you."

He reached out to tuck a piece of hair behind her ear, letting his hand linger on her face. His body hummed with pleasure at the silky texture of her skin. God, how he'd missed her. "I'm sorry I lied, Harper. All I ever wanted was to make the lodge viable again. I wanted to bring all your ideas to life. I know how important your lodge is to you."

"I think I started to believe that if I kept the lodge alive, somehow I'd be able to keep my parents and grandparents alive, too. But as much as I love the place, it doesn't have magical powers."

"Still, it's important to you. You were so adamant that ownership of the lodge stay in your family. What's changed?"

"Your sister told me about some of the things that happened to you after you won the lottery. She told me about Bree, and the baby."

A sense of disappointment assailed him. She was here because she pitied him. He let his hand drop from her face and looked away. "She told you about that?"

"Yes. Don't be angry with Lydia. She thought I should know the truth, and she was right. She made me understand why you didn't talk about the money, why you were afraid to tell me who you really were."

"I wanted to tell you the truth from the beginning, but I couldn't. I planned to tell you when you got back from your shopping trip with Maggie, the day after we made love. I couldn't lie to you anymore, not after that."

She gripped his hand again. "But then my sisters told me what they'd found out about you and I wouldn't listen. I was stubborn and selfish, and I wouldn't look at things from your point of view. I'm so sorry for what you went through. Especially the baby. I can't imagine how hurt you were."

He swallowed and looked down at their joined hands. Losing his unborn child was something he was never going to forget. Or forgive.

"I love you, Ethan. Even with everything we've been through, I never stopped loving you. I think I've loved you since you walked through my door in that blizzard."

His heart overflowed with relief. And love for her. "I love you, too."

She caressed his face, a smile of happiness blossoming on her lips. "You mean so much to me. I loved you when I thought you were an ordinary working man. It wouldn't matter to me if you didn't have a dime. I hope you can believe that."

"I do. I swear to you, I'll never keep another secret from you again." A thought occurred to him. There was still one lie he had to make good on.

"About Mr. Hainstock's brother—"

"I know. *Your* brother," she said with a laugh.

Ethan shook his head, relieved. Everything was out in open now. "I promise I'll tell you every day how much you mean to me."

"It's a deal. So, will you sign the new contract and become my business partner and join me in this crazy venture we've embarked on?"

He kissed the back of her hand. "I will. And will you join your life with mine and be my wife?"

She blinked in surprise. Tears filled her eyes but her smile brimmed with happiness. "I will."

Ethan softly kissed her lips to seal the deal.

Epilogue

HARPER AND HER SISTERS walked around the lake to The Point, the thin piece of land jutting out into Solace Lake. They stepped onto the dock and walked to the end. The sun was beginning to set, painting the western sky in shades of pink and red. Harper inhaled the pine scented air and listened to the croaking of the frogs hiding amongst the reeds along the lakeshore.

It didn't get much better than this. Her sisters were home and for the next five months, they'd all be together. And in a week, she'd be marrying the man she loved. She was truly blessed.

Scarlet draped her arm over Harper's shoulders. "Happy?"

Harper linked her fingers with her sister's. "Ecstatic. Especially now that you two are home."

Maggie put her arm around her waist and rested her head against her shoulder. "You're going to be a beautiful bride. Your dress is perfect."

"Thank goodness the one off the rack fit you so well. There wouldn't have been time to order a custom dress." Scarlet gently tugged on a lock of Harper's hair. "Of course, this wouldn't have happened if you two had waited a few months to plan your wedding instead of springing it on us so quickly."

"We didn't want to wait. We want a simple wedding with our friends and family. If I hadn't found my dress yesterday, I would have been happy to wear jeans and a flannel shirt." Harper put her arms around both her sisters. "All I want is to marry Ethan."

"He's perfect for you. You're going to be very happy together."

"Yes, we are. I just wish..." She shook her head, not wanting to spoil this perfect moment with sad thoughts.

"What? Spit it out."

She should have known Scarlet wouldn't let her be evasive. "I wish Mom and Daddy could be here on my wedding day."

"Yes, that would be truly perfect," Maggie said. "I often wonder what our lives would have been like if they'd lived. If Daddy hadn't..." She bowed her head.

Harper squeezed her waist. "After all these years, I still can't believe he killed her, no matter what the police said. I wish there was some way of knowing what really happened that last day."

"We know what happened, Harper." Scarlet's voice had a rough edge. "There was a witness, remember? Willy saw Rob hit Miranda with the oar, and she fell into the lake and drowned. For whatever reason, Rob jumped in after her and he drowned, too. End of story."

"Yes, but we don't know why it happened. What had gone so wrong that it led to murder? I've never been able to understand or make sense of it. I tried talking to Grandma and Grampa and Willy when I was a kid, but they never wanted to talk about our parents. Maybe they thought what we didn't know wouldn't hurt us. But they were wrong."

"I'd like to find out what happened, too," Maggie said. "I never had a chance to know them in life. Maybe learning about them now will help me discover who they were."

"Let's not talk about this anymore," Scarlet said. "Your wedding is supposed to be a happy occasion. Let's not ruin it with sad old memories."

Scarlet had never been able to talk about their parents. For her sake especially, it was essential to unravel the secrets that had kept them in the dark for so long. Harper needed to find a way to do that. If there was one thing she'd learned in the last few weeks, it was that healing could only begin if secrets and lies were brought out into the light.

"You're right. My wedding is a very happy occasion. And it's also a happy occasion that the three of us are together."

"It's good to be home." Scarlet kissed her hair. "It's getting late. Time to head back."

Harper nodded and turned around to walk back down the dock to the shore. She glanced over her shoulder, needing one last look at the lake. A yellow canoe glistened in the sun, two people paddling toward the opposite shore. She grasped Maggie's arm, her heart in her throat. "Look!"

"What?" Maggie turned in the direction Harper pointed, shading her eyes from the sun's glare. "What do you see?"

The canoe was gone. Harper blinked into the sun and then shook her head. "Nothing. A trick of the light."

But she knew what she saw. Harper sent a silent prayer out over the lake as she'd done so many times in the past. *I love you, Mom and Daddy. I hope you're both at peace.*

"Let's go back to the cottage," she said. "Ethan is waiting for me."

Hand in hand, they walked the length of the dock back to the shore.

The End

Thank you for reading "Lies and Solace." Are you ready for Scarlet and Cameron's story? Check out the blurb from "Secrets and Solace", book two in the Love at Solace Lake Series:

NO MATTER HOW DEEPLY buried, secrets rise to the surface.

Scarlet Lindquist has agreed to help her sisters rebuild the dilapidated fishing lodge in Minnesota they inherited from their grandparents. Although the lengthy restoration is bringing the three sisters closer together, Scarlet's support is temporary. Her leave of absence from her job in Chicago is temporary and she has no intention of staying at Solace Lake Lodge, where the lake holds dark secrets. When frightening childhood memories resurface, they are tempered by her fascination with an irritating contractor. If only she could trust her feelings for him. If only he could trust her.

Cameron Hainstock meets Scarlet at his brother's wedding to her sister and their attraction is instantaneous. But Cam avoids the beautiful marketing executive. All his efforts are aimed at battling for custody of his only child.

When the unimaginable happens and Cam faces the biggest challenge of his life, he's reluctant to accept help to halt his downward spiral. Can they learn to trust each other and fight for a future together or will they go their separate ways?

Scan the QR code for your copy of SECRETS AND SOLACE!

A Note from Jana

REVIEWS ARE THE LIFE BLOOD for authors. I hope you enjoyed I'LL BE SEEING YOU, and if you did, I would appreciate you letting other readers know. Please leave a review at the retailer where you purchased the book, on Goodreads, or on your own blog. If you leave a review, I would love to read it! Please email me the link at Jana@JanaRichards.com.

You can stay up to date with me and my upcoming new releases, sales, giveaways and contests by joining my newsletter. You'll receive a FREE ecopy of **HOME TO SOLACE LAKE** as a thank you for signing up. This romantic novella is available only to newsletter subscribers. I'd love to have you on board! Here's the blurb for **HOME TO SOLACE LAKE**:

> After Jerry Fields buried his mother twenty-two years ago, he cut all ties to the small town in Minnesota where he grew up. He swore he'd never return. But when his biological father, a man who never acknowledged him, leaves Jerry his entire estate, curiosity has him returning to Minnewasta. Why did Earl Rogers will him

everything he owned when during his lifetime he didn't give Jerry a minute of his time?

Denise Rogers wants to save the business that her deceased husband loved so much. But when her father-in-law Earl leaves all his property to his illegitimate son, saving the business gets much more complicated. Denise is determined to buy the property from Jerry Fields to keep it from being demolished and turned into condos. She wants to continue to run the business as a marine repair shop, knowing it's what her husband would have wanted. But events throw her plans into disarray and she has to give up on her dream. Until Jerry offers to work with her over the summer to help her buy the property.

Jerry can't stomach the idea of putting his half-brother's widow out of a job and a home, so he decides to stay in Minnewasta to help her. At the end of the summer, Denise will purchase the property from him and they'll go their separate ways. But as they work together, their feelings for each other deepen into love, and they uncover long-held secrets that force Jerry to question everything he thought he knew about his parents. Can Jerry overcome past hurts and fears for a chance at love?

Sign up using the QR code below for Jana's newsletter and receive your FREE copy of **HOME TO SOLACE LAKE!**

Don't miss out!

Visit the website below and you can sign up to receive emails whenever Jana Richards publishes a new book. There's no charge and no obligation.

https://books2read.com/r/B-A-YISD-GNLZC

BOOKS 2 READ

Connecting independent readers to independent writers.

Also by Jana Richards

A Left at the Altar Romance

Her Best Man

There Goes the Groom

Always a Bridesmaid

Love at Solace Lake

Lies and Solace

Secrets and Solace

Truth and Solace

Christmas at Solace Lake

The Victorian Mansion Series

Rescue Me

Take a Chance on Me

Twice in a Lifetime Series

I'll Be Seeing You
Never Can Say Goodbye
When I Was Your Man

Standalone
A Long Way From Eden
Seeing Things

Watch for more at https://www.janarichards.com/.

About the Author

When Jana Richards read her first romance novel, she immediately knew two things: she had to commit the stories running through her head to paper, and they had to end with a happily ever after. She also knew she'd found what she was meant to do. Since then she's never met a romance genre she didn't like. She writes contemporary romance, romantic suspense, and historical romance set in World War Two, in lengths ranging from short story to full length novel. Just for fun, she throws in generous helpings of humor, and the occasional dash of the paranormal.

In her life away from writing, Jana is a mother to two grown daughters, grandmother to an amazing granddaughter, and a wife to her husband Warren. She enjoys golf, yoga, movies, concerts, travel and reading, not necessarily in that order. She and her husband live in western Canada with a senior calico cat named Layla and an acquarium full of unnamed fish. She loves to hear from readers and can be reached through her website.

Read more at https://www.janarichards.com/.